Since early childhood, Don-Michael Smith has been a lover of literature. He is currently a contemporary literature teacher at a high school in East Harlem. Don-Michael grew up in Hampton, Virginia, before attending Virginia Tech, where he received a bachelor's of science degree in 2001. Upon graduating from VT, Don-Michael moved to Atlanta, Georgia, where he obtained his master's degree in education and began his career teaching.

A Roommate's Promise is his first novel.

To Mom and Dad,
my wild imagination finally paid off!

Don-Michael Smith

A ROOMMATE'S PROMISE

AUSTIN MACAULEY PUBLISHERS™

LONDON • CAMBRIDGE • NEW YORK • SHARJAH

Ordering Information
Quantity sales: Special discounts are available on quantity purchases by corporations, associations, and others. For details, contact the publisher at the address below.

Publisher's Cataloging-in-Publication data
Smith, Don-Michael
A Roommate's Promise

ISBN 9781645753681 (Paperback)
ISBN 9781645753674 (Hardback)
ISBN 9781645753698 (ePub e-book)

Library of Congress Control Number: 2020924217

www.austinmacauley.com/us

First Published (2021)
Austin Macauley Publishers LLC
40 Wall Street, 33rd Floor, Suite 3302
New York, NY 10005
USA

mail-usa@austinmacauley.com
+1 (646) 5125767

Army, Armo, Ms. Blue, Amy T, Dhonielle—you guys had eyes on this work when I couldn't stand to look at it. Thanks for all the glows and grows you provided. This would not be possible without you. Ms. Ferguson and Ms. Wampler, my favorite writing teachers who never gave me an *A* because I deserved it, but *B*s because I could always be better. Thank you!

Chapter 1

I tossed an old yearbook into a box labeled *attic* before standing up to survey the damage. The past four years of my life were sprawled out everywhere with sparse glimpses of carpet peeking desperately through the rummage. No wonder my bedroom is completely trashed, I've been struggling to get things into boxes for weeks. My dilemma—filtering unnecessary items of teenage obsession from articles deemed as college appropriate. Truth be told, it's not as easy as I thought it would be.

To date, my life can pretty much be summed up by the brimming, attic-bound box in front of me bursting at the seams from old science fair ribbons, graded papers, horrifying school pictures, and a Keyboarding Club T-shirt! No doubt, that has definitely got to go into the *Relics of Loserville Past* box. I mean damn, I'm about to be a college freshman for all that's good and holy!

It's hard to believe that the much-anticipated summer after my senior year has ended and that I'm really headed to Southern California University tomorrow morning. Getting accepted was not a total surprise because both of my parents are alumni. Speaking for my own contribution, I've always done pretty well in school. I don't know why, but for some reason, high school just got easier as I passed from one grade to the next. But don't misunderstand me, I'm by no means a genius. I wasn't Valedictorian or Salutatorian either. I'm just Lewis *Lewis*, with the 3.5 GPA, ranked 53 in a class of 315, and the son of two college lovebirds who insisted that I attend their glorious alma mater of SoCafo (that's what privy folks call Southern California University). Non-privy folks often confuse SoCafo with *The* University of Southern California, which is actually in Los Angeles and better known as the research snooze fest, USC… if I had to go there you could shoot me between the eyes right now. SoCafo is further south, just an hour east of San Diego. And yep, you heard me—I was given an unusual punishment at birth by two seemingly sane parents, identical first and last names. My mom always wanted to name her firstborn son after her Grandpa Lewis, who died shortly after she married my dad. She has this humiliating and over-told monologue about how she just *knew it was meant to be* with Dad after she found out his last name was

Lewis. Now fast-forward eighteen years and *I*, Lewis Emmanuel Lewis, am reaping the absolutely ridiculous brunt of a well-rehearsed yet mediocre love story.

I'm an only child, so lucky for my hypothetical sibling(s) my mom didn't get to name any more Lewis's. And lucky for me, my best friend, Dean, has been my brother through all the painful years of life a guy loathes talking to his parents about. Dean got accepted to UCLA, so I'm hoping to get a cool roommate in his absence.

Across my room on the desk, the only visibly clear surface remaining, my phone vibrated with what I can only imagine being a text from Dean. After stepping over my sloppily packaged high school life, I discovered that sure enough, it was.

CU @ Sharkey's n 10.

With tonight being my last night in town, Dean and I made plans to go to Sharkey's, our young-adult hangout with a bowling alley, arcade, dancefloor, and the best pizza on the West Coast. I've been so caught up with packing that our plans totally slipped my mind. I have a shit ton left to pack but certainly could use this break from the monotony. My only concern is that Dean is not exactly a guy of moderation. If I'm not careful that troublemaker will have me out all night, and then I'll never finish packing before tomorrow.

In addition to being a magnet for trouble, Dean also has this incredible talent for talking his way into *and* out of any situation. To say that Dean is mischievous would be beyond an understatement. It's really nothing legally harmful, just stuff like sliding down the bowling lanes on his stomach, unplugging the videogames, breakdancing very badly on a crowded dance floor, and throwing slices of the best pizza on the West Coast across a very frustrated arcade.

Harold Sharkey would have long ago stripped Dean the privilege to step foot inside of his establishment if it weren't for Dean's aforementioned ability to talk himself out of all unfavorable circumstances. However, most Vedadonians attribute Mr. Sharkey's continued graciousness to the obvious—Dean Eddleston Senior is the most successful public relations attorney in Vedado, California, and Harold Sharkey is one of his oldest clients.

I do lovingly pity Dean. One day, when he finds himself in a situation at UCLA without daddy in his corner and too drunk to articulate himself, he is going to suffer an imperial wakeup call. I just hope that I'm not there to witness it. Not to mention he'll probably need someone to bail him out, and I'm sure that I won't be able to foot that bill. But let's not think that situation into existence.

It was already 8:15 when I shot a short text back.

Meet ya n 30, SSS.

I could probably be out of the door in twenty minutes if I finish packing this last box quickly. So, after about twenty seconds of hurriedly throwing random objects that were within reach into a half-full cardboard box, I stood up again to look at the remaining task. There was a clear circular space of carpet in the middle of the floor from where I'd been sitting for hours enclosed by a mass of unpacked destruction…it would have to wait until I got back to be addressed.

I waded through the boxes blocking my bathroom door and skirted them out of the way pulling it open. I was masterful at an efficient SSS therefore on my way by 8:40. Oh, and FYI SSS stands for *shit, shower, and shave.* I don't have my own car, so I share the minivan with my mom. To be honest, it's more humiliating than my name. She's a stay-at-home-mom and thus insisted on getting a Dodge Caravan because of the dual sliding doors and grocery storage space in the back. Mom has a degree in Elementary Education and used to be a teacher, but she and Dad agreed that she was needed more at home when I was six. I think she may start working again once I'm out of the house though. I just hope that she realizes an SUV would be just as spacious as and ten times more fashionable than that janky minivan (or disgrace on wheels as Dean calls it).

But I digress… So, by the time I got to Sharkey's Dean had already managed to sneak-guzzle a pitcher of beer. I guess he was serious about me being here at 8:25. It was now 8:50, and he was tapdancing, in bowling shoes, on the back bar in front of a seventy-two-inch television. Mr. Sharkey must not be managing tonight because he'd *on no account* let Dean get away with these crowd menacing shenanigans. Harold Sharkey is a nice guy: heartily Scottish, in his late fifties, widower, grown children (I think two girls), with a harsh Scottish accent that guards an overprotective and loving heart. I think I should stop Dean for *his* sake, poor old man.

"Dean! C'mon dude, get down from there. Mr. Sharkey doesn't need this for business. Besides, you're making me look bad," I pleaded half-heartedly.

Harold Sharkey, who had been stacking glasses underneath the bar, grumbled, "Ha! The lad's making UCLA look good," in his usual disapproving tone.

Surprised that he was actually allowing this scene to take place, "Mr. Sharkey! How are you, sir?" I said.

"I'm *glad*, Mister Lewis! Glad this here is Dean's last weeken' in town, so he can go erupt on some other hard worrkin' man's establishment," he retorted with a robust chuckle. "Yeah, I figured I'd let'em go all out tonight without calling the patrol or his pop, aye? Since I won't be seein' the lihil crritter 'till winter," Harold Sharkey stared at Dean and a wan smile grazed his lips as he shook his head.

"Oh, well that's umm…nice of you," I was slightly uncomfortable and majorly shocked. Harold Sharkey NEVER tolerates Dean's performances, but I suppose he's a tolerable and forbearing man in the face of hope, at least until winter break.

"So, I guess I can let him stay up there then?" I asked, half-joking and half-serious.

"Hell, no boy! Rubbish all-the-way-round! Get that clown down from thur'nd take him to the arcade or somewhere he can't pirate any more spirits from me!" he barked.

"Dean, come on down man! I've got to leave early tomorrow morning, and I want you to at least be able to *remember* my last night in Vedado as a pre-SoCafo student," I beckoned with more urgency.

"I'm SoCafoking sick of hearing about SoCafo! Get up here Loser Loser! I swear I'll remember you grooving on the bar your last night here," Dean shouted, and I knew this was going to be a tough sell.

Dean tapped and gyrated clumsily while trying to keep his 5'10" frame from toppling off the bar. As his feet shuffled, his shaggy brown hair swayed uncontrollably from side-to-side and his sloppy hand attempted to keep it from falling over his eyes.

"Not tonight dude, winter break for sure. There are some girls from school hanging out in the arcade. Let's go chill in there," I said.

Girls are and probably always will be Dean's Achilles' heel. Abruptly pausing his dancing, he asked, "Seriously? Who?"

Damn, I didn't think that far ahead. "Uh, you know, those sophomore girls who always eat lunch in The Square when it's not raining."

When it's not raining, there are dozens of girls who eat lunch in The Square. The Square is just what we call Vedado High School's picnic area, but Dean wouldn't know the distinction of girls because he's always eating lunch in detention.

But he acquiesced with slurred obstinacy, "Damn dude, buzz-kill. Alright, alright, I'm coming."

"Here man," I offered my hand.

Swatting my hand away, "Get that outta here, Lewis. I'll get down the same way I got up," Dean said belligerently. After setting down his pitcher, he leaped from the bar to the floor landing first on his feet, then on his hands and knees. It was almost graceful, had it not been for the topple there at the end.

My hand remained extended from tracking his flight, "You alright?" I asked.

"Ooooh the pain...I'm dead, can't you tell? Somebody call the coroner!" Dean joked. "C'mon let's go," he said as he put me in a playful headlock.

Wrestling my way out of his grip I asked, "So when you headed to UCLA?"

"Ugh, I don't know. It's in a letter somewhere," Dean said nonchalantly. I was amazed at how unconcerned he was with the topic of college. "So, who's in the arcade?" he asked.

"You know, the sophomore chicks," I said, quickening my steps as if I were anxious to see the hypothetical tenth graders.

"No, I don't know. That's why I'm asking you, genius," Dean replied smugly.

"I don't know, I just said that to get you down. Sharkey was nursing a hernia." I couldn't keep up the charade, I never can with Dean.

"You bum," he shouted while punching me on the shoulder, pretty hard too.

"Ow," I matched his volume and returned the punch. "Since when do we need girls to have a good time anyway?"

"Ahhh, since we co-wrote the Carnal Constitution in ninth grade. Do you remember that? Ha! That was the single-most insightfully awesome accomplishment of our lives!

"Aha, 1st Amendment: *No girls, no fun*! Hmm, that your new motto? Guess I'll go home and finish packing then," I said feigning disappointment.

Pushing me lightly, "get over yourself. You know what I mean," Dean said. Suddenly, Dean paused mid-stride. "Lewis look! It's Camille Harris. Oh duuude, she is smokin' hot," he said in awe.

Alright, so where do I begin on the topic of Camille Harris? First off, she's not your typical California girl. Camille Harris is more what I'd call your *All African-American Girl Next Door*. Her skin literally looks like churned caramel, and her eyes are like two dazzling sapphires dancing gracefully across her gorgeous face. But here's the crazy part, she's not only just beautiful, but she was also on the varsity tennis team, in the National Honor Society, Keyboarding Club, Student Council, and Prom Queen. And get this, she's our Class Valedictorian! Camille tested out of calculus in tenth grade and was accepted to SoCafo on a full scholarship. It almost seemed unfair: genius, gorgeous and genuine—whoever got to date her was getting the total package.

Camille was with a couple of her girlfriends, Ebony Copeland and Olivia Wendell, who both seemed as if they had other places they'd rather be. I had a couple of classes with both of them, but we weren't friends or even acquaintances. As a matter of fact, we were in entirely different social circles, so their being in Sharkey's is sort of odd. Regardless of why, they were here, and I had a feeling that Dean's wanna-be-down white boy routine while under the influence was not going to go over well with these undeniably down brown girls.

I said a silent prayer that Dean didn't use his typical and offensive misogyny to try to play her. "Yo, what's up Camille?" he was philandering.

"Hey, Dean…Lewis," she said with a smile revealing her perfect teeth.

"Yo," I said trying to make my voice sound as deep as possible.

YO? Really Lewis? I might as well have said, "AYE, WHAT IT IS SOUL SISTA?" But 'YO' did manage to get a girlish chuckle out of her, and her friends were too busy talking to each other to notice my blunder.

"You all packed and ready to go?" she asked me. I wasn't prepared for this; our worlds are so different. I never expected her to speak to me, let alone know I'm also attending SoCafo.

Stunned, I managed to relay a delayed response, "Not even close, it's going to be an all-nighter. I just came out for a break to keep this one out of trouble," I said tilting my head toward Dean.

I knew that Dean would retaliate at my using him to promote my own cause. "What? You mean you still have to go buy a set of plastic sheets to accommodate your bedwetting problem, and Sharkey's is on the way," he snapped.

"Oh, you got jokes," I said trying to conceal my embarrassment. Not that I have a bedwetting problem, but this was a deliberately slick, foul, and tactical move. If I deny it, the fact that it was mentioned still lingers, and if I admit it, then what type of self-respecting sane person would that make me? Dean was skilled in the art of dickhead.

I had to think quickly, "Yeah, you lucked out! Plastic sheets and bedpans come standard in UCLA dorms. Let me know what you get in Partying 101," I retorted.

I surprised myself with that one and stifled a laugh. To my surprise, Camille was giggling too, and for a moment her eyes flickered. When my eyes met hers, she stopped, but my chuckle lingered awkwardly.

"Ha ha ha, good one. Guess you'll be majoring in standup comedy," Dean grunted while punching my shoulder, harder than before. This time I returned a scowl instead of the 'ow' and the punch, and Camille pretended not to see the obviously painful display of masculinity.

"Thanks, bro," I smirked in sarcasm. "So, you ready?" I asked Camille, returning attention back to our conversation.

"I've been ready since first semester. I started packing the day I got my acceptance letter. I can't wait to get out of here, oh-my-gosh," she said. Her vulnerability was surprising and candid.

"I hear that. You had a great run though, Miss All-star Tennis Seed *and* Valedictorian. Great speech by the way," I said.

"Thanks. Yeah, high school was great, but I'm ready to start my life, you know?" she asked rhetorically.

But I *do* know. I feel the exact same way. I love Vedado, and Dean, but this is all I know. I am ready for the metaphorical next chapter: one that doesn't involve pulling drunken best friends off of bars, parents' control, or high school Keyboarding Club meetings. I wish I knew what I wanted to do with my life or could see some purpose in it. But there's one thing that I do know, and that's if I stay here then I'll never figure it out.

"Right on," I said casually.

Suddenly Olivia interrupted, "Um, Camille? We gotta go, girl. Shawn just texted and they're waiting for us," she said with a coating of utter boredom.

Ebony, who was chewing her gum loudly and examining her cuticles, managed a hurried, "Yeah Cam, we got-to-go girl. He's rolling with Bernard Watson tonight, from Summit High, and he is fiiiiine!"

"Oh. OK, girl, you stupid," Camille said nonchalantly. "Well Lewis, ahh…why don't you take my number or something? I mean, I'm sure we'll have *some* freshman class together, and I don't know a soul at SoCafo, so it'd be nice to see a familiar face from home. You know until we acclimate or whatever?"

I wasn't prepared for this either, this girl is full of surprises. "Yeah sure," I said, fumbling clumsily to retrieve my phone from my pocket. "Go 'head."

"310," she paused, "865," another pause, "0882."

"Got it," I said confidently.

"Alright, see you soon," she said grinning coyly. "Bye Dean."

Newly frustrated, "Later," Dean mumbled.

Camille turned and walked away. When she was out of earshot Dean began his harangue, "And the award for *Cock Block of the Night* goes to…ladies and gentlemen, it's an upset! It's Lewis Lewis, I mean Loser Loser of Vedado, California!" Dean imitated the audience applause with his hands cupping his mouth. "You douche," he said.

"Dude, what was I supposed to do? Ignore her?"

"Yes! I do it all the time, girls love being ignored," Dean said.

"You're insane," I laughed.

Crossing his eyes, "That's what they tell me," he joked. "You want to go lane surfing?"

"Ah, yeah right. Sharkey won't go too crazy," I said. "Let's get some pizza, I'm starving. Then I gotta get back and finish packing."

"Pizza, perfect. Packing, pathetic," Dean said rolling his eyes.

Chapter 2

I arrived home to find my mom and dad watching the eleven o'clock news in the den, spellbound. My dad didn't even notice me standing there, and my mom spoke to me without turning her attention from the television.

"Hey Lewis, how's Dean?" she asked, her voice void of inflection or emotion.

"Dean is Dean," I replied.

"Oh hey, Lew. You all set to go, champ?" My dad said in the same robotic tone.

"Just about, Dad. What's going on in the world?" I asked, not expecting an answer.

"They're finding missing persons," Mom said.

"Body count up to seventeen now," Dad added.

"Out in Shasta, upstate," Mom finalized.

"Oh. Turn it up," I said, stepping into the den.

Dad flickered the volume button on the remote, not breaking his focus from the attractive reporter.

Victims, both male and female, have been between the ages of 18 and 25. Several of the bodies present multiple bite wounds on the upper neck and face. In more gruesome cases, the deceased suffered extreme blood loss from a horizontal gash in the neck. Local authorities have issued an animal watch and dusk curfew until further notice. This is Vanessa Hargrave reminding you all to stay safe. Reporting live from Shasta, California. Channel 9 News. Thanks, Andrew.

"My word," Mom sighed.

"It's a crazy world. Those poor families," Dad said, "I'm so glad the people I love most are right here where I can hold and kiss 'em," he joked, breaking his television trance and planting a light-hearted peck on my mom's cheek. Dad always jokes when things are serious or emotional. It's some type of coping thing he has to do, but Mom and I are used to it.

"Gross," I said wincing. "Not that I want the kiss, but you'll be losing a loved one tomorrow, Dad."

"Oh, my baby boy, you can't leave me here alone with this lunatic, honey," Mom said, repelling Dad's boyish flirtations with a harmless elbow to his abdomen. "Well, you'd better finish up your packing and get to sleep, you've got quite a day tomorrow, Lew Lew."

"I know Mom, I'm headed up now. Goodnight." P.S. I hate it when she calls me that.

"Goodnight," they harmonized.

"Love you," Mom soloed.

"Love you too, Mom."

"Hey, what about me? Don't make me get up and kiss you, boy!" Dad joked.

"Good God, love you too Dad," I said while hastily backing out of the room.

Skipping every other step, I charged up the stairs to resume packing. Damn, I had forgotten about the wreckage! It looked as if Vedado High School had exploded in my bedroom…I still had some serious work left to do. I took my position in the middle of the floor and began to rifle through the closest items. As I settled into a rhythm of sorting and boxing, my mind began to drift over the events of the last few hours.

Considering that Dean's predictable antics were somewhat humorous at times, I am beginning to tire of always having to clean up his messes. I love Dean, and I know that I'll miss him, but this space may be exactly what our friendship needs. I know it's wrong, but ever since that mortifying scene at Woody Newman's graduation party, I've actually been counting down the days to separation from him.

I'd been looking forward to Woody's party for weeks, I mean everyone had been. Dean, a few other guys, and I even got there early to help Woody set up the food, move furniture around, put out Solo cups, and tap the kegs. True to form, Dean began binge drinking, so by the time the party got going he was three-sheets-to-the-wind. I'm talking W-A-S-T-E-D: spilling beer, knocking into people, groping girls, yelling all loud and crazy, close-talking—just belligerent. Several people had commented to me that he needed to go, but when Woody finally suggested that I take him home and come back, I had no choice.

Dean fought me tooth-and-nail, hollering nonsense about how nobody cuts off Dean Eddleston and how he wasn't even all that drunk. The louder he got, the more people began to stare, and then he yelled that he wasn't going fucking anywhere. *Humiliating* doesn't even begin to define the scene. But bad went to worse when Dean shoved me and yelled to leave him the hell alone. At this point, all eyes were on us.

Woody came to seal the deal, again and told Dean that if he didn't let me take him home, he would have to ask his parents to call his dad to come to pick him up. Dean knew that if Woody's parents, who were allegedly (in case the cops showed up) at a dinner party when really, they were turning a blind eye in the pool house, had to call his father, that his friendship with Woody was as good as over. Begrudgingly, he agreed to go home with me. The embarrassment had subsided by the time I pulled into Dean's driveway, but anger settled in when I discovered that he was vomiting all over himself in the front seat of my mom's minivan! Chunks went everywhere. The floor, on the glove compartment, his shirt…it was disgusting. He hadn't even bothered to try to roll the window down. My yelling his name and putting the window down was futile, he was done. I had to carry his puke-covered, funky, dead weight to the front door, reach into his soiled pocket for the key, and let him inside. Luckily his parents were asleep, so getting him to his room, cleaning him up, and putting him to bed went undetected. But going back to Woody's was a non-possibility. I had to find an open carwash at 12:23 am!

I hadn't confronted Dean about that night because he never remembers anything when he gets like that, so I convinced myself that none of it would matter after I left for SoCafo. So, it was perfect timing that I should run into Camille the last night we were both in town. It's a comforting thought that I will actually know someone sober and responsible on campus, even though we don't *really* know each other that well. I mean, Camille spends her time preparing speeches and winning scholarships, while I'm designated driving for Dean or watching the news with my parents.

If tonight hadn't happened and our paths crossed at SoCafo, I doubt if I'd even speak. Out of shyness or embarrassment, I know I probably would've pretended not to see her. But now, even if I don't call and we happen to bump into each other, I won't have to pretend. *Whatever,* she said she wanted a study partner and didn't know anyone else. But she is Valedictorian, and wouldn't that be like studying down? Besides, I'm pretty sure that Camille Harris will have no problem 'acclimating' to life as a beautiful, smart, and cool freshman in college without me. Damn, I'm zoning!

Realizing how tired I was, my mind refocused on the boxes and luggage in front of me. I was about seventy percent done, which motivated me to continue packing through my exhaustion.

Hmmm, I wonder if Dean is still out or if he got himself home alive. I hope Mr. Sharkey called him a cab and not his dad. Thank goodness there are no bloodthirsty, savage animals stalking around Vedado because Dean would be a sitting duck in some of the incoherent states he gets himself into. Man, that news story was so freaky. And Shasta is such a remote, mountainous town. What type of wild animal tears people's necks open? Maybe a bear? I guess that would explain it…I guess. I hope they figure it out, seventeen dead, that's like a whole soccer team.

Drifting back to packing and fighting sleep, I admitted to myself that I had expired about twenty minutes ago. I had put a pretty good dent in the remaining thirty percent. I'm sure I'll be able to finish what's left tomorrow morning. It's time for me to stare at the back of my eyelids.

I woke up to a fantastic California sun. The rays were casting a triangular beam right through my window onto the floor beside my bed. The warmth felt good on my arms, and the quiet morning was reassuring that the day was going to be awesome. It's finally the day that I've been emotionally counting down to for months, and I still can't believe that it's here. I've been scared of the move, nervous about the possibility of failure, and ambivalent because of all of the conflicting emotions. But today, I'm just excited because today I'm *actually* going to Southern California University! These types of rushes make getting up so much easier than usual.

"Lewis! Wake up, champ! Breakfast is ready, Mom made omelets and pancakes," Dad hollered through my bedroom door.

"Alright, Dad, I'll be down in a minute," I moaned.

"OK. Don't go back to sleep, Lew. You've got a big day ahead of you. The early bird…"

"I'm up," I said groggily while opening the door.

"Alright then. How you feeling?" he asked.

"I'm more excited than nervous, if that's what you mean, Dad."

He nodded, "Well, your mom's a nervous wreck. Take it easy on her, OK?"

"What are you talking about?" I asked.

"You know Lew, pretend you're sick about leaving, you're going to miss her terribly, promise to call every day, and all of that *Mom* stuff," Dad deliberately drew out his words and had this weird, endearing smirk resting on his cheekbones. "This missing person mess has her all wound up with you going away." Now he looked serious, yet I felt like he was still joking.

"Yeah, OK Dad. I'll mush it up, but when Mom's tears start, remember you asked for it," I said jokingly, but totally serious.

"Fair enough, champ. Come on down when you're ready."

He put his hand on my shoulder and ruffled it vigorously. Hell! It was as if I was five again and had won a T-ball game! It's strange how a simple gesture can take you back in time to a place where happiness was defined by something as simple as winning or losing a game. And presently, I'll be on my way to college in a matter of hours.

Mustering a smile, I responded, "OK. I'll be right down after I throw some water on my face."

"OK, hustle. After we eat, Mom and I have a surprise for you, and then I've got to head to the office," he said with a wink.

The words landed on my ears and were processed through my brain like a nuclear bomb detonation. Shocked and alarmed, "The office!" I shriek uncontrollably and had it been anyone but my father present, I would've been completely embarrassed by the soprano range of it. Restoring my voice to normal, "But I thought you and Mom were gonna help move me to SoCafo," I pleaded.

Now I know that my dad has always been a workaholic architect, but this was just fucking negligent. He scoffed and shrugged, "I know it champ, but we're working on the new Emerson building, and the clients have moved the deadline forward. You don't understand this, Lewis, but there are a lot of investors on this project, and I've got a lot riding on it. This is my career, but we can talk about it more over breakfast."

"Dad!" I said, annoyed.

Sternly, he replied to my angst, "Just come downstairs, we'll discuss it with Mom too."

"Alright," I said obediently.

Three hours in a car with a sobbing and hysterical Mom playing Paul Simon and warning of impending danger... Great! It looks like I'll be mushing it up and dealing with the tears too. What a mess. Well, I might as well hurry downstairs so that I can get this party started because the sooner it begins, the sooner it can end. My mother is going to be totally embarrassing with her bon voyage hysterics, not to mention no help at all carrying boxes. How could Dad go to work today? And so much for the sun being a harbinger of an awesome day, it might as well be raining.

By the time I got downstairs, my parents were already eating. Mom looked up and said, "Good morning Mr. SoCafo freshman," with a warm smile. "Did you sleep well?"

"Yeah Mom, now all I need is some sustenance as only you can provide," I said while kissing her cheek. The mush had begun.

"Aww, thank you, honey. Now eat up, your father and I have a surprise for you," she said.

"Well, Dad's already dropped the first one on me," I said, cutting my eyes at him.

"Now don't go blame your father, his job is the reason your room and board are paid for young man," she admonished.

"Yeah, thanks, Dad," I said dully.

I sat down and took a long and continuous gulp of orange juice. My eyes shut by reflex, and I sighed, "Ahhhh." Savagely, I began to cut into my omelet and shovel it into my mouth. The last thing I had eaten was a slice of pizza with Dean, and I was hungrier than I thought. The eggs felt flakey and cushioned my cheeks as I chewed ravenously.

"Slow down, son," Dad requested.

"Why? I can't wait to see this *other* surprise you have for me," I said sarcastically while pouring a hearty amount of syrup over my perfectly bronzed pancakes. My parents glanced at one another out of the corners of their eyes and grinned mischievously. They were up to something. Their lack of consideration for the recent blow storm that Dad couldn't help me move in *and* that I was dealing with "first-day" nerves caused me to explode.

Irritated, I barked, "Is this what you two do, sit around and plot how to make my life miserable? Well, congratulations, I'm miserable!" I shoveled a mouthful of the fluffy and delicious pancake into my mouth and then chewed while trying to display the evilest eyes I could muster.

"Oh, come on now, Lew. It's not my fault. You'll understand deadlines a little bit better in about three weeks," Dad recycled his insult from earlier, and squeezed it out effortlessly.

"Yeah. Whatever," I managed to say from behind a mouthful of pancake. "I mean, what kind of father doesn't take his only son to college to help him move in? Who'd have known I've been living under the same roof as *Father of the Year* my entire life?" I said sarcastically. And so much for me mushing it up too, I thought. If he broke his promise to drive me to school, why should I keep mine? I'll just consider this karma.

"Lewis, calm down," Mom said firmly, "You're being fresh, and it's quite unbecoming of a college freshman."

Twirling my fork into the plate, "Well isn't that ironic," I grumbled.

I could feel my mom's eyes on me, "Cliff, I can't take it anymore. Look at our baby, he's so upset. Can we show him now?" she asked looking at Dad with a pursed lip.

"Alright Lewis, put your fork down and come with us," Dad demanded, yet his voice was non-threatening.

I was annoyed, but whatever this surprise was had suddenly become intriguing. We never interrupted meals. I could feel those three wrinkles that appear on my forehead when I'm confused pushing my eyebrows together. My fork unintentionally fell from my hand; it was almost as if I forgot I was even holding it. Cautiously, I stood up and followed my parents out of the kitchen into the foyer. We were headed toward the front door, so clearly they have been hiding whatever this surprise is outside. Knowing them, they have probably spray painted the minivan with all sorts of embarrassing graffiti to celebrate my arrival on campus with my mother! This just might turn out to be the shittiest day of my life.

My mom abruptly stopped and allowed me to pass her. "Mom, what the heck is going on?" I asked.

"You'll see precious," she said in a shrilly and faux comforting voice.

She stood still, waiting beside the front door, refusing to budge until I passed her. Once I did, she put her hands over my eyes. Dad grabbed my hands and ushered me through the door, and I could sense from the decline under my flip-flops that we were heading down the driveway.

"Now, Cliff?" Mom asked Dad.

"Hmmmmmm. Now, Patricia!" Dad boomed.

My mother's fingers lifted from my face, and I opened my eyes. Parked in front of me was a brand new, champagne colored, Jeep Grand Cherokee 4x4, with a bright and gaudy red bow on the roof. I was in a state of temporary shock, my knees buckled, and my hands began to shake uncontrollably.

I hollered, "Oh My God! An SUV! Seriously! It's mine?"

"Yes!" my parents shouted in unison.

"Congratulations, we are so proud of you Lew Lew," Mom said.

Shocked, I stammered, "But…I, but…it's NEW!"

"Well, so is our only kid leaving for college, champ," Dad added.

"Well hop in, let's see how you look in it," Mom said pulling her camera out of her pocket.

"Oh my God, Ooooooh my God. Dean is gonna shit! Ooo, sorry Mom," I said. She smiled and tilted her head in understanding admonishment.

My dad handed me the key fob and said, "We'll go on and get in," with a pleasing smile.

I pulled open the driver-side door and took in the overwhelming new-car-scent. The blemish-free surface of the leather compelled me to delicately slide myself into the driver's seat as if my weight would ruin it forever. My skin immediately sunk into the soft and warm, pristine leather.

"*Leather*," I belted.

"Yep," Dad answered.

I traced the wood grain of the center console and took notice of the GPS navigation screen, which was covered in a protective piece of plastic.

"Navigation," I gasped.

"Now you can always find your way home," Mom joked.

Pressing open the sunroof, I decided not to be shocked any further, as this was obviously the fully loaded option.

"You don't even have to put the key fob in the ignition, just push the *start* button and viola!" Dad explained.

I followed his instructions. The clean, virgin engine reverberated a robust roar. The console lit up all of its digital glory, and I sat back with an ear-to-ear grin. I began my mental checklist of awesomeness: iPod docking station, deluxe sound system, digital everything, dual climate control, four-wheel drive, cruise control, six-disc changer, Bluetooth capability, On Star, and it was all brand spanking new, *and* entirely mine. This is Lewis Emmanuel Lewis's ride! For the first time in my life, I was in love with my name and wouldn't want to have any other name on earth. The sun's beckoning of an awesome day had been fulfilled.

I pushed the *start/stop* button, silencing the engine, and sighed again. Stepping out of the SUV, I nearly lost one of my flip-flops...and with the door ajar, I threw myself (open armed) at my parents—my right arm around my dad's shoulder and my left arm around my mom's. Suddenly, uncontrollably, and without expectation, I began to cry. This burst of spontaneous sentiment sent my mom into an emotional wreckage of her own.

Wailing, "We are going to miss you so much, Lewis!" she said.

"Oh, come on now you two," Dad begged.

Stifling my emotion, "Thank you, I love you," I whispered.

"We love you too, champ," Dad said, "Now get your butt upstairs and get ready to go! Let me know when you're ready, and I'll help you bring down some boxes before I go into work. I've only got a few minutes, so make it quick, Lew."

"Alright Dad," I responded and ran inside letting out a wild yell, "YES! Jeep Grand Cherokee, WOOOO!"

I turned back to give my parents one more 'thank you,' but they weren't paying any attention to me. They were lost in each other, just standing there, frozen in their weird *Mom and Dad* embrace. My 'thank you' would've fallen on deaf ears or prematurely unfrozen them, so I just went inside, smiling gleefully.

The house appeared to be full of sunlight now. I sat down at the table and tried to finish my breakfast, realizing that I was too overjoyed and no longer hungry. Looking down at the plate that my mom had put so much love and care into preparing for me, I decided to eat as much as I could anyhow. I chewed each bite melodically, fantasizing about the reception I would have arriving on SoCafo's campus in my undeniably hot ride. I looked down at a suddenly empty plate, and my stomach confirmed that I was full. The front door creaked open, and I could hear my parents talking, speculating how shocked and happy I was. They always do that on Christmas morning, and this was by far nicer than any gift I had ever received. I listened to them coo-hoo down memory lane before the present reality uppercut me!

"Shit! I'm going to college today!" I said aloud.

I sprang from the table, carried my plate to the sink, and rinsed it out. "Don't worry about that, Lew Lew, I'll get it. Go on upstairs and get yourself ready to go. You've got a long drive ahead of you in your new car," Mom said, ignoring having witnessed my 'come to Jesus moment.'

"Wait a minute, so *you're* not coming with me either?" I asked, suddenly realizing the jeep and I were going alone.

"How would I get back, Lewis? No, we'll say our goodbyes here and you'll call us as soon as you get settled," Mom answered sounding more confident in her emotional grip of my leaving home.

In agreement, "Right. OK, well I need to shower and get going then," I answered.

Concerned, "I mean, unless you *want* me to come, and Dad can drive out and pick me up after work later tonight," Mom replied. I looked behind her at my dad who was profusely shaking his head as she went on, "Then we can hang out, I can set up your dorm room, and meet your hall mates, and…"

The thought of my new hall mates and prospective friends witnessing my mother fluffing my pillows and crying every other minute was enough for me to interrupt her fantasy, "Oh no, Mom, that's OK. You don't have to do that. It's too much of an inconvenience for you and Dad. I'll stick with plan A."

Dad's shoulders dropped in relief, "I'll pack the car while you're showering then," he said.

Feeling like the brand-new SUV was service enough, "You don't have to do that Dad, you're already running late," I said.

"Nonsense, go on upstairs and get ready. I'll tell Oliver and Associates I had to see my son off to college this morning," he said proudly.

Shocked at his rare and rebellious behavior, "Well OK Dad!" I said, making an overly dramatic attempt to appear hurried.

Skipping every other step, I rushed back to my room. Too excited to monitor my own strength, I accidentally slammed the door and stumbled over boxes to the window so that I could get another look at *my* brand-new jeep in the driveway. My parents had removed the bow. Closing the curtain that had let so much sun into my morning, I grinned boyishly though I'm not sure why. I'm guessing that this is what it feels like to be completely thankful.

My shower was superfluous. Knowing that I would be moving boxes in the hot California sun made thorough bathing seem futile. When I walked out of my bathroom, I noticed that my room was box free, save the ones labeled *attic*; Dad had packed everything! I threw on a pair of cargo shorts, a T-shirt, and my flip-flops. After grabbing my wallet and cell phone, I gave my room one last glance in nostalgic recognition of the years spent enclosed by its walls. I'll be sharing four walls with a total stranger soon. I've never had to share anything in my life. God, I pray he's sane and cool.

I shut the door behind me, realizing that I wouldn't reopen it until early winter. Mom and Dad were waiting for me at the foot of the stairs, cuddling and bracing themselves for our last goodbye. Descending the steps, my brain took a mental photo of the people that had given me all the comforts I could ever want or need. They were excellent parents, despite my frustration with them at times.

Exhaling, "I guess this is it," I said.

"I can't believe he's really going to college, Cliff," Mom began to sob.

"Yeah, and taking my salary with him," Dad joked as he tends to do in emotional climates.

I hugged my mom and felt her clenching vivacity not wanting to let go, "Mom, I'll be back, and I'll call as much as possible. I promise," I said.

"Promise," she begged while balling dramatically.

"Promise," I reassured her, melodramatically.

Breaking us up, "Alright champ, give your old man a hug why don't cha?" Dad said. I hugged him and he squeezed so tightly that I gasped.

"Love you Dad," I croaked.

"Love you too, champ," he said solemnly.

Waiting for Dad to release his emotional clutch, I patted his back awkwardly. After he did, I headed toward the front door. It felt strange leaving them. I began to imagine what their life together was like before me and how different it would be once I was gone. I guess to them they aren't just parents because they were once my age and in love. Now they are twice my age and in life. Well maybe they are a bit older than twice my age, but that just places them further into life's grasp. They'll have to completely redefine who they are in an empty nest. That's got to feel peculiar. Now I do kind of wish that I had a younger sibling, so I didn't have to worry about them as much. But I'll make peace with that wish because my younger sibling may have financially inhibited me from being gifted with my devastatingly nice ride.

Opening the door to the jeep, I saw that in my excitement I had left the key fob in the cupholder. I have to be sure *not* to do that again. I got in and pushed the engine-start button. This was it—I'm officially beginning my collegiate life. Looking through the window, my parents were like a new picture frame stock photograph: side-by-side in an emotional trance, holding one another lovingly. I searched the door for one of many little gadgets that would let the window down so that I could say my final goodbye. There was a slight moment of panic before I found the correct switch amongst the sea of dials on the door panel. If I left my parents trapped in that pose for another minute, I may burst into tears again too.

I pressed the little lever aligned with the driver's seat, and the window went all the way down automatically, sending another surge of *my new car* enthrallment through my veins.

"So, this is it, I'm off," I said, placing my right hand on the top of the steering wheel.

"You have your phone and wallet?" Mom asked.

"Yep," I said, anxious to get going before another display of sentiment ensued.

"Here, take this," Dad said pulling his wallet out of his back pocket. He fumbled through crisp folds before handing me several twenty-dollar-bills, "for gas."

"Thanks, Dad. I'll call you guys once I'm all settled in," I said putting the gear shifter into reverse.

"You'd better," Mom said.

"Bye! Love you," I yelled while rolling backward slowly.

"Bye, love you," they chimed in unison.

I backed out of the driveway and shifted into the drive position and watched my parents step into the space the jeep previously occupied. They were still embracing, and I could see my mom's tearstained face in the rearview mirror. Dad looked at peace and confidently strong. My mom raised her left arm, and my dad raised his right, and they both began to wave gracefully. I raised my hand to the rearview mirror and returned the loving wave goodbye. Stepping on the accelerator, unfamiliar with the horsepower of my chariot, I unintentionally sped down the quiet suburban street that I knew so well. As soon as I turned right out of my complex, I used my brand-new Bluetooth to call Dean.

He was groggy and disturbed, "Emm…hey. What's up?"

Excited and energetic, I hollered, "DUDE!"

"Awe man, not so loud," Dean begged.

Apologetically, "My bad, man. Are you still asleep?"

"I was," he responded annoyed.

"Normally I wouldn't call you this early, however being that I am on my way to college in my brand-new Jeep Grand Cherokee, I figured I'd make an exception," I boasted.

"No way!" Dean said suddenly excited.

"Yes way, man! My parents surprised me with it this morning before I left. Dude, fully loaded, four-wheel-drive, the works," I bragged.

"Damn, Lewis. That's awesome! Looks like you won't be sporting Disgrace On Wheels anymore!"

I laughed, "Nope!"

"Well stop by and take me for a ride," he asked.

"Awe man, can't. I've got to check in on campus by noon, get the keys to my dorm, ID, and all that. I'm already running late," I said.

"Boooooo," Dean teased. "That's cool. I'm not ready to get up anyway. Well, don't junk it up too badly before Thanksgiving Break. And no chicks in shotgun before me," he requested.

I laughed, "Alright man, go back to sleep. I'll call you when I'm there," I said.

"Alright brother. And hey, drive safely idiot," Dean hung up before I could cut back, and a resonating static buzzed through the speakers.

In an attempt to kill the white noise, I began to search for the radio controls. There were so many buttons, switches, and dials, that it took longer than I expected (I should definitely read the owner's manual before I get behind the wheel again). After locating the power button, I delicately pressed it and placed my phone into the port. Scrolling through my playlist, I recklessly swerved off of the road for a second before regaining control. Damn, I am an idiot. I probably should direct more of my attention to driving, but I need some good road-trip music. Something with energy and *badly sing along really loudly* lyrics. I continued to scroll through the artists, glancing back at the road every millisecond, until Lenny Kravitz. Who could go wrong with Lenny Kravitz?

"Are You Gonna Go My Way" blasted through the crisp, new speakers. I sank into the leather seat, grinning again at the sheer awesomeness of my new SUV. My new chapter was beginning and listening to Lenny's words, I couldn't help but think that *life* was gonna go my way.

Chapter 3

SoCafo's campus was immense. If it weren't for this GPS, the chances of me finding the North Quad check-in location before sundown would have been extremely questionable. Thankfully, the robotic female voice led me right up to the designated unloading area. I parked and applied the hazard lights, grabbed my key fob, and braced myself for my next task of checking in. North campus was a mass of chaos. Students, parents, campus security, and upper-class student aides were bustling to ensure their endeavors were all accomplished with ease. I got out of the jeep, intending to open the hatch to the cargo area, but I was temporarily derailed. The air was unfamiliarly fresh, and the sounds of the bustling were mesmerizing. The campus was so clean and green, and the architecture seemed to blend together like a painting. The buildings were all forged from the same stone and towering above me. I pivoted 360 degrees beside the truck before realizing that I was directly in the way of a father and son hauling the heavy looking pieces of a wooden loft bed into a dormitory hall.

"Watch out!" The son announced urgently.

More politely, "Coming through son," the father warned.

Throwing myself against the side of the jeep, "Excuse me. My bad," I said. "You need some help?"

"Nah, we got it. Thanks though," the son answered, beads of sweat dripping from his forehead.

I carefully stepped toward the rear cargo hatch to retrieve the check-in instructions from my satchel. My dad had packed meticulously. In the structured way of an architect, every box was symmetrically aligned and had a similarly sized piece of luggage on top; the larger boxes were closest to the back door, and the smaller ones were packed up against the rear seats. I smiled, thinking about the care that Dad had put into making sure my move went as smoothly as possible in his absence. My satchel was tucked down into a space created by the gap between the hatch door and a column of boxes. Effortlessly, I removed it and headed into the sea of chaos.

This frantic scene of scattered movement had created a cacophony of sound: people inquiring directions, others giving them, students meeting one another and sharing their background stories, a security warning against illegal parking zones and where to find legal alternatives. I followed the moving mass toward an unknown destination, hoping that I would end up somewhere near the check-in location. This was probably exactly what cattle being herded felt like. The crowd was moving slower than my excitement to finally be on campus was comfortable with, so I attempted to push my way through. It was pointless because the crowd just returned my impatience by pushing back. I have to say that after this clusterfuck, I definitely have a newfound appreciation for ants.

After the herd had migrated about twenty-five steps, I began to see signs with arrows directing people to check-in sites, dorms, food, and restrooms. The check-in tables were in a grassy courtyard between two lofty dorm buildings and were set up by last name: letters A-G, H-M, N-S, and T-Z. Behind each table there were two campus resident advisors, one male and one female, all seemingly bubbly and all conventionally attractive. I skimmed the posters duck-taped to the ends of the tables for where the L's would be.

H, I, J, K, *L(ewis)*…H-M, the middle table, and of course the longest line. To secure my place in the somewhat lengthy line, I jogged around the crowd. I felt a bit awkward standing there alone. Most of the other incoming students were with their parents, siblings, or classmates. I was pleasantly surprised when an eager, yet cool looking guy began to make small talk with me on the line.

"Hey man, making the move solo, huh?" he asked while observing my *Southern California University Check-in Instructions* folder gripped tightly in my hand.

I glanced down at the folder myself as if I didn't know I had been carrying it for the past fifteen minutes, "Oh yeah," I said nonchalantly.

He nodded, "Me too. I'm Brant," he extended a friendly hand, "Brant Manderson."

"Nice to meet you," I shook his hand firmly, "I'm Lewis…uh…Lewis," I said.

First and last name introductions are always the worst. It usually takes repeating myself before people finally understand that my first and last names are Lewis. And then once they get that, they start asking questions, in which case I'm forced to explain the absurdity of my parents in naming me. Brant Manderson felt compelled to disclose his first and last names, so my wager is questions are impending.

"Nice to meet you too, man. So, *Lewis Lewis,* that's got to be a conversation starter," he said.

I scoffed, "Yeah. How did you know my last name was Lewis?" and how did I end up the one asking the questions?

"You told me," he said.

"Yeah, but people usually don't get it," I admitted.

"Well, you *were* hesitant to say Lewis the second time, but being that you *are* in the H-M line, I figured Lewis was your last name and you were just…" he stopped himself.

"Embarrassed?" I finished.

"Yeeaaah…Awk-waaaaard," he laughed. "Lewis *squared*," he joked, "Hey, I get it. I have an embarrassing name too, bro."

"Brant Manderson? What's so embarrassing about that?" I asked

In amazement and open-mouthed he whispered, "Brant Manderson? Seriously? My initials are B.M. dude."

Genuinely confused I shrugged, "Yeah, so?"

He looked more embarrassed than annoyed (or some combination of both) and whispered again, "*Bowel Movement.*"

Louder than I anticipated, I began to laugh. I was partially surprised that I didn't piece that together myself and majorly entertained at Brant's whole-hearted mortification of his initials.

"OK, OK. Get it out now, but keep it down," he urged dismally.

Regaining my composure, I asked, "So where're you from *number two*?"

Feigning laughter, he responded, "Haha…Crockett, north of San Fran. You?"

"Vedado, south of Hell," I grinned jokingly, and he cracked an earnest smile.

Brant was a tall and muscular guy, probably from playing football for his high school. He had a slight California surfer's drawl and disposition, but not in a dim-witted way. His hair was scruffy and dark, dark brown, almost black if not for the highlighting agents of the California sun, and his eyes were a lazily contrasting grey. He was a couple of inches taller than me, which would put him at 6'2"; however, he appeared much more massive due to his ridiculously broad shoulders and chest. I knew this guy was going to be a serious drinker and diehard fraternity pledge of any cheesy Greek order that would have him.

The line had moved considerably, so I tried to ask questions that could be answered quickly. "So, what's your major?"

"Engineering," he said with a tinge of disappointment. His face and shoulders shrunk slightly from what I assumed was disdain for engineers.

"What's wrong with engineering?" I asked, genuinely concerned.

"Well, it's not my dad's choice of major for me if that's what you mean. I really do *want* to be an engineer, it's that all the damn engineering courses are at night, and that puts a major curtail on my social life…aka partying," he said.

"*All* of the classes?" I asked in disbelief.

"Every lab, lecture, and elective. It's been like that since the inception of the program. No classes on Fridays and all classes at night," he said defeated.

"Hey, that's awesome!" I said.

"It is?" Brant's face was twisted with puzzled bemusement.

"Sure. See, you'll get out of class late but certainly not after all the parties have winded down. In fact, they'll be at their peak. So, after your classes, you can let yourself have it the rest of the night and then sleep *all day long*. Then come Thursday night, you can be a total animal since you won't see the inside of an academic building again until Monday night!" I explained.

Pleased and nodding, he said, "Yo, you are absolutely right! I can't believe I hadn't thought of that. Lewis Squared, you're a fucking genius…even though you laughed at my name."

Bowing my head, "Glad I could be of some service to you, Number Two," I joked.

"Next in line please," the bubbly female resident assistant summoned me out of the conversation. "Hi and welcome to SoCafo," she beamed ecstatically. I could tell that she was forcing her enthusiasm, but the effect made me feel welcomed anyhow.

Turning my attention from Brant, I managed a much less enthusiastic, "Thanks."

Brant nudged me in the back with his elbow, so I turned around. Brant's forehead was wavy, and his lips were spread across his face. His eyes were ping-ponging back and forth from me to the resident welcoming girl. So, I guess this is his supposedly discreet way of saying, 'she's hot dude.' Teetering my head from side-to-side, I cracked a smile to insinuate that she was just alright. She wasn't that bad at all, but I'm not into the bright and bubbly type. In my limited yet impressionable experience, I've learned that the bubble wrapping conceals so much that when the wrath finally is triggered and does escape, it's like releasing a caged dragon. When I turned back around, I knew for sure that she had caught the entire exchange by her obvious attempt to pretend like she hadn't. So, I guess after I get checked in, I'll stick around to see how Brant's interaction with her works out/or not.

Clearing her throat, "Em Emmm…it's a beautiful day on campus today, isn't it?" She smiled. I nodded. "Hi, I'm Stephanie Masters, I'm one of two resident assistants at Franklin Hall," she said. Clearly, this introduction was rehearsed. Even the extension of her index finger toward Franklin Hall seemed like a directional gesture mandated by the powers that be. "If I could have your name, I'd be happy to get you the keys to your new home," she smiled so hard I became intrigued by how long she could keep up this charade.

"I'm Lewis *Lewis.*" I noticed that she noticed the identical names, but she didn't let it slow her down. She nodded and managed a 'thanks' and began to fumble through sealed, manila envelopes that had been separated by the last name.

Finding my envelope almost immediately, she handed it to me with purpose, "Here you are Mr. Lewis. You'll be staying in 1004 Ponce West. Your resident advisor is *this* handsome gentleman to my right, Mr. Jonathan Greene."

Jonathan Greene was a slim and waspy guy, so it was obvious that her compliment was playful flattery. He took it as it was intended and while multitasking, Jonathan Greene managed a joking southern drawl, "Why thank'ya Ma'am," a wink at Stephanie Masters, a friendly smile at me, and a sealed envelope passing to an eager and homely blonde standing in front of him. Yooo, these people are serious!

Stephanie continued with her rehearsed, informative sermon, "There's a mandatory meet-and-greet in Ponce Hall's recreation room tomorrow night where you'll get to go over our campus-living guidelines, which you received in your orientation packet." She motioned with her head at my check-in folder. "Once you have unpacked and settled in, you're going to need to go to the student center, Bell Hall, and get your photo taken for your student passport. This is very important because…"

I had to interrupt her, "I'm sorry, what's with the names of all these buildings? Um, Ponce…Bell?"

Stephanie Masters leaned carefully over the table as if she were about to divulge the secret ingredient to a recipe that had been in her family for years and whispered, "We usually make the Freshmen figure it out on their own, but in your case, you can figure it out with your little friend." She glanced at Brant and then flashed a superiorly smug lip pursing before belting, "Next in line please!"

Much to his disappointment and probably my fault, Brant had been called by Jonathan Greene and was in the introductory phase of his check-in process. I decided to step off the line and wait. I tore open my envelope and inside, there were many papers and two keys—a large bronze one and a smaller silver one. I pulled out the papers first and skimmed through them in search of the information that seemed most important. I found a paper with the familiar Southern California University letterhead on it and began to read.

Welcome to Southern California University. We are thrilled to have you and know that this year will be an exciting new experience for you both academically and socially. Enclosed you will find the key to your dorm room and mailbox for 1004 Ponce De Leon Hall West. You have a doubles suite and have been assigned a roommate based on the interests you submitted on your on-campus housing application.

After move-in, it is imperative that you go to Alexander Graham Bell Hall today to have your picture taken for your student identification passport. This card will be your access to activities, sporting events, courses, dining halls, residential buildings, etc. The university is not checking passports today, but beginning tomorrow you will be required to scan this card.

Please plan tomorrow evening around a mandatory meet-and-greet for your residential hall that will begin promptly at 7:30 pm. This will give you the opportunity to meet your neighbors and ask any further questions regarding your check-in and residential rules.
Welcome again,
Jonathan Green-CRA (Chief Resident Advisor)

Slipping the letter back into the envelope, I noticed a colorful pamphlet on waxed cardstock, the campus map and directory. SoCafo looked too overwhelming to study the map, so I just mentally noted that Alexander Graham Bell Hall was almost in the center of the campus, and Ponce De Leon Hall, the northern quadrant. Determined to figure out the secret behind the building names, I began to read over the key's building list: Eli Whitney Hall, Benjamin Thompson Dining Hall, Wright Hall, Benjamin Franklin Hall… I get it, I get it, I get it…all the buildings are named after someone who discovered or invented something. I looked at some of the other names of buildings on the map: Richter Hall, Banneker Hall, oh wow—Christopher Columbus Hall, now that's shameless.

Checking to see where Brant was in the check-in process, I looked up. He was receiving his envelope and shaking hands with Jonathan, who had no doubt introduced him to Stephanie as *this beautiful girl to my left*. Brant's height allowed him to locate me quickly over the crowd, so he gave an acknowledging wave and headed my way. In addition to the map, there were so many other papers that I hadn't had the opportunity to read, so I promised myself that I'd look at them later and tucked everything neatly back inside the envelope.

"So what dorm are you in?" I asked.

"3006 Franklin Hall East," he said, "you?"

"1004 Ponce West. That guy that checked you in is my RA," I said.

"That's cool. Your girl is mine, and in more ways than one: resident advisor and resident ass!" he said.

His comment reminded me of something sexually crass that Dean would say. I don't know why, but I really didn't like it. It made me think that I wouldn't appreciate someone saying that about my hypothetical little sister, and definitely would be infuriated by someone saying that about my *very real* mother. But despite this ping, I laughed anyhow, shaking my head the same way I do with Dean. And yeah, I am slightly ashamed by my faux-enjoyment of Brant's womanizing banter. Due to this odd comparison to Dean, and my desire for a fresh start, I felt like befriending Brant could be a slight conflict of interest. But he is the first and only person that I've met, and even though I may not share his taste or view on girls, he still seems pretty cool.

"Lewis, check out that piece in the line," Brant said as we walked away from the crowd. I looked in the direction he was pointing and saw Camille gripping her check-in folder against her chest.

"Dude, I know her," I said, trying not to sound protective. "She's the valedictorian of my graduating class."

"Smart *and* gorgeous...Niiiice. Let's go talk to her," Brant suggested.

"What? No fucking way. Why?" I protested. I didn't want him preying on or anywhere near Camille.

"She's all alone and has to wait in this line by herself, poor girl. Come on," he said in a false, compassionate tone. Open-mouthed, I stared at Brant Manderson, thinking that his personality was an exact replica of Dean Eddleston Junior. As much as I hate to admit it, like Dean, Brant had a point, *and* he was right. Camille was alone in line; it was the right thing to do. Also, I promised myself that when this very moment occurred, I wouldn't ignore her.

"OK, OK!" I agreed and excused myself through the line of freshmen. I could feel the harsh eyeballs of people wondering if I was trying to cut them in line, so I made my unsealed *check(ed)-in* envelope as visible as possible.

"Camille, hey," I said when Brant and I were a few steps away.

"Lewis, oh-my-gosh! Hey! How are you?" she asked.

"I'm great, you?" I said.

"I'm alright, trying to get checked in. My mom couldn't find a parking space, so she's waiting with the car. It's crazy out here," Camille said.

"Oh, I know. It's absolutely nuts. I just got checked in, thank God. The line does go by fast though."

"Hey, I'm Brant," he interrupted.

"Oh Camille, this is Brant. Brant…Camille," I said.

I moved slightly to my left to allow room for Brant to step in and form a small, triangular conversation space. Brant extended his hand while stepping forward.

"Hi, I'm Camille," she took Brant's hand underneath hers and gripped it femininely while giving it two firm shakes. She was smiling kindly, and her eyes were jumping with excitement.

"Hey Camille, nice to meet you," Brant said making uninterrupted eye contact before looking at me. "So, you two went to high school together?"

"Yep," Camille said, also looking at me to continue the conversation.

"Yeah, VHS Phantoms. Go! Fight! Win!" I pantomimed a masked ghoul playing a sinister air-organ. My goofiness was successful in its purpose to lighten the air because both Camille and Brant chuckled. "So you must be living in the North Quad," I asked immediately realizing that of course, she was living in the North Quad if she was in line to check in here, at the North Quad check-in site, and of course she'd be in the H-M line, her last name being Harris.

She nodded while biting her bottom lip and raising a brow. "Yeah, I'm hoping to be in Franklin, it's supposed to be the newest and nicest dorm."

"Oh really? I lucked out then, I'm in Franklin," Brant said.

"That's awesome. I hope I luck out too," she said looking perplexed. "You know, I never quite understood that saying, *lucked out*," she admitted, curling her index and middle fingers on both hands. "It sounds like, like your luck actually ran out, right? Shouldn't it be *lucked in*?"

"I see your point," Brant said nodding in agreement. "Because we say, 'you're in luck' or 'you're out of luck,' right? It doesn't make any sense that you'd luck out if you actually get lucky. Kind of like it doesn't make sense that we park in the driveway and drive on the parkway."

Camille nodded and smiled in agreement, "Yes!" she said enthusiastically, "it's totally oxymoronic."

"Hold on though," I said in rebuttal. "I think it could mean that you've gotten *so* lucky that you've absolutely run *out* of all the luck you could possibly get like you couldn't have gotten *any* luckier."

Camille and Brant looked at each other and then back at me, "Naaaaah," they said shaking their heads.

"I'm just playing devil's advocate."

"Yeah, well nobody likes the devil," Brant joked.

"No, but I can kind of see your point, Lewis. But that argument is definitely a stretch," Camille said.

Putting my hands up, "Alright, alright, I tried," I said smiling.

"That you did," Camille said sarcastically. "So, where did you luck *into* staying?"

Brant laughed out loud acknowledging Camille's subtle joke.

"Hahaaa, funny," I said, "I lucked *out*. Unfortunately, I didn't get Franklin. I'm in Ponce."

"Oh, OK," Camille nodded.

Suddenly, Jonathan Green interrupted our conversation. "Next in line please!"

We had conversed our way to the front of the line, and it was time for Camille to receive her check-in spiel and sealed envelope.

"Well, that's me. I guess I'll see you guys around campus then?" Camille proposed.

"OK, yeah, for sure. Good luck," I said with a wave.

"It was nice to meet you, Camille," Brant said.

"Nice to meet you too, Brant. Bye Lewis," she said waving back.

We walked away, but as soon as we were out of Camille's range, Brant began his accolades. "Dude, she is gorgeous! And cool, *and* funny."

"Yeah, she is," I said, trying to sound neutrally affable.

"We've definitely got to get up with her sometime."

"For sure," I said feeling another surge of protectiveness.

Sooooooo, it's time for me to admit to myself that I kind of like Camille for some crazy-ass reason. I suppose it's that inexplicable and self-destructive reason that guys *always* like girls who are out of their league. But more importantly, I had just made an empty promise to Brant that we'd hang out with her. If anyone is going to hang out with Camille, it will definitely be me. But it also wouldn't be too bad chilling with Brant, Camille free.

"Hey, let me get your number. I'll call you after I get settled. Maybe we can go to the student center to get our passports and stuff," I offered.

"Yeah, man! It's 510," he paused, "766…0208…you got it?"

"Yep. I'll call you in a few hours then," I said, typing *Number Two* into the contact field.

I turned the phone around to show Brant what I saved his name as, "Dick," he laughed, "talk to you later man."

"Alright Brant, talk to you later," I said.

Brant walked toward Franklin, which was directly across the courtyard from Ponce, and I headed back to the jeep. The excitement of the morning quickly wore off when I remembered that I had an SUV, packed to the max with cardboard boxes that I had to unpack alone. I silently cursed my dad for not being here because it would take me several trips to unload all that shit by myself. I slowly approached the jeep dreading the next few hours of my life and hoping that the manual labor would be over soon.

Chapter 4

1004 Ponce De Leon West was an approximately 375 square foot space enclosed by four cinderblock walls. On the wall across from the entrance, there was a decently sized window that divided the room in half. Each side was a mirror image of the other: cedar closet, cedar desk and chair, and cedar shelving units above the desk, obviously intended for books. Directly beside the window were iron twin beds with cedar storage trunks at each foot. To the right of the door was a small iron entertainment unit, and to the left was a sink atop a cedar storage cabinet. It's pretty cool that the dorm had a sink and mirror because this would allow me to achieve the shaving portion of an SSS without having to leave the room! Above the mirror, there was a small rectangular light fixture with a chain hanging from the center. With the exception of the window, this was the only other source of light in the room. And the floor, a hideous, taupe tile splotched with black specks that gave off the appearance of splattered paint.

My roommate hadn't yet arrived, so I had the luxury of choosing which side of the room I wanted. I settled on the side that the sink was on, figuring the fewer steps I had to take in the morning to brush my teeth, the better. After strenuously working to get the room set up, I stood with my back against the door admiring my handy work. The bed was made up with a horrific green comforter that my mom had purchased from Bed Bath and Beyond. I didn't have the heart to tell her it was hideous when she gifted it to me, so there it was staring me in the face. All of my clothes were hung or folded in the closet, and my toiletries were under the sink to one side of the storage cabinet. My blue-shag rug was in the center of the room clashing horribly with the green comforter set. I set my laptop up on the desk and made the overhead shelf the printer's new home. The stereo and TV were strategically placed on the wobbly, iron entertainment stand. Positioning the television in the corner was genius because it would allow my future roommate and me to *both* be able to watch TV from bed. So, four hours later, I had managed to unload the jeep, unpack all my clothes, break down the boxes, and get my side of the room set up.

Inviting the Southern California sunlight and air into the room, I opened the window. I could hear the cars and people still in full force despite the mid-afternoon time. I wondered if Jonathan Green or Stephanie Masters had become derelict in their enthusiasm from hours of repeat benedictions.

I found myself peering vapidly into the mirror. My hair was a jostled mass of dirty blond that appeared as if it hadn't been brushed in days. I didn't look tired though; my honey-brown eyes were alert and bright in the sun reflecting off of the mirror. My skin looked slightly sun-baked from being outside moving boxes too, but it rarely gives me any problems other than that. It's peachy and free of acne, (most of the time) thank goodness. Come to think of it, the only time I had a problem with my skin was when I got poison oak on a trip to Georgia with Dean to visit his Aunt Florence, Uncle Morris, and cousin, Chris. It was so messed up I couldn't see for two days because my eyes were swollen shut from the allergic reaction. Dean and Chris kept calling me Buddha, those dickheads. I should be emotionally scarred and probably would be if I hadn't come such a long way since braces and puberty. Not that I'm God's gift to anything, but I think I'm a decent looking guy. Overall, I'm a pretty confident and self-respecting person too. I mean, you won't find me doing drugs or sleeping with anything that hits on me. I have pretty high standards for my mental and physical health. I could use a little more muscle mass, although I'd never want to be as big as Brant per se...which reminds me! I told him that I'd call. Shit, I lost track of time and totally forgot that we planned on going to Bell Hall to get passports.

Staring at the telephone, I realized that it was a prehistoric fossil. To start, there were too many buttons. Campus security and all of the most dialed buildings, like the infirmary and student center, were mint green rectangles protruding from the archaic vessel. The LED voicemail indicator was a hazardous red, and the speakerphone button was the same egg-like, cream color as the phone. There was also a matching, stretched out cord that attached the headset and base. Seriously, a residential, wired landline? This dinosaur will never, in a million years, call Brant's long-distance cell phone number without an epic hassle. I hope I can do dorm-to-dorm calling, like in hotels.

I scanned the campus directory for Franklin Hall and punched the code. I was prompted to enter Brant's dorm room number, and then the phone rang a few times before his machismo outgoing message chimed.

Yoooo, this is Brant and Phil, we can't get to the phone right now. You know what to do... BEEEEP.

"Hey Brant, it's Lewis. Uh, I'm all done here but could use a shower, so I'll probably be ready to head to Bell Hall in about half an hour or so. Um, if I don't hear from you by the time I've showered, I guess I'll try your cell. Later," I hung up the phone.

So, I guess he's already met his roommate. I don't know why, but an inexplicable peg of jealousy shot up my neck for a split second. Was it because I hadn't met *my* roommate? Or maybe that I bonded with Brant rommateless, and now I have to meet this Phil character? Whatever…I shook it off, grabbed my key and toiletries, and headed to the shower.

Actually, getting to the showers was a creeped-out and ominous experience. The corridor that connects the East and West wings of Ponce Hall was a poorly lit one, which made the walk down it seem perilous. The lights (that still worked) flickered for life and buzzed from the higher wattage and poorer electric current. The old door to the shower room was a massive chunk of weathered wood with a rusty metal plate instead of a knob. I pushed it open to discover a completely tiled space with rusted metal draining grates sporadically nailed to the floor. There were about a dozen showers across from one another and mildewed shower curtains for privacy. I now understood Camille's desire to stay in one of the newer dorms. This was atrocious. Staring down at the moldy tiles, I was suddenly much more appreciative of the ragged flip-flops that I slipped on.

Stepping cautiously toward the stalls, dripping noises echoed from the faucets and showerheads. I can't imagine a place this disgusting being where one goes to get clean. I put my things on a wooden bench between the showers that had been drilled into the moldy, cracked tiles with orange, rusted metal nails. The wooden part of the bench was dry, despite the consistently wet look that old wood gives off. After pulling back the shower curtain, I was shocked and relieved to see a clean shower. I made a mental note of which shower stall it was; *the third on the left*. I will most definitely be a repeat customer. Removing my towel, I leaned in and turned the shower knob to warm. It took a few minutes for the water to become an endurable temperature, but eventually, my finger test approved, and I stepped in. My flip-flops squeaked and chirped on the tile floor while I quickly bathed. Being in this space alone gave me the creeps, and the sooner I was clean, the sooner I could bounce.

In an effort to get out of the dingy space as fast as possible, I barely dried off and darted back to my room dripping wet with the slippery water lingering in the cloth straps of my flip-flops and under my feet. I made loud chirping noises and thought I was going to fall on my ass every time I took a step, so in an attempt to avoid that, I ended up walking on my tip-toes the rest of the way to my room.

I put on the same outfit from this morning, except I did put on clean underwear. I groomed my hair, brushed my teeth, and checked to see if Brant had called. The voicemail indicator was flashing, so I pushed it, and the speaker projected Brant's voice through the amplifier.

Yo Lewis, it's Brant. Sorry, I missed you, Phil and I were pimping our pad. You've got to come by and check it out. Why don't you call me when you're done showering and then head over? We can go to Bell from here. Alright man, talk to you later.

I called him back, this time from my cell so that he had my number too. "Hello," Brant said.

"Hey Brant, it's Lewis."

"Oh, hey man. You all showered up and ready to go?"

"Yeah, I was just about to head your way. I can't wait to see what you've done with the place," I said jokingly.

"Oooh, you are going to flip man, it's pretty dope if I do say so myself. C'mon over whenever."

"Alright, I'll be there in a minute," I hung up the phone, checked my reflection in the mirror, and grabbed my set of keys before leaving.

The walk to Brant's was *literally* a minute. Franklin was directly across the yard from Ponce, I just walked diagonally over the courtyard, dodging frisbees, footballs, hacky-sackers, and incoming tenants carrying luggage and furniture. When I stepped inside, the newness of Franklin Hall was envy-inspiring beyond containment.

I let out a reflex gasp and said, "What?" aloud.

There was actually a lobby *and* information desk. No one was manning it at the moment, but I'm sure that in the future, a RA will be there asking to see ids or doing after hour check-ins on a regular basis. The fresh drywall, lighting, carpet, furniture, and elevators all screamed 'new! New! NEW!' I scrolled down the directory on the information desk for room 3006. It says that I need to go up to the third floor, then to the left. I can't imagine what he possibly could have done to his sparkly, new dorm room to make it any nicer than it was prior to his pimping.

I ended up sharing the elevator with a nice-looking family. The mom and dad were moving the older of their two daughters in. Their younger daughter kept asking her sister asinine questions about college and why she had to move away and live here. Her older sister reassured her that she too would someday be going off to college and would be leaving Mom and Dad to live on campus as well. The younger sister shook her head furiously, denying her older sister's prophesy and revealing her own fortune that she would *never* leave her dolls and Mommy and Daddy behind and that her older sister should be ashamed of herself for leaving. I smiled at the mom, dad, and older sister; I was obviously bemused by the dissension caused due to the older sibling's desire for higher education.

Noticing my attention, the mother spoke, "We have been trying to prepare her for this for weeks."

"Oh," I said nodding sympathetically.

"Do you have brothers or sisters?" The older daughter asked.

"Nope, just me," I answered.

"Lucky," the younger daughter pouted.

We all let out a laugh as she looked around at us, frustrated by our finding humor in her most vicious attempt to hurt her sister. The elevator door opened, and I stepped off and said goodbye to the upward bound family. Due to the smoldering look on her face, I felt certain that the mother was going to say something about me to the older daughter as soon as the elevator doors shut.

The plates on the wall reaffirmed the directory that rooms 3000-3020 were to the left. I could hear the techno music blaring from the third door before I could see the vertically painted number on the metallic plate. Sure enough, it read 3006. I knocked hard, to be heard over the thumping bass. The volume on the stereo lowered, and I knocked again. A tall blonde opened the door, assumedly Phil; he had a shaggy beach do and pale blue eyes. This guy was too tanned to be naturally tan, and too muscular to be naturally muscular. He's definitely going to have a hard time squeezing classes in between the tanning salon and gym. And why is he wearing red khaki cut off shorts, Sperry boating shoes, and a white Ralph Lauren Polo shirt? This is a college campus, not a yacht. What a tool.

Everything about him made me want to call him Ken, but I extended my hand and said, "You must be Phil, I'm Lewis."

"Yeah, man. Nice to meet you," he replied taking my hand and firmly shaking it, "come on in."

Brant was not joking about pimping he and Phil's dorm room, it was pimptastic! For starters, it was twice the size of mine, and instead of plain cedar, the wood was chocolate stained with frosted glass. The closets were roughly the same size as mine, and the floor was also the same tile, but in this room, it didn't seem nearly as hideous. In fact, the splotches now appeared to be purposeful and artistic. The sink and vanity were much newer, and the window much larger, but being that it was still a dorm, to make the most of the space limitation Brant and Phil had both gotten loft beds. The ample space underneath the beds housed their desks and personal computers. Their entertainment area had a much newer iron stand, but they didn't even need it. What was probably a forty-two-inch flatscreen was mounted on the wall and in the stand where the television should have been, was a tiny refrigerator with a microwave on top! The stand was caddy-corner on top of some sort of cowskin or rawhide rug, and a nice, but obviously not brand new, brown futon was purposefully positioned directly in front. All hate aside, the positioning of everything was aesthetically very well done.

I stood in the middle of the room equal parts jealous and impressed. But then I was just astonished. The unnecessary yet fiery as hell cherry on top of the cake—a disco ball hanging from the ceiling! How had I not noticed that when I came in? At this point, I looked at Brant and said, "Really?"

"What do you think?" Brant asked.

"I love it and hate you, dude. My room is like a roach motel compared to this. This is awesome. I've got to admit, I'm a little jlo," I said nodding my head.

"Jealousy's a sickness, get well soon," Phil commented slyly. I wasn't quite sure how to take his remark, so I pretended not to hear him.

"But hey, I may have a roach motel to myself though," I said.

Brant and Phil's mouths dropped, and Brant said, "What? Where's your roommate?"

"Don't know, dude. I mean, I've been unpacking all day and haven't seen a sign of him."

"Maybe he dropped out. A ton of incoming students accept admission when they're waitlisted at their first choice. If they get into where they really want to go, they drop the backup plan like a bad habit," Phil offered.

"Yeah, you lucked *in*," Brant said with a nod. Phil scrunched his brow and looked back and forth as us incredulously.

"Don't you mean *out*, dude? He lucked out?" he said smugly. Phil was clueless, and I egotistically felt cool sharing the inside joke with Brant.

"Hey, do you have what's her name's number? You should call and see if she wants to come with us," Brant suggested.

"What? Who, Camille? Noooo. We aren't really friends. She's probably getting her room set up anyway, you know how girls unpack. Phil, are you coming?" I divertingly asked.

"Fo' sho'," he responded, "what girl?"

"This banging chick we ran into at check-in, they went to high school together. Dude, she is gorgeous!" Brant answered before I could say 'nobody.'

"Tick fucking tock. Yeah, she's hot, out of all of our leagues. I don't have her number, so I can't call her, and this conversation is making me sick, so let's go before I throw up on your cow's ass," I said. We all laughed hysterically in agreement and headed out of the room.

"So, Lewis, where're you from man?" Phil asked.

"Vedado. Small town, mid –"

Phil interrupted, "I know where that is, I'm from LA! I have family there. Nice area…it's quiet."

"Seriously, cool. I guessed you more of a coastal breed," I said eying his nautical ensemble up and down. "I'm a little over an hour from LA. I don't get there much though."

Against the slowly fading sun, a Bowel Movement, Ken doll, and Lewis squared walked and talked. Before this moment, I can't remember ever feeling this free. I doubt I even knew what being free or independent really was. It was almost like that feeling I had in sixth grade when I realized-slash-thought I was cool for owning a Baja pullover when no one else had one. I know this probably sounds strange, but let me explain… It's like when a person's perception of his or herself is challenged by new people or situations, and they're still able to find internal security despite peer influence or environmental situations. It's those moments that a person realizes that they are beyond-a-doubt *cool.* I didn't care that I was the only one wearing my scratchy, ill-fitting top, but Dean soon after got one, and before I knew it, I had set a fashion trend without receiving any credit.

Glancing at Brant and Phil, I noticed that they were also taking in this moment. No matter what we were in our old hometowns, we were all cool here because *now* we were hours away from parents, navigating an immense college campus, and on the way to obtain SoCafo student passports…now *that* is cool!

The scenery wasn't bad either. Cars sped by with their systems blasting old school hip-hop or top twenty beats, girls in summer attire cooed and chuckled as we walked by, special interests groups handed out flyers soliciting new membership, vendors sold wearables and second-hand books, and a massive jock stood on the corner physically and verbally assaulting his girlfriend. What a minute! What? The proverbial record player scratched, my mind imagined fingernails on a screeching chalkboard, and it seemed as if every cricket within a file mile radius was suddenly chirping with vehement disdain. Brant, Phil, and I immediately closed in.

45

"You stupid slut! I never should have gotten involved with you!" the guy shoved his girlfriend, but not hard enough to cause her to fall over.

"I'm sorry Kevin, I'm sorry!" she pleaded.

"I don't give a shit! I'm going to kill you," he punched her in the stomach causing her to double over in pain. "I want you out of my apartment, tonight!" After she stood up, he slapped her across the face and called her a bitch.

Brant stepped in his face, "Dude! What's your problem?"

I sidestepped and asked the girl if she needed any help. She shook her head nervously, not breaking her staring contest with the sidewalk. As I attempted to console her, I could hear Brant really going in on the guy.

"Are you crazy? You don't handle a female that way, punk! You wanna hit somebody, hit me, bitch-ass!" Brant pushed the guy, HARD!

He careened backward, hit the pavement, and yelled, "Dude!"

The girl shoved me out of the way and ran toward him screaming, "Leave him alone!"

"What?" Phil asked looking confused. "He was just kicking your ass."

She reached in her pocket and pulled out something small and white. She gripped it protectively like it was her living will and testament. But I knew exactly what it was as soon as she offered it to Brant. Oddly, it was a business card.

"Hi, I'm Sharon Preedy, Sociology major, and that's Kevin Thacker, Psychology. We are doing a study on human behavior. You see, by simulating a dangerous situation, we hope to get people to step in. You'd be amazed at how many people walk by and ignore us. You are only the third subject to intervene," she said looking at Brant as if he were a heroic figure from a fairytale.

"Yeah, and the first two were girls," A now chipper Kevin Thacker said as he dusted himself off. "And I had her down on the ground kicking her at one point," he added. It was amazing how his tone had suddenly gone from volatile to civil.

"I'm padded," Sharon added, punching herself in the stomach to show her layer of protection. I looked at Brant and Phil who were both looking like they had just been punked.

"So, take my card, I'd like to ask some follow up questions when we are finished with the first round of research and have collected a little more data," she said to Brant.

"You're freaking nuts!" Brant said, but I noticed that he put the card in his pocket.

Turning to walk away, "What was that?" I asked.

"I haven't the slightest flippin'clue! I thought I was going to have to lay that guy out!" Brant said panting, all of the veins in his arms and neck bulging through his skin ferociously like The Incredible Hulk.

"I know!" Phil yelled. "I was like, *not a fight on the first day of school...please.*"

I laughed, "That wouldn't have been right, expelled before your first course. I wonder if admissions would return your tuition."

"Hells no," Phil answered finger-combing the hair out of his face.

"Then you wouldn't have a roommate either, Phil," I said sadly, making a puppy dog face at Brant.

Agitated, "It's not funny you jackasses," Brant grumbled. "You losers were just going to stand there and watch that girl get beat up. It's you people she should be doing a study on."

"I had your back," Phil winced.

"Yeah, *way* back," Brant joked, "but Sharon Preedy was mighty pretty," Brant said putting his left arm around my shoulder and his right around Phil's.

"Aww man, I knew it!" I said pushing Brant off. "I knew it when you kept her card!"

"You're a mess," Phil said. "So, Lewis, you gonna pledge a fraternity?"

"I don't know. I haven't really thought about it. I'm taking this whole experience one step at a time," I said. But I was thinking, 'paying to have friends haze me and force me to binge drink until I'm o.d. wasted before finals is not a step I foresee taking.'

"OK, fair enough. So, you've moved in, what is the next step then?" Phil asked.

I thought about his question trying to make sure I avoided the topic of frats, "Um, for now, I'm going to go into this building and get this picture taken so that I can officially be a SoCafo student."

"Right on," Number Two confirmed as he pulled open the door to Alexander Graham Bell Hall and held it for a Ken doll and Lewis squared.

Chapter 5

That Sunday I awoke to another brilliant California sun. I peaked at the blazing crimson numbers on my digital alarm clock and the flashing colon between the nine and eight-teen before turning over to notice that the other bed was still empty. Maybe Phil was right about all that last-minute dis enrollment stuff. A slight smile creased my lips, and I felt the dryness from a full night's sleep in the corners of my mouth. I stretched out on the bed and stared up at the ceiling, enjoying the silence and soaking in the newness of my first collegiate morning. Realizing that I hadn't called my parents yet, I picked up my cell phone and saw that there was a missed call from home at 10:30 last night. I was passed all-the-way out an hour before that.

Bracing myself for the guilt evoking voicemail, I was pleasantly surprised to hear that it was actually from my dad. In his usual, casual tone: 'champ' at the end of everything and a corny 'okey-dokey' to finish the message, he expressed interest in how the move had gone. I'm sure that if the message had been from Mom, there would have been an accusatory tone for not having called, coupled with a fit of *is everything alright* hysteria. I hit *callback* and waited for the phone to ring.

Mom answered, "Hello."

"Hey, Mom."

"Lew Lew! Hey love. We missed you yesterday, is everything OK?" she asked.

"Yeah, everything is fine Mom. I just had a ton of things to do on campus, you know, with the checking in, unpacking, going to the bookstore, and all that."

"Good, so everything is fine?"

"Yeah Mom, everything is great."

"So what dorm are you in?" she asked.

"Ponce."

"Oh, Ponce! You're in the North Quad," she gasped in nostalgic recognition, "I lived in the East Quad, in Earhart. Your father lived in the

North Quad. Oh, that's so exciting! Have you met any friends? How's the car?"

"Which question do you want me to answer first, Mom?"

"Did you get your ID? Tell me about your roommate. Why aren't you more excited, Lewis?"

"I just woke up Mom," and can't get a word in edgewise. "I met two cool guys yesterday, the car is great, they're calling them passports now, and I got mine yesterday, and my roommate disenrolled last minute."

"Good, I'm so glad Lewis," she hadn't heard a word I said past 'I met.' She was just happy to confirm (by the sound of my voice) that I hadn't gone missing.

"Where's Dad?" I asked, seeking a listening party to actually converse with.

"Either still asleep or in the shower. He hasn't come down yet. This Emerson deal has been so stressful for him, on his days off he sleeps in really late."

"Hmmm, OK. He called me last night, so I wanted to let him know that everything went smoothly yesterday. Should I call back later tonight? You sound busy."

"That sounds perfect. I'm in the middle of a really interesting docu-drama about abducted children. These parents' testimonies are so powerful. They-"

Oh boy, I had to cut this short. "Mom, I gotta go, but I'll call you guys tonight."

"Oh, alright honey, talk to you then. Love you, Lewis."

"Love you too, Mom."

"Muah. Bye," she hung up.

However short the conversation, I was relieved to have spoken to her because at least the guilt for not having called yesterday could be postponed until I forgot again. I glanced at the alarm clock, 9:25, still pretty darn early. I could snooze for another hour or so before getting up to go explore the campus. I closed my eyes and thought about whether or not I'd have a roommate. Suddenly my eyes sprang open at the thought of having a room to myself all year!

Lying there, I stared at the empty bed for a few more moments before beginning to drift back to sleep. Through slit eyes, I was becoming more and more comfortable with my drowsiness and loss of consciousness until the landline rang so loudly it startled me. The jarring sound sprang me up like a terrified startle. The ring echoed and bounced off of the narrow cinderblock walls, and I was pretty sure that it could be heard in neighboring rooms. I crawled over to the desk and looked at the phone to see who could be calling, but there was no caller identification screen. Wtf...all those damn buttons and lights and no caller id?

I picked up the handpiece and reluctantly answered, "Hello?"

"Lewis?" Camille's voice asked uncertainly.

"Yeah, this is he," I said.

"Hi, it's Camille Harris, did I wake you?"

I decided to play along and muttered a groggy, "Em, no. Not at all."

Calling my faux-bluff she responded, "Yeah, OK. Well, you sound like you just woke up."

"No, it's OK. How did you know my dorm number?" I asked.

"Campus directory," she said immediately.

"Oh, sweet. So, what's up?" I asked as if we had known each other our entire lives.

"Well I would have slept in this morning too, but my mom left to go back to Vedado early and I couldn't get back to sleep. So, I figured...never mind. Anyhow, have you heard of The Cascades?"

"No. What's that?"

Camille exhaled dramatically, "*They* are San Bernardino's natural waterfalls and supposedly they are beautiful. My roommate's from this area, and she said I must see them. Besides, it's a good omen to stand under the tallest one before your first academic course."

"Really?" I asked skeptically. "Why?"

"Yeah, it's a school tradition. So, they say that the legendary waters grant you passing powers or some foolishness like that. Anyhow, I have absolutely nothing to do today, so I was wondering if you wanted any scholarly luck as only mystic waters can bestow."

"I didn't peg you for the superficial," I said.

"You mean superstitious?" she corrected with a playful attitude. "I'm not. I just like waterfalls. I'm a girl," she responded. She was witty and a little sassy, but it made my heart tingle a little. We were flirting, and I liked it.

"Easy now, I like waterfalls too, and I'm not a girl. You may not be superficial or superstitious, but I'm hearing some super-sexism for sure," I flirted back.

"Wow, Lewis. OK, go back to sleep. I'm *not* sorry I woke you," she was laughing through her words.

"OK. So, how about this? I will do *your* superstitious college success ritual if you promise to do one that I've heard about...deal?" I wagered.

"Sure. Is it a unicorn I get to pet after the waterfall? You know how much girls *love* unicorns and waterfalls. Throw in a rainbow and my hair may automatically ponytail," she joked, and she was actually funny.

I laughed, "Nope, not a unicorn. So, I'll pick you up if you tell me when and where."

"Hoffmann."

"Oh, I'm sorry you didn't get Franklin."

"Yeah, but Hoffmann isn't bad. It's an all-girls dorm, and since I'm on a super-sexist streak, we tend to keep things a little nicer than you boys."

"Oh, you went there," I said, although I totally agreed with her.

When Aunt Sal, my mom's sister, had back surgery and Mom left town to be with her, Dad and I were left to our own devices. The house began to show signs of squalor within days, and by the time she returned, we were eating out for every meal because neither of us knew how to boil water and all of the leftovers and microwavable meals had been devoured. Not to mention that Mom was no stranger to telling us about our slovenly male living habits on a daily basis. If it wasn't dirty dishes, it was dirty clothes on the floor. If it wasn't dirty clothes, it was dirty shoes. She often referred to herself as a one-woman cleaning show, so I had nothing to throw back at Camille's joke.

"Yes, I did go there," Camille said smugly, "OK, so get yourself together, and I'll meet you out front of Hoffmann at 10:30?"

"Sounds great, see you then." I hung up the phone too excited to remember to say goodbye. How could I help but be this amped? I, Lewis Lewis, am going to The Cascades with Camille Harris in my new jeep!

Postponing the daunting task of those showers, I took my time brushing my teeth and shaving. After I had conjured the spirit to go, my shower (the third on the left) was vacant and still immaculate, so I was psyched. I quickly showered and chirped back to my dorm room on wet flip-flops. I noticed that Ponce Hall was way more vibrant than yesterday because everyone had moved in. There were sounds of conversation, music, and setting up of rooms. I desperately wanted to make friends with my hall mates, but dripping wet in a towel and flip-flops was not the appropriate time, so I squeaked past the open doors. The sound of my waterlogged flip-flops became shrill as I hastily passed doorways, noticing guys in exercise shorts and sweatpants playing an Xbox in one room, cards in another, eating cold pizza in the next with beer cans strewn everywhere. It was a classic college scene and I loved that I was a part of it.

Camille has never been a prospective friend, let alone an interest of mine, and now I could hardly wait to see her. Envisioning the striking contrast of her caramel skin and sapphire eyes, my face relaxed into a smile. My mind had become a picture of her: full, thick, dark, shoulder-length hair, it was always perfect, always lovely. That smile...so natural yet radiant, and her

51

curves…so voluptuous, yet not overtly sexual. Camille Harris had been under my nose for the past four years, and I am just now beginning to notice her humor, wit, and gorgeousness.

Nervously fumbling with my keys, I struggled to get into my room. Once inside, I breathed deeply in an effort to calm myself down. The room was now fully lit with morning sunlight, and the clock was flashing 10:15. I disrobed and bolted over to my closet where I grabbed a clean pair of underwear, plaid green Old Navy board shorts, a yellow tank, and a baseball cap. After slipping on nicer flip-flops, I was ready.

I gave myself one last glance over in the mirror before I grabbed my keys, wallet, and cell. On-campus parking for residents was in a huge lot directly behind Ponce, so I only had a short walk and a few minutes before I would be face-to-face with Camille. I wondered if she was feeling the same excitement and if so, I hope that today is everything.

I brought the jeep to a stop on the street in front of Hoffmann Hall at 10:29. I sat for what seemed to be the longest four minutes of my life, and at 10:33, Camille emerged from the glass doors of Hoffmann Hall. I could not stop watching her. Every inch of my skin felt like it was being tickled with feathers. She was stunning in a white, which looked to be terrycloth, beach dress. I could see the yellow straps of her bikini top around her neck and her hair was pulled back in a brisk ponytail. She wasn't wearing any makeup at all, and her skin was glowing as if she had lived on a Caribbean island her entire life. She descended the steps carefully, her plain black flip-flops and polished toes leading her toward the street. But her face was not as confident, and it struck me that I hadn't told her what vehicle to look for. She stopped a few yards from the street and stood there looking perplexed and clutching her oversized lime green beach bag. She flipped a loose piece of her bang from her face, and I watched from the short distance, falling in love with the pretty picture. Should I honk the horn and ruin the scene, or get out and escort her like a chivalrous knight or duke or whatever noble gentry men are? Or how about both?

I gave the horn two light taps and caught her attention immediately. Waving, I got out of the jeep and headed her way. Almost yelling, "Good morning, sunshine. You're late," I said.

"Am I?" she asked with her nose and lips bunched together.

"Naaah, not at all. I was early actually. Let me get your bag for you," I offered.

"I got it, thank you though," she said dipping her shoulder as if to show the bag weighed nothing at all. Rolled up and sticking out of her bag, I could see that she had packed a multi-colored, striped beach towel. Oops, I hadn't packed one at all. "Is this you?" she asked looking at the jeep in amazement.

"Oh, yeah," I answered trying to sound like I wasn't totally obsessed with it. "Well, my parents surprised me with it right before I left yesterday."

"Seriously? Wow, Lewis. This is some going-away present," she said, "And they did a great job picking out the color too! It's sparkly, like champagne."

I laughed and opened the passenger door for her. A refreshing gust of air conditioning blew us in the face. That was nice, however, I had left an old and depressing Radiohead song playing when I got out of the car, and the mood (I felt) was unhinged a bit by it.

"Thanks," she said smiling.

"Anytime."

I walked around to the driver's side and got in. The Radiohead needed to be terminated immediately.

"You can change the music if you want," I offered.

Reaching over to turn the volume up, "Oh my gosh, are you kidding? I love Radiohead," Camille said.

Completely taken aback by her awareness and love of a rather obscure 90's alternative rock band, I put the car in drive, and we rolled off. Camille began to move her head melodically to the music. Looking at her out of the corner of my eye, I couldn't help smiling. She looked back and returned the smile. The moment was perfection as if she were made to sit in shotgun at this very moment, in this car, with Radiohead's *High and Dry* creeping through the speakers. I'll just be sure not to mention to Dean that a girl rode in shotgun before he did, and Camille Harris of all girls.

I turned the volume down to ask, "Do you know where we're going?"

"Oh yeah! Sandra, my roommate, gave me an address. It's for the park site, but we park and then hike from there."

"Hike? I have on flip-flops," I said, regretting my thoughtless choice.

"Not *hike* like Marin Headlands hike…*hike* like Laguna Beach hike," she laughed, "You are so funny."

"That's awesome, you're a pretty funny one too," I said.

She glanced at me and said, "Thanks."

Camille continued staring at me and it was slightly awkward for a second. Then she said, "Sooo, do you actually want the address or not?"

"Oh, yeah. Just um…read it to me and I'll put it in here," I said tapping the navigation screen.

"Really? No Lewis, that's OK. I can put it in, and you just concentrate on the road."

"That's actually a great idea," I admitted. "I promised myself that I wouldn't get behind the wheel again until I read the owner's manual. Let's just say that I shouldn't trust myself, at least not in this particular situation."

"Well, that's unfortunate," she said fumbling with the dials and buttons. "Because I was going to ask you how to work this thing," she laughed. "And at least now I know that if you can't trust yourself, then I shouldn't trust you either."

"Of course, you should, I mean *can* trust me. I only break promises to myself. It's a self-destructive thing, I…I should see a therapist, really."

I was serious, but she must have thought I was joking because she laughed out loud, "Oh my gosh, you are hilarious. But honestly, I hear you. It's like one of those humanly flawed things, you know? Like, we don't value ourselves as much as we should or as much as we value others who don't really value us. Like—I can give really good advice to my girls, but when confronted with the same, exact situation…I'm a total mess. In those moments I feel like the world's biggest hypocrite. It's like, how can I not follow my own advice? What is that?"

I nodded in agreement, "I know exactly what you mean."

"And the self-destructive thing, what is that? I don't know how many times I have walked right back into a situation I knew was going to end horribly. Or like, knew something was wrong, yet did it anyway. Oh, it's the worst!"

"How about when you witness something you know is wrong and want to speak up but don't and then immediately after it's too late or the situation has been resolved, a million thoughts of what-"

"You could have said miraculously come to mind! Yes!" Camille said excitedly.

OK, so she actually finished my sentence—SWEET!

"Then you cry the 'would have, could have, should have' blues," I said.

"And beat yourself *all kinds of up*. But honestly, don't you think that everybody is like that in some way?" Camille asked.

"Yeah, it's like what you said about being tragically human or flawed or whatever," I confirmed.

"*I* said humanly flawed, but I like *tragically human* better. It's darker," she said.

I looked at her in shock, "What happened to the unicorns, rainbows, and waterfalls girl?"

"Don't get it twisted boy, this girl has got a dark side," she smirked naughtily. Whew, and man she looked sexy as hell doing it.

"Just put in the address, Cruella D'evil," I joked.

"OK, Mr. *I don't know how to work my car*."

"Aye! I do know how to work the GPS, but you insisted on entering it yourself," I joked.

"I'm trying, but this thing is like a spaceship from the future. I don't even know what this button means?" she pointed to a button that had a weird fork like symbol on it.

"I think you plug computer stuff up in there, but really I have no clue."

She laughed, "And what is this button with the dog on it that says SIRIUS?" She asked.

"I think that's Sirius radio—I don't know how to work that either," I admitted.

"What? Oh-my-gosh," Camille laughed sinking down into the seat.

"Hit the NAV button. It's above the MAP/GUIDE dial on the right."

"Oh. OK, I got it. Enter address. Cool." She fumbled with the knobs some more and then announced that we were set, and any further navigational failures would be entirely my fault.

"Thanks," I said.

Placing her bag on the floor, she responded, "Yep."

"What would you like to listen to?" I asked.

"I'm cool with whatever. What would you listen to if you were alone?" she said.

"Damn, good question," I love this girl, "Let's see…um, maybe some Bob Marley?"

"OK. Three seconds to answer: *Uprising, Legend, Kaya,* or *Babylon by Bus*—GO!"

I was caught off guard, but said the most familiar choice, "*Legend*."

"*Legend,* huh? OK," she responded.

"Well, what would you choose?" I asked.

She hesitated before responding, "I mean, I'm a fan all-day-everyday so *Legend* is cool, I just prefer *Babylon by Bus. Legend* is more of a feel-good slash pop album, *Babylon by Bus* actually has a voice and a message, you know?"

"Never heard it," I admitted.

"What? Plug this in," she said while picking her bag up.

Camille stuck her hand in the bag and felt around for a few seconds. After finding her phone, she scrolled through the music library and handed it to me. Luckily, I knew how to dock it, so *Babylon by Bus* immediately began to play. Camille put her head back against the headrest and closed her eyes in total bliss.

"It sounds like it's live," I said trying to sound like I knew what I was talking about, "especially the acoustics, you know?"

"Yeah, it's not the best recording, but the song, the words...positive vibration...it's all about radiating good thoughts and rendering good karma. I wish I was someone who could stay in that feeling forever."

"Well there are people that can, they're called potheads," I jabbed.

She swung the back of her left hand against my shoulder lightly and said, "No, but you know what I mean. Without the drugs. Drugs are just ersatz good times. We have the ability to create happiness naturally, and we squander it on things that won't matter in a week."

"Like what?" I asked.

"Like obsessing over being the best at everything. I always wanted my mom to know that it didn't matter that I was the best, just that I enjoyed what I was doing. She was never having that. It was always, 'That is what losers tell themselves, Camille.' So, I was kind of forced to find personal fulfillment in being the best, which is stressful...not happy or positive. But no more of that," Camille threw her hands up, snapping her fingers and began singing along with the track, "because I'm feeling a positive vibration, yeah! POSITIVE! Rastaman vibration yeah! POSITIVE!"

"Wow, you must really be comfortable," I said glancing over at her totally captivated.

"I am," she shrugged. "So, what about you, Lewis Lewis? Why SoCafo?"

No one has ever made my name sound so glorious. It sounded fluid and natural coming from her lips. I wanted to playback her saying my name in my mind over and over again.

But instead, I decided to answer her question, "My parents met at SoCafo. I really didn't have a choice."

Camille frowned, "What do you mean?"

"I mean...I don't know," I said uncomfortably.

"Oh c'mon, Lewis! You do too know!" she smiled.

"OK, but don't laugh!"

"I won't, I promise," she said.

"So, my mom took this picture of me when I was seven. I was wearing this extra ridiculously large SoCafo sweatshirt, and nothing else, and sitting on my Dad's lap at a football game. It has been on his desk in his office since it was taken, the same tacky frame and all. It was like an unspoken truth that I was going to college at Southern California University. I'd feel like the prodigal son if I went anywhere else."

"That's sweet. Why would I laugh at that?" she looked at me and I shrugged. "But what do *you* want?" she asked probing for more truth.

"The truth is that I don't know what I want. To some degree, I really don't care. But I do know that I want to please my parents, and this is a sure way to do it. SoCafo is a great school, except for the showers, and I'm glad I have the opportunity to attend."

She grimaced, "Fair enough. So, you must get insane alumni scholarships? And what's wrong with the showers?"

"Partial, my dad has to pay room and board and book fees, but all academics are gratis. And the showers are revolting, but I found the nicest one. My beauty, the third on the left baby."

She laughed, "That's funny," she said tidying her ponytail. "And at least you don't have to pay tuition to a school with gross showers," she laughed again.

"It ain't a full ride Ms. Valedictorian," I teased.

"Ah, don't even go there. The pressure to get the best grades has followed me to college too. It sucks."

"I don't understand how the pressure followed you," I said.

"I have to maintain above a three-point seven in order to keep the scholarship. That's like a ninety-three percent average or above in every single course I take until I graduate," she sighed.

"That does sound challenging, but I know you can do it."

She grinned, "I appreciate that, Lewis," she said with complete sincerity. "So, what's your major?"

"I'm undeclared. You," I asked feeling slightly bummy.

"Communications. So, when do you have to decide?"

"By the end of next semester. I'm taking all the 101's now though: Biology, English Social Sciences, and stuff. I figured I'd get the requisites out of the way so that I can focus on in-major courses, if and whenever I figure out what *that* even is." I felt redeemed.

"Smart," she approved.

I drove for roughly forty-five minutes, yet it seemed like forty-five seconds because of the seamlessly stitched conversations Camille and I were having. We rattled on about our high school experiences, common friends from home, and our parents. Camille disclosed that her father had died from a heart attack when she was eleven. She confessed to missing him every day. I was shocked when Camille told me the death of her father changed her mother; that she tried to become a mother *and* father and, in the process, lost her nurturing vulnerability. I was amazed that she was so emotionally aware. She had been exposed to a trauma at age eleven that I could never imagine. I didn't know what to say, so I just said I'm sorry and allowed her to change the subject.

Camille introduced me to the *Yes or No* game. It's simple: someone says something random like, 'Tattoo,' and the other person has to say 'yes' or 'no' without hesitation. She seemed to like those rapid response games, shooting out categories like Christianity, breast implants, snow, and the Lakers. To which my responses were: yes, no, yes, no. I was not quite as good coming up with the categories, so mine were pretty wack. I wanted to say Lewis Lewis, but I thought that might be a bit premature, and I may not be ready for the answer.

We arrived at the park site at 11:43, and the sun was trying hard to make its presence felt through the obstinate clouds. I got out of the jeep and stretched my torso. Camille was making sure she had everything, so I checked to make sure I did too. The key fob was secure inside my pocket, and I had forgotten a towel, so I was set to go.

I walked around to the passenger side and said, "You ready to chase some waterfalls and rainbows, girl?"

Camille smiled, "I was born ready, boy. Let's do it," she mocked.

At first glance, the park didn't look like much. It appeared to be a typical tree and bench scene with a few families scattered here and there utilizing the play apparatuses and picnic areas. There were old wooden signs that served as directors and mile markers, so Camille and I followed those toward a narrow dirt path that ducked in between a covering of trees.

Mimicking the iconic *Friday the 13th* soundtrack, I whispered, "Chhh chhh chhh…Ha ha ha."

"Uh uh, not funny," she said stepping over crisp leaves and dirt.

Laughing, I realized that we were alone on the worn path. I could hear scurrying animals hiding from us in the woods but no other people. The trees had become so thick that I couldn't even find the sun, and the sky was now trying to make its presence felt through the obstinate leaves and branches. Camille threw her bag over her shoulder and moved in closer to my side. Her bare shoulder accidentally grazed against my chest, so she moved a little further to her right, but maintained an intimate distance. I was in heaven.

"Yes or No, horror movies…Go!" I said.

"No! Um…cold pizza," she snapped.

"No. Motorcycles," I said.

"Yes. Michael Jackson."

"Wait a minute, wait a minute. Let's raise the stakes a bit. Can we make it a choice, like Michael Jackson or Prince?" I suggested.

"Oh, I like that. But you know it's gonna turn into a debate every time we disagree."

"Well, that's OK. To each his own," I said.

She looked me up and down, "To each her own too. Who's sexist now?" Camille playfully tossed her ponytail and sashayed ahead of me.

"Ahhhh. C'mon! It's a saying," I protested.

Not turning back to look at me, "It's a sexist saying," she snapped.

"Well then to each his or her own," I said.

I quickened my steps and put my clammy palms inside my pockets, drying them against the mesh inner liner of my trunks. Camille wasn't really mad because her cheeks were bulging from stifling a grin.

Suddenly Camille stopped and said, "Listen."

I stood silent trying to see what had startled her, "I don't hear anything," I said.

She grabbed my arm and pulled me toward her. "You don't hear that...the water?"

I squinted my eyes as if that would help me hear more effectively, but surprisingly the steady cadence of rushing water became faintly audible.

"I hear it!" I said.

"We must be close to the first cascade, let's go!"

Camille began quickly pacing down the path, and I followed in excitement. We came to a stone bridge that carried us over a rushing stream. On the far side of the small bridge, the path widened, and the ground was more damp and rocky. The directional post had a faded, white arrow pointing to the right, so we followed it. After a few anxious steps, we were standing directly in front of a fifteen-foot stone wall with fiercely white water cascading down it into a small cove. Camille took out her phone and took a picture.

"Wow, it's like a natural fountain. If this is the smallest fall, then I can't wait to see the other ones. Come on," she belted as if she were a schoolgirl in an amusement park.

As we walked alongside the cascade, droplets from the runoff splashed up against our ankles. Camille was beautiful. She skipped over her heels and let out shallow calls of fake anguish. Avoiding the falls became a game for her, the objective—being girly and free in the struggle to maintain her dry beauty. Getting wet would have equaled disaster, staying dry...perfection. I watched her skip and jump over the wet patches of earth and smiled. I wanted to kiss her desperately, but I felt that the timing was way off...too soon. But against my better judgment, I grabbed her, pulled her toward me, and stared into her gleaming grey eyes. I let the back of my hand acquaint itself with the skin on her cheeks, and then I pressed my lips against hers.

I blinked hard, Camille was several feet ahead of me shouting, "Come on!" I landed my flight of imagination and boarded reality. When I caught up to her, she asked, "What was that all about?"

"Nothing," I responded casually. "I was just taking it all in. I've never seen a waterfall before."

"Yeah, I know. Just wait until we see the taller ones. This is amazing, thanks so much for doing this with me, Lewis."

"Thanks for inviting me," I said.

The trail became a series of uphill twists and turns with helpful stone steps along with the steeper climbs. It wasn't a bad hike at all, but I figured it would be easier without the flip-flops.

"Flip-flops or bare feet?" I asked, reprising the Yes or No game.

Camille turned her head sharply with a devious smile parting her lips, "Bare feet," she said kicking off her flip-flops.

I pulled my flip-flops off one at a time, and Camille offered to put them in her bag with hers. After she tucked our footwear down underneath her beach towel, she pivoted quickly and charged up a row of stone steps screaming, "Race you to the top!"

"Hey! Cheater!" I yelled, charging after her.

I skipped every other step (the way I do at home) and was on Camille's heels in no time, but the stone stairwell was too narrow for me to pass her. I attempted to slip around on the right, but she moved closer to the guardrail blocking me out. She giggled mischievously and continued swiftly upward. Aiming to slow her down, I grabbed her bag by the strap and tugged on it. Apparently, I tugged too hard because Camille lost all her momentum and balance. Struggling, she barely cleared the top step and thrust her weight forward, which threw me off balance too. Camille jerked her shoulder in an effort to release my grip on her bag. This maneuver worked, however, Camille accidentally swung around 180 degrees, and I clumsily continued charging forward. Unable to stop, I knocked her backward. It almost seemed to happen in slow motion, and there was nothing either of us could do to stop the collapse from happening. The look on Camille's face was sheer terror as she was falling, unable to see the ground. She clamored at my arms and shirt, trying to grab onto something in one last attempt to prevent the plunge. Gravity's only choice for me was to topple, down, and on top of her. So...down we went until the thump of impact. Luckily, the cushiony bag took the brunt of the collision. I had extended my arms aside her shoulders to break my fall, so I was fine.

"Are you OK?" I asked.

She covered her face with her hands, and I began to feel her chest shake. Sighs and deep inhaling soon followed. I stared at her completely frozen.

"Oh my God, Camille, are you OK?" I asked more urgently.

I could see tears streaming down her temples. I didn't know what to do. I said a silent prayer that she hadn't sprained or broken anything. She moved her hands from her face and put one on each of my shoulders. She was laughing so uncontrollably that she had induced a fit of tears. She wailed hysterically and I just shook my head. I couldn't help but to submit to her contagious laughing spell too, so I dropped my head and lost myself in the moment.

I laughed until my face hurt and could laugh no longer. When I looked up, I noticed that Camille was fixated on something else. Her head was tilted back, and her eyes were entranced. I raised my head and discovered that water was gushing from a height of at least twenty-five feet. It was breathtaking, especially from this angle. The water poured down to the base of the fall and became a current rushing to an unknown destination. The sound of the falling water combined with the spectacle of its transparent blanket lulled me into a state of hypnosis; when I came out of it, I noticed that Camille was there waiting for me to finish taking it all in. Her face was serious, and she was staring directly into my eyes. Her fingers began to trace the curve of my biceps, and her lips parted slightly. I was locked under her spell, paralyzed. Something tingly and magnetic pulled our faces closer and closer together. Our lips caressed lightly as we maintained our gaze. I applied gentle pressure to her lips, kissing her slowly and softly. Camille closed her eyes and parted her lips which were now reciprocating every caress of mine. Her tongue toyed with my lips, not quite sure it was ready to come out and play. I closed my eyes and let my head reel. She gripped my lower lip lightly with her teeth and puckered her lips. She surrendered two sensual kisses, the softness of her lips making every hair on my arm stand at attention. At that moment, she had complete control of me and I was her slave. I could no longer feel the warmth of her mouth, so I slowly opened my eyes. Camille had cast another contagious spell and allowed me to pace my recovery.

She bit her bottom lip into an adorable grin and said, "I think we can get up now."

"I think you're right," I said smirking back.

"Boy, you are so damn cute," she said.

"Girl, you are cute, *damn*," I flirted and she giggled.

I got up with ease and extended my arm to help Camille. We wiped the collected pine needles and foliage from our clothes and continued down the path. I hooked my index finger and dropped it by Camille's side. She made a hook with her index finger and clasped it with mine, and we walked, hooked together, toward the distant sound of heavily cascading water.

Chapter 6

The last waterfall was truly one of the most beautiful things that I had ever seen. Camille and I stood gaping at the fifty feet of down-pouring water. I pulled off my tank top, and Camille stepped out of her beach dress. I could not believe how toned her legs and arms were. I commented on what great shape she was in, and she attributed it to tennis. She told me I was in good shape too. I attributed it to genetics.

We walked over huge, slippery plates of rock to get closer to the waterfall, and I could hear laughter and conversation of other people beyond the blanket of water. I was slightly disappointed because I was enjoying no one else being around, but I knew that it was unrealistic to think Camille and I were the only students that were going to capitalize on the *so-called* cerebral powers of The Cascades. We stared at each other, realizing the next step in our adventure was actually running through the intimidating waterfall to be granted collegiate success.

I said, "On three," and Camille nodded. "One…Twooo…Three!"

With our fingers still linked together, we bolted through the gravity-worshipping blanket of water. The frigid and heavy-hitting stream pricked my skin, inciting instant goose pimples. Camille let out a shriek as she leapt (very agilely) through the deluge; it was definitely a tennis player's lunge. Wiping the water out of my face, I noticed how different it was behind the waterfall. It was like crossing into another world, dark and cavernous—nothing like I would have expected. The glossy and wet rock was decorated with patches of bright green moss. All sounds and sights were now blurred by the waterfall, so I couldn't audibly distinguish anything that had been perfectly clear a moment ago. It was one of those weird yet intriguing pockets of nature. Before crossing, I had to strain just to hear the pounding inundation, and even up close it seemed like a peripheral soundtrack to the larger than life falls. Now, the sound of the water seemed to be trapped and resonating to the point where the others were yelling at one another in order to be heard. This made their presence even more irritating. Immediately,

Camille and I exchanged a glance and there was an unspoken understanding that we both would've preferred for them to be anywhere but here.

Patting away stubborn droplets from her face, Camille's awestruck expression revealed that she was mesmerized by the cove as well. "It's absolutely beautiful, isn't it?" she said.

"Absolutely," I agreed.

"Did you want to use this?" she asked, offering me her towel.

Taking it from her hand, "Yeah! Thanks," I said.

Camille smiled, "Of course, I noticed you didn't pack one. Hey, can you do me a favor?" She asked, rummaging in her bag for something. "Here," she handed me her phone. "Can you take a picture of me standing in front of the cascade?"

"Sure," I grabbed the phone more eagerly than I would have liked.

"Oh, and you'll have to make sure the flash is on because it..." she said pointing at the phone.

I interrupted her need to micromanage the photoshoot, "I got this," I laughed.

Throwing Camille's towel over my shoulder, I observed her as she got into position. She stood in front of the cascading water, raised both of her palms (parting the blanket), and bent her left knee slightly in front of her right. Her posed hand placement created two narrow slits in the waterfall, and tiny misting prisms meshed with the sun to produce two narrow rainbows beside her shadow. All I needed now was a unicorn, and the magic of this moment would be sealed.

Camille adjusted her head so that her ponytail escaped the flow of water, then she flashed her smile. Not a coy grin, or a mischievous smirk, but the smile that I had seen the night Dean and I ran into her, Ebony, and Olivia at Sharkey's. The one that made her eyes become dancing sapphires...the smile that beautifully framed the symmetry of her teeth, the smile that had forever changed how I would feel about her as she waved goodbye in the H-M line, and the smile that presently confirmed that I had fallen in love.

I steadied the camera and checked the phone to perfect the image before snapping the picture. The screen captured the waterfall *and* Camille impeccably. It was the most captivating thing I had ever witnessed, for real. I was looking at two of the most beautiful of God's creations in one, single, solitary frame. If my brain hadn't forced my finger to push, my awe would have caused my reflex to miss the opportunity to document this flawless vision. The flash lit up the cove like lightening, and the screen confirmed what I already knew to be true—that the photograph would be breathtaking.

***

Camille and I arrived on campus slightly later than I had expected. The jeep slowly rolled into an off-street parking space across from Hoffmann Hall, and I turned off the ignition. Letting down the windows halfway, I invited the setting sunlight into the jeep to create its intimate and quixotic mood. Camille removed her seatbelt and wriggled her body to face me, so it sort of looked like she was riding shotgun sidesaddle.

Nervously tracing the steering wheel, I awaited the beginning of what was seemingly going to be an awkward conversation. Perhaps we had moved too quickly, and she had changed her mind. Maybe now is terrible timing for her? She had mentioned the stress of the scholarship and its academic demands. She could be apprehensive about the whole black and white thing too, although it doesn't bother me at all. Why should it be strange now though? Nothing about the ride home was different. We talked and alternated song choices just like on the way there. Camille fixed her mouth into the shape of a sideways O, so I knew that she was about to say something. I shifted my weight to the right side and made eye contact with her, bracing myself against the silence.

"Sooooo, what now?" Camille's voice was low and emotionally unreadable.

"Um, what do you mean?" I said, trying to detect some hint as to how she wanted me to respond.

"I mean, classes start tomorrow, we are going to be busy." She gave me nothing.

I relented with a casual head nod, "Yep."

"Ugh," she sighed.

"What?" Stubbornly, I was not giving her an inch of vulnerability. It seemed too dangerous and too uncertain…too soon.

Agitated, "Did you have fun today?" she asked.

"Yeah, I had a blast," I said as neutrally as possible.

I knew it wasn't fair, but for some reason, I was feeling that I had more to lose than she did. I felt that I was feeling her way too much to let it be known. If she knew that I wanted to scream out of the window that I was in infatuated with her, she might run, full speed, in the opposite direction. So, I did what I guess many insecure guys would do to a girl they like, I shut down my true feelings and turned on my façade.

"So, I'll give you a call sometime," I said nonchalantly.

"Yeah, OK," She grabbed her bag off of the floor and got out of the jeep.

She closed the door softly, avoiding eye contact with me, and turned toward her dorm, shoulders sunken. I sat there, watching her walk away, feeling like an idiot. The rational part of me wanted to call her back, but the irrational part stole my confidence away. When she had gone inside the building, I started the ignition and headed to Ponce feeling like I ruined everything. The sun had promised and delivered an unbelievable day, and as it set, given it away to whatever lay beyond the horizon on that heartbreaking hue of purple and pink.

I thought about my parents' first date here: had my dad picked up my mother and taken her somewhere magical just to become an idiot and choke? Blocking out the thought that Camille probably now thinks that I'm the Earth's biggest asshole, I pressed the Bluetooth button. The same robotic navigation woman asked me *who would you like to call?* I told her to call home, and my parents' number appeared on the GPS screen, accompanied by an outgoing ring.

"Hey champ," Dad answered. "How goes it out there?"

"It's alright," I said solemnly.

"Just alright?" he asked, concerned, and listening.

In an effort to not have him worry, I reversed my tone, "It's great as far as school goes, there's just this girl –"

Dad interrupted, "Already? Lewis, you just got there yesterday!"

"Dad, she's from Vedado. We graduated together. I've known her for like four years," I said trying to soften the blow.

"OK, but Lew, you've got the rest of your life for that. College is a time to focus on academics," he scolded.

"Didn't you and Mom meet here?" I asked brazenly.

"Hey! Don't be fresh, boy."

"Yes sir," I said in obedience, "I'm sorry."

"It's OK, champ, but you're right. I did meet Mom at SoCafo, and we knew right away that we were going to get married, but we also knew that we wanted to graduate first. Our degrees were a priority. Lewis listen, all I'm saying is to stay focused. You've got forever for girls, but only one transcript."

Somehow his analogy was humorously hypocritical to me. I thought for sure he was going to say, 'only one life.' Mom and I are his life, and if it weren't for college none of it would even exist. I accepted his advice kindly, but the conversation had become entirely too paternal, so I changed the subject and began to small talk about the move-in process. I told him about meeting Brant and Phil, and all about Sharon Preedy and Kevin Thacker's dramatic display turned social experiment.

The Emerson project was heavily weighing on Dad, so he mostly talked about having to redo drafts and resubmit expense reports to the finance department. Mom was taking a nap, so I told Dad to make up whatever mush he wanted to tell her that I had said. He laughed heartily, which made me immediately regret giving him that liberty. Dad has been known to purposefully induce emotional fits and happy tears from Mom. I told him to be nice and he promised.

"OK, Dad. I've gotta go now. I have this thing, this meet-and-greet for the dorm. I just wanted to call you back since I told Mom I would."

"OK champ. Don't stay up too late though, big day tomorrow."

"I know, Dad. Tell Mom I called, she seemed a bit off this morning when I talked to her."

"Yeah, she's just trying not to worry about you too much."

"Well, I'm fine."

"I know Lew, I know."

"Alright Dad, love you."

"Right back at ya, bud…talk soon."

"Bye." I pushed the Bluetooth button to end the call.

After pulling into a parking space, I sat in the jeep for a few moments and thought about what Dad had said. I understand his point and also know that he has the best intentions, but I just don't think that I'm in a place where I can continue to be lectured about my choices. If I decide to develop a romantic relationship with Camille, that decision is entirely my prerogative. My Dad needs to recognize that I am my own man, and although I appreciate his advice, I can't help feeling like it was entirely unsolicited. But none of it may matter at this point anyway, Camille may never speak to me again after the legendary cop-out I just arrested her with.

Zoning off into the blurry, campus landscape, I sat for a few more moments shaking off the insecurity of my epic fail. I pressed the windows up, the engine off, and collected what was left of my pride before getting out of the jeep to head to Ponce (which was now officially home).

Chapter 7

Following my much needed and scary as hell shower, I threw on some exercise shorts and a white T-shirt. There was still no sign of my roommate and with classes starting tomorrow, it seemed certain that Phil's drop out theory had proven to be accurate as hell. But unfortunately, this means that I'll be braving the 7:30 meet-and-greet roommateless. I checked my reflection and noticed that I had picked up a little more sun on my face. My cheeks were gleaming orange-bronze and tingling with comfortable warmth. I just hope they maintain this and don't burn off into a dried-up peel. Shuffling my hair around with my hand, I positioned it into its shaggy *I'm not too concerned* look and headed to the recreation room.

The halls were alive with residents in route to the meeting. Some of the guys looked familiar from this morning when I was frantically running by their open doorways. I also recognized the guy that told me to get out of his way yesterday when I first arrived on campus. He was conversing with (whom I assume is) his roommate and apparently someone he knew from his hometown. They were both wearing identical, blue North Springs High School Lacrosse shorts. I followed the crowd down the spooky connecting corridor, past the wretched showers, and into a huge open space in the middle of the building. There were old, salmon-colored, plaid couches and matching chairs in three of the four corners of the room. In front of each of the matching seating arrangements there was an aged television. The room also had foosball, pool, and air hockey tables set up in the center, where some Ponce residents were rowdily engaged in games. There was a door on the far wall of the space that had *Ponce East & Washroom* painted in black letters above it, and beside that door the wall was floor to ceiling glass wherein a row of shiny washing machines and dryers could be seen. I scanned the enormous space until I saw Jonathan Greene standing in the far corner on an amphitheater stylized sitting area. There were five large platform steps built along the walls that extended outward, and each row of stairs was covered in the same salmon/plaid upholstery of the couches.

Jonathan stood waving his arms, so I hurried in that direction to secure a salmon-seat. When the gamers and conversing residents saw that the crowd was migrating, people began to bum rush the area. I got there in time to secure a spot on one of the rows, but unlucky latecomers stood, sat on the floor, or dragged a chair over from one of the TV sitting areas.

Jonathan began in a crisp and comfortable speaking voice, and the crowd decrescendoed and shushed each other to silence. "Gather round, take a seat where you can, we will be getting started momentarily... Alright, so welcome to Southern California University gentlemen!"

Jonathan threw his hands up in a gesture of liberation and excitement. We all roared, clapped, screamed, and hollered in anticipation.

"Alright, SoCafo! I'm going to keep this short-and-sweet, guys. As you probably can guess, we have a few dorm rules here: Number one—no drugs, *ever.* Number two— guests after dark check-in, *always.* Number three— no halogen lamps, light bulbs, screens, or devices, *ever.* Four— no radio's or TV at an audible volume after 10:30 Sunday-Thursday night, *ever.* But Friday and Saturday night, you can blast whatever the hell you want, *always!"*

"YAAAAAAS!" A slim and charismatic Asian guy stood up and fist-pumped. Chuckles could be heard amongst the group. Jonathan nodded and smiled.

"Also, limit showers to ten minutes. Laundry days are odd-numbered rooms are on odd days of the month and even-numbered rooms are even days. Don't try to trick us, you have to swipe your passport to get access to the washroom, and the system knows your address. If you are drinking and not twenty-one, I don't want to know about it. And guys, please no parties in the rooms larger than ten. That's the Fire Marshall's rule, not mine. This rec room is for residents of Ponce only, just leave the space in the same condition as you found it. I take that back fellas, leave it better than you found it. We want to keep our common areas nice and clean, got it?"

"Yeah," multiple handfuls of guys said nodding in understanding agreement.

"You will receive three citations for breaking rules before you are asked to move off-campus. So, with that being said, please be respectful of your roommates and neighbors. We are a community, so standard communal rules apply, *always.* Any questions?"

I thought about asking about missing roommates but quickly dislodged the urge. Drawing attention to my situation could result in being reassigned to someone, and not sharing is definitely my comfort zone. What an absurd idea to purposefully make Jonathan aware of the fact that I am a single occupying a double's room, despite the minor guilt of doing something wrong. Obviously, I kept my mouth shut. A few guys asked asinine questions like if they were allowed to copy keys for their girlfriends, or why a fire hazard such as halogen wasn't allowed. My focus was fading until I heard someone ask…

"Why are all the buildings named after all these old, dead people?"

"Does anyone know?" Jonathan asked the group. Everyone looked around the room for a taker, but there were none. "Nobody?" Jonathan challenged.

I raised my hand slowly, "You! In the white T-shirt, what's your name?" Jonathan asked.

"Lewis."

"Lewis what?" he asked.

My heart dropped. The last thing I considered necessary for answering this question was to recite my humiliating name in front of my entire residence hall. But here we are. "Lewis," I said loud and clear.

"Yeah, I heard that part, what's your last name, Lewis?"

"That is my last name," I said calmly.

"Oh, so what's your first name then?"

"Lewis." At this point, people began to laugh out loud and Jonathan became frustrated.

Rolling his eyes, "OK, on three you are going to say your first and last names. Got it?" he said.

"Yeah," I said shaking my head at the snickering guys close by.

Jonathan counted quickly, "one, two, three, go."

"My first name is Lewis, and my last name is also Lewis." At this, the entire room fell out in hysterical laughter. But I have to admit, the situation was a bit ridiculous, so I laughed as well.

Not amused, Jonathan looked my name up on a piece of paper that materialized from his pants pocket and said, "So… Lewis Lewis, 1004 Ponce West, go ahead and tell me what the rationale is behind the building names."

"They are named after innovators," I said just barely loud enough to be heard.

Surprised, "That is correct," Jonathan affirmed.

Some members of the audience gave my answer some consideration and began to nod their heads while some teeth sucking could be heard throughout the rest of the horde.

"Do I get some sort of prize?" I asked jokingly.

Jonathan stifled a laugh, "Ahh, sorry bro. But that's not a bad idea for next year."

"BOOOOOOO," charismatic *YAAAAAAS* guy reasserted himself.

By this point, side conversations had begun, and laughter was becoming louder, so Jonathan adjourned the meeting, and we all went our separate ways. I considered being social and joining the table games, but my mind was somewhere else, so I joined the Ponce West exit processional. Some of the guys made friendly faces in acknowledgment that I was the guy with identical first and last names that had solved the building name mystery, so it was nice to know that my public humiliation wasn't entirely in vain. I followed the mob of residents back through the shower hall of horrors before it dispersed up stairwells and onto alternate corridors.

Sauntering back to my dorm room down an empty hall, my mind began to revisit all of the wrong turns that I had taken earlier with Camille. Ironically, after setting the destination, Camille had even joked that any further navigational error would be my fault. And she had given me every sign that her final destination was something more than friends. Hadn't she? Had I strung her along just to drop her off back at home? Of course I did, I know I did! I totally took the punk-ass detour.

I need to fix this stat. But how? I can't just call her; I at least owe her a face-to-face explanation of my cowardice. But what if she doesn't want to face me? She has every right to be pissed, or hurt, or whatever it is that girls feel when they are rejected. Especially considering that *she* invited *me* to the cascades today. Why am I being such a wuss? I have nothing to lose by being assertive. I could just go to her dorm room and assert myself and let the chips fall where they may. So, I'll just go there, and I'll say… What the hell am I going to say? I can't even worry about what to say right now. I'll just get there and be honest. Being genuine in the moment has always worked out for me in the past. Or has it?

Bypassing my room, I continued through an exit at the end of the hallway, curious to see where it would lead. The door was incredibly hard to open, not because it stuck, but because it was solid metal, huge, and ridiculously heavy. I forced the door open with both hands and then found myself on a stoop a few steps from the ground, which was odd being that my dorm room was on the first floor. The exit ended up bringing me out on the side of the building which was vacant and poorly lit. In terms of direction, I had no idea where I was because I was below street level and facing nothing of familiarity. This side of Ponce was actually built on a slope and partially underground, but there was a row of about twenty steps to the right of the door, so I ascended the mystery stairwell, oscillating my head in search of a familiar landmark.

I recognized the main street after reaching the top step, Central Campus Concourse, or something like that, but I had no idea which direction was north or south, so I tried to gather my bearings by turning around. All of the buildings looked identical at night, so this journey seemed impossible to even begin. Feeling hopeless, I asked a passing couple where Hoffmann Hall was. They directed me east, which was opposite of where I had come out—damn my sense of direction.

Finally, in route to Hoffmann, I began to feel something bizarre, like my heart was knocking on my chest for admittance to an exclusive party. I stopped walking and tried to familiarize myself with the thudding in my chest, but my heart just began to knock harder and louder. I swear I could almost hear it. After listening for a second, I decided that I absolutely could *not* hear my heart beating and continued toward Hoffmann.

Approximately one hundred heart wrenching and emotionally excruciating steps later, I noticed that an annoying caterpillar had spun a cocoon in my stomach. I stopped again, hoping to pacify the spawning butterfly that was determined to emerge from its incasing. The anxious wings began tickling my abdomen. This nauseating little nuisance was forcing me to feel its new and nervous existence. I refused and tried to ignore it, so it split into two or three more butterflies, and they became determined to seek permanent residence in the pit of my stomach. Walking a few more feet, the butterflies became bored with just fluttering, so they decided to take up breakdancing! The dancing anxiety became increasingly more nerve-wrecking and my palms began to clam up. Slowing to a stop again (I know I must look crazy), I tried to think of some sort of conversation starter, but nothing came to mind except 'I'm sorry.' If that's all I got I'll try it, but honestly, does that even work anymore?

Finally arriving at Hoffmann with my sweaty palms tucked as deep inside of my shallow exercise short's pockets as they could go, I reluctantly entered the building. Entering this dorm was like entering into a fabled land of pink; *A Pink Palace*. There wasn't a single male in sight. The Pink Palace oozed with such femininity that I immediately felt my presence was unwanted, out of place, and discomforting. The tiles on the floor were pink, the study lounges had pink chairs and couches, the walls, the guest check-in counter, the elevator door...all pink!

I approached the not-so-pink looking personality holding vigil at the guest-check-in-kiosk, "Hi. I'm here to see Camille Harris."

Point blank, "I need to see your passport, or you ain't seein' nobody," she said.

Damn, I didn't bring it. I hadn't planned on coming here after the meet-and-greet. I began my plea, "I went to high school with her, and I live in Ponce, I –"

"I don't care if you went to Sunday school with her and if you live next door to Jesus. You ain't seeing *nobody* without your student passport."

She wasn't pink at all, she was RED! Deep and dark crimson!

"I understand. It's just that you would be doing me a huge favor if you could make an exception just this once. Um…see…I just moved in yesterday and forgot that passports would be needed today."

"Mm-hm," she hummed with skeptical eyes. Reaching into the top drawer of her desk, she pulled out a nail file and proceeded to go to work on creating perfect parabolas.

"Camille and I are friends from back home, so I know she'd be happy to see me. Could I call her from this phone and at least let her know I'm here? Maybe she could come down and get me? That would save me the walk back just to get the passport."

"What's your name?" she asked.

"Lewis Lewis."

"Lewis *huh*?" she asked again.

"Lewis Lewis, my first and last names are Lewis."

"Oh, that's messed up. You know my momma told me never to trust anybody with no two first names! Oh, you gotta go."

"Could you at least look me up in the student directory? I live in Ponce. I promise I go to school here," I pleaded with the red girl.

"Emhmm," she said not breaking her attention from her nails.

"Please?"

Looking up, "Look, I'm gonna do this one time because you ain't fittin' to stand here all night and get on the *last nerve* I have left in the world. And listen L.L. Fool J., or Lew Lew, or Louis Gossett Louis the third, or whoever you are… Do not bring your pasty behind in here again without your passport, or you will be snatched all the way up and turned all the way around! Do you hear me?"

"Yes Ma'am," I said trying to stifle laughter.

"What did you call me, fool? Do I really look like a one-hundred-year-old madam to you? I ain't anybody's Ma'am."

"I'm sorry," I offered.

"Yeah, me too." Then the red girl went back to her nail filing and entered into a mumbling monologue, "Couldn't go to med school at UCLA, hell. Had to come all the way out here where it was remote. This is some bullshit."

"Med school, huh? That's awesome. What kind of doctor you want to be?"

She glanced at me, hesitant to answer, "A hematologist," she said in a more comforting tone.

I looked on the floor beside her desk and noticed the stack of papers and books with titles I couldn't even pronounce piled up. Then I looked back at the weary-looking soul who was overwhelmed in her attempt to achieve personal excellence. And I offered, "It won't be a problem for me to walk back and get my passport. I take it you'll still be here?"

The corners of her lips turned upward, "You ain't got to do all of that. I believed you when you offered to call that girl. Ain't no serial rapist going to extend no calling card. Go 'head, Lewis."

"Thanks...um?"

"Katrina."

"Katrina, could you, I mean would you mind telling me what room she's in?"

"Damn, you need a personal escort too?"

I laughed, "No, just Camille's dorm room number. I'm sorry for the trouble, seriously."

"Em hmm, you said her last name is Harris, right?"

"Yes Ma'am, I mean Katrina."

"Emhm." She typed something into the computer and then announced, "Oh, I've seen her 'round here, she's really pretty! Sweet too," Katrina continued, "7007. Up the elevator to the 7th floor, on your right."

"Thanks, Katrina."

"You're welcome, fool. And you aren't pasty. Especially if you're here to see her," She eyed me up and down.

I smiled and continued past the desk toward the elevator. Totally gender-conscious and getting on the elevator with girls in their loungewear, I felt like a leper. I pushed the *seven* button and eased myself into the back, right corner. The interior of the elevator was one monstrous cork board with flyers with phone number tassels thumb tacked to it. Girls looking for roommates, selling furniture, offering tutoring services, needing tutoring services, piano lessons, designer bags, and clothing for sale. I braced myself for the jolting, upward lift of the elevator. Girls got on and off the elevator, and they all seemed to become immediately aware of my serial presence. The awkward ride was plagued by whispers and giggles that I am assuming were centered on some sort of conversation about the awkward boy standing in the corner with his hands in his pockets staring at the floor—Me.

When the elevator arrived on the seventh floor, I pulled in my shoulders and shyly excused myself to the front, avoiding eye contact with anything except the floor. Stepping out, the oppression of discomfort dissipated, and I noticed that the walls and ceiling on Camille's floor were a powdery yellow, not pink. I was relieved as if the neutrality of the color gave my misfortune of being born male a fighting chance. Following Katrina's direction, I turned right and felt a resurgence of the breakdancing butterflies that our interaction helped to stifle. Staring at Camille's door, I suddenly became apprehensive, but this time I was determined not to let my confidence be stolen. I knocked heavily like I had come to reclaim a lost possession, and curtly a pretty girl wearing a T-shirt with the Japanese flag on it answered.

"Hi," she said, with *who are you and what do you want* stamped across her forehead.

"Is Camille here?" I asked in a tiny, almost juvenile voice.

"Yeah, she's on the phone though. Hold on a sec," she turned her head and called, "Camille, you have a visitor." Turning back to me she smiled with her lips together and tilted her head.

Behind her roommate, I could see Camille pacing the room with the archaic telephone base in one hand and the headpiece held up to her ear with the other. She was telling whomever was on the other end of the call something about how she didn't know who it could possibly be visiting her and to hold on.

When she saw that it was me, she paused mid-sentence and said, "Let me call you back Ebony, girl it's him... Yeah... Girl, I don't know. OK! Girl, you are so stupid, bye!" Looking up at me, she forced a smile, and I was not such a fan of this smile. This smile was unreadable, definitely phony, and almost a scowl. "Hi Lewis," she said.

"Uh, hey Camille."

"What are you doing here?" she asked flatly.

"I wanted to talk to you about what happened earlier."

"What happened earlier?"

I knew that she knew exactly what happened earlier and was being illusive. Yes, and absolutely, I deserve it, but this aloof attitude is what got us here in the first place. Refusing to play anymore games, I asserted myself.

"You know damn well what happened earlier. Neither one of us said what we wanted," I declared, much more forcefully than I anticipated (no doubt an effect of breakdancing butterflies).

She put the phone down on her desk and approached me, squaring her shoulders. "I tried to."

"You tried to get *me* to tell *you* how I felt, and I tried to get *you* to tell *me*. It's all so petty. I like you, Camille. It actually kind of scares me how much. I've wondered how you've been right under my nose for four years, and I never realized it," My voice shook, "Scary or weird as it may sound, I think I may have fallen in love with you, and only in one day. I don't know what love goes around pretending to be with other people, but I know that it's real

75

when I'm with you. I was scared! OK? I was. You make me feel like it doesn't matter that I haven't chosen a major, or that I'm a pasty white boy, or that I don't particularly care for Radiohead because you see me, I mean the real me. And I couldn't handle you seeing the real me and then not wanting it. Look, Camille, I'm sorry if I was scared. No pretense, no games, I just want to be real with you about everything. I want you to be my girlfriend…and…and I like you. A lot!"

I watched Camille's scowl transform into something much less formidable, it was almost expressionless. "Lewis," she said no longer looking termagant, but almost flustered and caught against which words to say next. "So, no pretense? Well then, here goes…Lewis, I've liked you since the day I joined the Keyboarding Club. You were wearing that awful T-shirt with the keyboard on it…you know the one where the only keys with letters on them are the ones that spell *Keyboarding Club?*" I nodded in shame. "Yeah, it was pretty terrible. Mine immediately became the cover for my tennis racquet. But you asked what the difference between backspace and delete was." I dropped my head recalling the exact day and felt embarrassed, yet flattered that she remembered.

We both laughed, Camille at herself, and me at the nerves caused by what I was hearing. I was in total shock. Standing there listening to her, I had a hard time hearing anything beyond, 'I have liked you…' Camille gracefully fumbled through her admittance of feelings as I stood there completely dumbfounded.

"So, when we had to stand up and explain our rationale for joining the club, you admitted that your mom made you," she said as I felt my face go red. "You said that she said you could learn how to type without wasting an elective credit on an actual class, which I thought was genius by the way. But I was so nervous because I had to stand up and say why I joined, and I just knew that I could say anything except for the truth…that I joined because I was desperately crushing on you."

"You had a crush on me?" I asked. This conversation was like something out of the twilight zone: weird, true but unknown, and awesome!

"Lewis, please! Wasn't it obvious? I joined the Keyboarding Club. I drag Olivia and Ebony to Sharkey's because I know you and Dean hang out there, and it's our last night in town. Think about it, really. *Me*, at Sharkey's? Oh, I give you my number! I call and invite you to The Cascades! Are you kidding me, Lewis?"

Shit! I have been completely oblivious. And what's worse, Camille just confessed her love for me and I'm standing here questioning it, still!

Terminating doubt, disengaging dwelling, and without hesitation, I grabbed her by the shoulders, pulled her body into mine, and kissed her hard and long. The force and intensity of my lips ravished hers, and I could feel her entire body becoming limp. I pulled away violently and then looked into Camille's eyes. Now *she* was under *my* spell. Her dizzy lashes were blinking rapidly in attempts to catch up to Earth's frantic orbit. I gently nudged her chin with my thumb. Pleased with the effect and Camille's doe-eyed response, I did it again with my index finger and smiled, knowing that I was in complete control. I didn't know I had it in me to be so seductive, soft, or sensual. I grabbed her chin more playfully and shook it lightly.

"Hey. You OK?" I asked.

Steadying her eyes, she sighed, "Yeah, I'm fine. I'm better than fine, I'm..."

"In love?"

"Um... NO," she rolled her eyes and looked away embarrassed. Looking back at me, "*In like,* maybe," she whispered breathlessly.

"You guys make me sick!" The alarming shrill of her roommate's jealous disdain was jarring.

"Oh-my-gosh! I'm so sorry, Sandra. This is Lewis, my..." she paused and glanced back at me, "my boyfriend. Lewis, this is Sandra, my roommate."

"Hey, nice to meet you," I said.

"Pleasure," she joked and sucked her teeth before turning to go sit on her bed.

"So, remember when you promised to do one of my superstitious rituals?" I asked

"Yeah. Why?"

"Well, are you ready?"

"Now?" Camille looked skeptical.

"Well, it kind of *has* to be now," I said.

"But am I dressed OK?" she asked.

Camille was wearing a fuzzy-looking, powder-blue lounge suit with a hood, "It's perfect, in fact, anything you want to put on would be perfect." She made an incredulous face insinuating that she believed me to be full of crap. "Well, it's true," I said coyly.

"OK, let me grab my passport and keys. Sandra, I'll be back in, ummm?" she looked at me for a timeframe.

"Oh, within the hour," I said confidently.

"Alright. Don't forget we have class tomorrow," Sandra warned.

"Ugh, don't remind me," Camille said, "see you in a little bit."

"OK," Sandra replied.

I took Camille's hand in mine, and we headed to the elevator. The breakdancing butterflies had mellowed. They were back to only fluttering now, but they had migrated north to my chest, creating an invigorating flurry around my heart.

"So, when did you join Keyboarding Club, loser?" I asked.

Pushing the down arrow, "Sophomore year, way after you! Loser," she responded.

"Yeah, but you joined because I was in it, loser. It must have been my biceps in that T-shirt. Ha!" I joked.

"You think you are sooo cute, don't you?" Camille said elbowing me lightly. "I so did not *want* to be in the Keyboarding Club, but I guess I thought that I could get to know you without it becoming too real, and obvious. I mean, I always thought you were cute, but somehow it became this weird, unexplainable crush."

"Really?" I said.

Camille's voice was reflective, "Yeah, but it's sad considering that we barely even spoke in those terrible computer lab meetings," she said as the elevator doors opened.

Stepping on the empty elevator, "Well look at it this way, now you can probably type more words per minute than you would have been able to had you not been in Keyboarding Club," I joked.

She laughed and pushed the lobby button, "Yeah, that's true, I guess."

"So, why didn't you ever talk to me in those meetings?"

"I guess I was scared," Camille said.

"Scared? Of what?"

"You know, scared of…I don't know, being rejected I guess."

"What? Why would I reject you?" I asked, thoroughly confused.

"Hmm, I don't know. I guess I thought I wouldn't be your *type*, haha, get it?"

"Camille, that was terrible," I laughed.

Smiling, "But seriously, we are from different worlds," Camille's tone was serious.

"You mean you're black and I'm white? In case you hadn't noticed, we are both humans, from Earth, Camille," I said, distracted by the elevator doors opening. "And Camille, I don't care about that. I could feel the same way too, but how unfair would that be?" We both stepped off the elevator and moved to the side to finish our conversation in private.

"So, why me?" After hearing the question out loud, I felt like knowing the answer would appease every Camille related insecurity I had.

"I don't know," she shrugged. "Let's see, initially because I thought you were cute."

"OK, but then what?" I pressed.

"You have that whole nonchalant, understated, strong-but-silent thing going on. Couple that with those eyes and lips, and skin. Oh-my-gosh, you're gorgeous, Lewis. Everybody at school thought so! It's just that I assumed you were a jackass because you're best friends with *Dean Eddleston*." She winced like she had just taken a bite out of a lemon. "I'm sorry, I know that's your boy, but Lewis, he is horrible."

Camille's insulting Dean sent a current of hurt through my veins, but I shook my head and said, "No worries. Sure, I love Dean, he's like a brother to me, but he can be a bit much at times. I hate to say it, but I one hundred percent agree with you." I'd never admitted that to anyone, and never thought I would be able to without feeling an ounce of guilt. I knew that Dean would be crushed, me selling him out to Camille. I blocked out the thought and focused on Camille and me. "But I don't know that I agree with me being all of what you are saying and girls at school thinking that I'm hot."

"Well let's just put it this way, a lot of girls referred to Dean as your guard dog," Camille said with a stinging finality.

"What? No way! Girls love Dean! You're crazy!" I protested, "He dated so many more girls than I did."

"Yeah, and I know for a fact that three of them started talking to him by default because they all liked you first."

"No way," I said shaking my head.

"Courtney Haskins, Deb Schilling, and um…who was that brunette that was on the swim team?"

"Julie Ferris? I used to tutor her."

Camille interjected, "Then Dean met her, and *they* ended up dating for a little while. Anyhow, they were *all* into you at first."

"What?" I contested.

"Yes Lewis," she affirmed.

"Whatever. How do you know all of this anyway, were you even friends with those girls?" I asked.

"Let me explain something to you, Lewis. Girls, emotionally and socially speaking, live on an alternate planet than boys. We obsessively interpret all non-verbals, we're aware of intuitive needs which we usually try to change, fix, or nurture. We read moods and intonation, and we all communicate with each other whether we are friends or not. For example, the conversations that take place in the girls' locker room versus the boys' locker room. Tell me, what do boys talk about in the locker room?"

79

"I don't know, sports, cars, weekend plans, girls, I guess. Why?" I asked, seriously intrigued.

"So, let's focus on the latter, *girls*. What types of things do you guys say about us girls?" Camille inquired, but I got the sense that she was driving at a bigger picture.

"Ummm, who's hot and who's not, and who's nice, smart, and who…" I stopped myself.

"Emmm hmmm, go on."

"I mean, you know. Who they…you know."

"Had sex with," she said flatly.

"Yeah," I said dopily.

"OK, so now let's take a trip to the girls' locker room. Say it's third period and your besties have gym second. You have to mesh and find consolation in a group outside your clique. So, you aren't athletic, don't own a pair of Jordans, and have a bad haircut…girls don't care. We come together regardless, we listen, we cry, we discuss, we learn, and we move on. But, my point is that I've heard the heartbroken stories of girls who've thought some guy was into them and then gave up the goodies. And while you guys are bragging about it in your locker room, I'm getting toilet paper and drying tears in mine. For instance, Courtney Haskins, she knew she shouldn't have tried to make you jealous by hooking up with Dean, but she did anyway and ended up screwed, literally, and devastated."

"That's just one coincidental example. Besides, she really liked Dean, all she talked about to me was him," I rebutted.

"OK, take Julie Ferris for example then. She didn't need any tutoring in Latin, please. She met Dean and thought by flirting with him that you'd see her as more than just a study partner. Then, as you know, Dean charmed the pants off of her, again literally, and the rest is textbook. Lewis!" Camille paused to observe my vacant expression. "Oh-my-gosh, boys can be so blind. So, I have been a shoulder to cry on and then the same girls don't even speak to me in the hallway, but it's an understanding of sorts. A femme fatal code more or less. It's nothing personal, just high school bitchery I guess."

Sensing that the conversation had become less private, we began walking to the exit, "Well that certainly is eye-opening," I said as we bypassed the check-in counter. I waved at Katrina, but her nose was so far into one of her medical books that she didn't notice.

Camille continued, "Yeah, well I wasn't going to play those games. I guess I looked at it as a hopeless crush and tried to block it out. But I never could completely block you out for some reason. I think I totally get why now though."

"And why is that?"

"Well, timing is everything. It's like there are so many ways to get to one place, but you can't get there until the universe is ready for you to go," Camille answered.

"I get that," I said holding the door open for her.

"Speaking of going places, where are we going, Lewis?"

"You'll see."

"Oh, you're just full of surprises today," she joked.

We walked south toward the central campus hand-in-hand. The crescent moon was barely visible, and the stars flickered haphazardly. The nighttime air was tepid, but every Californian knows that the nights pale in comparison to the days. And still, Camille made the very bland evening seem luminous, and I felt I needed to tell her.

"You look beautiful."

"Thank you," she said grinning.

"My pleasure, babe," the term of endearment rolled off of my tongue impulsively, but I loved the way that it felt and sounded. Not knowing if Camille would love or hate it, I quickly launched a new topic before she could read me and vice versa. "So, what's your first class tomorrow," I asked.

"Biology lecture, eight am. Yours?" Camille began to swing my hand, and my arm gleefully followed.

"Calculus, also eight. It's a lab though."

"Calculus, OK. If you need any help, let me know. Calculus is tough, especially college level calc. I had to take that collegiate diagnostic to get exempt. I barely passed it."

I pretended like I didn't know any of this, although everyone knew that she had passed a college-level Calculus assessment in her sophomore year in high school. "Really? Wow. Check you out," I said.

"I'm serious Lewis, Calculus is no joke."

"I know," I said, "I'll be OK, but if not, I know your number," I winked.

"See! That was so sexy! How could you not know how cute you are?"

"OK, enough of that," I said, "Let's talk about you taking your clothes off right now."

Pulling her hand out of mine, "What?" Camille said stridently.

"You heard me. Check it out," I nodded my head to motion at the Central Campus Courtyard.

The Central Campus Courtyard also referred to as the CCC, is smack dab in the middle of SoCafo's campus. As the tradition goes, every student that has dared to streak across the CCC completely naked has graduated in four years or less. Presently, there were many young collegiate men and women who were determined to *only* be at SoCafo for four years. Needless to say, Camille Harris was not one of them. She stood ossified and flabbergasted by the entire scene.

"Um NO! Absolutely no way, under any circumstances. NO!" Camille was adamant.

"You promised," I said taking off my flip flops.

"Lewis, what are you doing? Look at these people, they could be arrested for indecency. I'm not doing it," she said shaking her head profusely.

"Yeah, and people could also spend the next five or six years of their lives here working toward an undergraduate degree," I rebutted smartly before pulling off my shirt.

"You're seriously going to do this?"

"Yep," I said twisting out of my shorts.

Putting her hands over her eyes, "Oh-my-gosh! Lewis, you're crazy! I'm dating a lunatic, an exhibitionist—an insane person!" Camille yelled.

"Quit your procrastinating and come on, pussy. Look at all these people," I said.

Camille drew her attention to the screams and clattering of many nude bodies running furiously, clinching their clothing, across the CCC. In the destined distance, people quickly redressed and proceeded to celebrate their success with yells of victory. Girls and guys, drunks and sobers, freshman and possibly second-year freshman who had neglected this tradition last year, were all enraptured by the frenzied madness, streaking together.

"Oh. My Gosh…ooooooh my gosh. I can't do this. Can I? I can't believe I'm saying this. I don't do these things. Why am I doing this? I can't believe I'm doing this. I'm *really* going to do this. Shit!" Camille babbled.

I pulled off my underwear and bundled all of my clothes together. They were the perfect shield to cover the essentials. However, my bare ass was entirely exposed.

"Are you coming?" I asked while trotting backward slowly.

Camille stared at the crescent moon for some sort of pardon and when there was none, she kicked off her flip-flops, unzipped her hooded lounge top, removed her bra and bottoms, and charged across the CCC after me, screaming like a crazed, exhibitionist lunatic.

Chapter 8

Running naked, in public, at a prestigious university after spending only one night on campus was probably not the best way to start the semester. But the superstitious tradition had gotten the best of us and there we were, in front of Hoffmann Hall, laughing hysterically at the recklessness of the last twenty minutes of our new collegiate lives. I couldn't believe she actually did it. Camille Harris, Vedado High School's Valedictorian, ran across the CCC butt-ass-naked!

"I can't believe I did that," she squawked.

"I know, I didn't think you would for a second there. So, it's not hard to believe that *I* would do it? What does that make me, some sort of sicko-nudist or something?" I asked jokingly.

"Yes! You probably loved it, freak!" Camille pushed my shoulder with her fingertips.

"You should be thanking me, now you're guaranteed to be scholarship-stress-free in four years."

"Or less! Speaking of, we should probably call it a night. It's getting kind of late, and we both have class in the morning."

I wasn't ready to let her go, but I agreed. "Yeah, eight am classes, gotta love that."

She winced, "I know right. But I'll call you tomorrow after I'm done, maybe we can check out one of the dining halls?"

"Sounds like a perfect plan," I said leaning in to kiss her.

She closed her eyes and kissed me back. "Have a wonderful slumber," she whispered.

"That was so freaking sexy, say it again," I whispered back.

She laughed, "Have a wonderful slumber, Lewis Lewis."

"Goodnight, Camille Harris."

"Goodnight," she said walking away.

I watched Camille disappear into Hoffmann before heading back to Ponce. We had a full day together, and the newness of the relationship was fresh and uplifting on my spirit. I controlled my steps back to my dorm, restraining the desire to skip and jump up in the air. The night had suddenly gone from lackluster to magical.

When I finally got back to the room, there was still no sign of a roommate. I had to have been the only student without one, but at this point, I didn't really care. Mischievously overjoyed at the thought of the privacy Camille and I would have in the absence of a roommate, I washed my face and brushed my teeth. I didn't realize how worn out I was until after I climbed into bed. The day was exhilarating yet exhausting; my mind was wide awake while my body was completely beat. I laid there, letting the anxiety over my first day of college courses race through my veins. This feeling was nothing like the night before the first day of school. Instead of nervous excitement, I mostly just felt fear. Until now, my teachers have always perpetuated this idea that they were more nurturing than college professors. They told us that by way of their omnipotent and gradual conditioning, by the time we succeeded in college we would be responsible, competent scholars. So, I undeniably have a lot riding on tomorrow because I finally have the opportunity to put the past thirteen years of my education to the test. Goodnight and good luck, Lewis.

***

Shuffling noises awoke me from a deep sleep. Blearily, I rolled over to glance at the alarm clock. It was 3:00 am on the dot, and someone was in my room!

Sitting up, "Who the hell are you?" I asked groggily.

"I do apologize, I'm Aden, your roommate. Pardon me for disturbing you, I am just moving in and will be done in a moment."

What in God's name? So, I do have a roommate, and this is his warm welcome? This bullshit has got to be the worst first impression in the history of first impressions.

Laying back down, "Do you need to turn the light on?" I asked, praying for a 'no' response.

"No, I can see perfectly. Please do go back to sleep, I'll try not to wake you again."

"Mmm…thanks bro," I rolled over.

I couldn't see Aden at all, but he was extremely well-spoken—almost blue blood sounding. He spoke with purpose and confidence, like a self-righteous adult. Despite the superior sounding tone, his consideration of my sleep, and having disturbed it seemed genuinely sincere.

I could have dreamt all of this because the next thing I knew, I was waking up. I didn't set an alarm, being a Californian, I've grown accustomed to waking up with the sun. But this morning was very bizarre; there wasn't a single beam of sunlight coming through the window. I glanced at the alarm clock to see if I had woken up in the middle of the night again. It was 7:30 am! The sun wouldn't be at full force at this hour, but unless there's an eclipse happening that I don't know about, there is no reason why it would be pitch dark in here.

Feeling my way through the darkness, I stumbled over to the window and drew the blinds. And still, no trace of light! Feeling for glass where the window should have been, I only felt the wall. It's inconceivable—the window was *gone*. Vanished, as if it never existed and had been a figment of my imagination the entire time. Where I distinctly remember the window being there was now, what felt like, a sheet of drywall. What is this?

"Aden, what happened to the window?" No answer. "Aden!" Still no answer. I don't have time for this, my first class is in less than half an hour. How am I supposed to get dressed? I can't even see my hand in front of my face.

I felt my way to the sink and turned on the light. The weak bulbs barely lit half of the room, but enough to brush my teeth, wash my face, and see my way to the closet. I could tell from the silhouette of blankets that Aden was knocked out cold.

"Asshole," I whispered under my breath. I definitely have to have a talk with him about this window situation when I got back from dinner with Camille.

I grabbed my bookbag, wallet, and cell phone and headed out. Before going to class, I decided to walk around to the south side of Ponce to see if the windows had been bricked in or something. None of them had, not even mine. I approached the building to get a better look and spotted my room. The drywall was visible through the glass. Aden had done this from the inside of our room! But why? If Aden doesn't have a good explanation for this, I'm reporting it to Jonathan. Covering a window has to be against some residential or fire safety code. And who the hell does he think he is, showing up in the middle of the night, waking me up, and then blocking out my natural alarm clock? Yeah, we definitely will be having a talk when I get back.

No thanks to Aden, I luckily arrived to Calculus in time for Professor Winn's introductory spew. Apparently, she was the very first tenured female professor at SoCafo and had been teaching at the university since God invented dirt. I mean, it's highly likely that both my mother *and* father were taught Calculus by this woman.

Dr. Rebecca Winn had this monstrous, U-shaped scar on her forehead. She disclosed to us that it was from being kicked by a horse. Prior to becoming tenured at SoCafo, she was a fierce equestrian. The incident occurred while trying to tame a young mare that retaliated against one of the other handlers. Per Dr. Winn, it was the only time in her life that she happened to be in the wrong place at the wrong time. Sadly, because of the trauma to her head, she was in a coma for several days and after regaining consciousness, she struggled with severe amnesia. After that, she developed a debilitating fear of horses and refuses to ever be in proximity of the beasts. And as a self-proclaimed equinophobic, she can't even bear to see them on television without losing her nerves. This poor woman. But the most fascinating part of Dr. Winn's biopic was when she told us that up until the accident, she was a horrific mathematician, however, after the coma, she could perform any operation of any digit in her head at the same rate of a calculator. Of course, we didn't believe her, so a few students challenged Professor Winn with random and ridiculously long numbers. The only part of the story that wasn't true was that it took her a little bit longer than a calculator, but I attribute that to her having to actually recite the number as opposed to display it.

Professor Winn's syllabus was insane, and her hair was even worse. We were required to take an assessment every time the class met, which was Monday, Wednesday, and Friday…at 8:00 in the morning! And the bob cut that she bobbed around as she spoke, it was like her hair functioned as the punctuation at the end of her sentences.

I sunk into my desk and observed the zany, little woman in her floral blouse and too long argyle skirt go on *and on* about how Calculus studies change and how the first assessment would be on limits and their relationship to our understanding of numerical values. The fact that she loved teaching Calculus was obvious and palpable because she wore a constant grin and was totally unaware of anything happening in the room that wasn't math-related. I had half the mind to facetime Camille and hold up the phone so that she could witness the madness for herself. In part, because I knew she wouldn't believe my description of Dr. Rebecca Winn, but mainly because she'd be more likely to help me prepare for Wednesday's test having seen that my Calc teacher is a math-obsessed-nut-job.

After Calculus, I had Freshman Lit with Dr. Ferguson. So far, he seemed to be pretty sane and normal. He was your prototypical college professor: overzealously excited about his area of content, corduroy pants, and golf shoes with a clashing tweed blazer, overgrown beard, and connecting moustache with thick tortoise shell glasses. His course, an in-depth, research-based study of Contemporary American Literature, already felt like it was going to be this semester's snooze fest. Fighting disinterest, I was forcing myself to listen to Dr. Ferguson's review of the syllabus when I felt two slight taps on my shoulder.

I looked back to see Phil. "Hey man, what's up?" I whispered.

"Yo. What do you think of Professor Fuck-your-son?" he joked.

"Aw man, you're the worst. He's not so bad, just boring. But at least it's contemporary. If I had to sit through his diatribes on some archaic Sophocles shit, I'd die."

"Wow, you're actually smart. And you're serious, aren't you?" Phil asked.

"Well look at it this way, hating the course will only make it harder to pass."

"Whatever. I just want the stupid Lit credit out of the way," he said.

"Yeah, well we actually have to have two. Sorry to flush while you're showering bro."

"Wow. Thanks for the inspiration Lew-zur, I mean Lew-is," his smile was a revelry of his own terrible pun. "Can you believe it's ten-thirty and Brant's still knocked out, lucky bastard. We went to a sorority mixer last night and got hammered."

A mousy brunette whipped her head around and hissed, "Shhh."

Phil and I both chuckled and Dr. Ferguson asked, "Is there a problem lady and gentlemen?"

"No sir," Phil said muffling his laughter. The brunette covered her face with her hand, so I did too.

Continuing on his infinite soapbox of differentiating modern authors from their contemporary counters, and why the post World War II setting was the end-all-be-all for both, Dr. Ferguson picked up a piece of chalk and slowly disappeared into my subconscious. Noticing my inattention, Phil passed me a post-it note.

> *So did your roommate ever show up?*
>
> YES! 3:00 this morning. He's weird. I'll tell you after class.
>
> *WTF? Seriously? Bummer man. But you might as well make the best of it.*

> *I mean, since he's going to be your roommate, you at least gotta try to keep things civil.*
>
> Yeah, I guess so.
>
> *We're going to a rager Friday night, you should invite him? We'll haze his ass.*
>
> Hmmm... We'll see. Let's talk

Phil nodded and I directed what was left of my attention back to Dr. Ferguson. He was deep into his tangent and was now name dropping. "Fitzgerald, Hemingway...*blah blah blah*." I was too preoccupied with Phil's invite and the thought of attending my first college party to focus. My mind drifted and I began to wonder if Camille was going to want to see me that night and if Aden and I would get along enough for me to even invite him. A lot could happen between now and Friday. Phil was right, I need to keep things civil with Aden and in the meantime ensure that I survive the Calculus crazed coo-coo and not die of boredom at the hands of Dr. Fuck-your-son.

Phil and I both had a break in our schedules, so we decided to grab lunch together. We went to Thompson Dining Hall and were lucky to find a table because it was beginning to get busy for the lunch rush. I got a bacon cheeseburger, fries, and a Sprite. Phil got a grilled chicken salad and Vitamin Water.

Chewing his salad, "Get out of here! No way dude, he actually dry-walled the freaking window? That's insane. Maybe he's going to hold you hostage and make you his sex slave."

"C'mon man, that's not even funny. We're talking about my roommate. What the hell am I supposed to do, for real? It's weird, right?"

"And why did he move in at three am? He's gonna have a rough day today, especially if he has morning classes. Was he asleep when you left?"

"Stone cold. I tried to wake him to ask about the window and he didn't even budge."

"Do you blame him? He moved from who knows where so he was probably driving all night. Hell, there's been plenty-a-mornings when I've wanted to drywall my window."

"Yeah, but you didn't. But touché to your point, your career in hangover renovation is promising." Phil put his middle finger up. "Seriously though, he'd better have a good ass reason for this," I said.

I took a bite out of the burger and listened to Phil's mocking speculation, "Or maybe he's from one of those black-out cults, you know, out in Oregon where they live their lives in darkness because they believe sin is blind or some shit."

"Well then, all I'm saying is that if I disappear, you tell the authorities about this conversation."

"For sure…can you imagine? Lewis, you need to talk to him. See what the window and bewitching hour move-in is all about. If it pans out, invite him out with us Friday. See if he's cool and what he's all about," Phil offered.

"I've got to check with my girlfriend first. She may want to hang Friday night."

Putting his fork down dramatically, "Girlfriend! What girlfriend?" Phil asked.

"Camille. We –"

"Since when," he questioned.

"Since yesterday, but we knew each other in high school." I took a sip of Sprite, embarrassed by the feeling that I needed to defend the fragile newness of the relationship.

"Is that the girl Brant was talking about meeting, she's super-hot?"

"That would be the one," I said regaining confidence.

Phil picked up his fork and stabbed a sliver of chicken breast, "That's why you didn't want to bring her around, afraid of a little competition, you cad!"

"It's not like that at all man, it's new and we're still figuring things out. It's definitely too soon to start meeting friends."

"Yeah, OK," he said. "But I'd still like to meet her sometime. We'll throw a girls-are-invited soiree or something. We can host it in our suite." Phil's eyes trailed off in awe of his future party.

I looked at my phone for a time check and realized that my Sociology lecture would be starting in fifteen minutes. Phil had to get to Economics, so we finished our lunches and went our separate ways. Being in the same Contemporary Lit lecture, I'd see Phil twice before Friday. That's plenty of time to figure out if I'm going with him and Brant to this raging party.

89

Sociology, my last class of the day, was on the southeast side of campus, so I had to cross the CCC to get to it. I immediately thought of Camille and an uncontainable smile planted itself on my face. It'll be just a couple of hours before I see her, and the thought of waiting that long made me jump with anxiety. People were staring at me grinning dazedly and writhing with excitement, but I knew it was from the thought of Camille, so I didn't care.

Sociology was such a constant stream of Camille obsessing that I have no recollection of which room of what building that I just spent the last ninety minutes of my life. All I know is that it's 4:00, I now get to see the most perfect of girlfriends and despite that burger, I'm hungry again.

I called Camille as soon as I stepped outside. "Hey Lewis," she said. Her voice was full of excitement. It made me feel loved in a way that I can't explain because I've never felt it before.

"Hey gorgeous, how was your day?" I said, beaming uncontrollably.

"Oh-my-gosh, so intense. I don't know if I am more tired or hungry."

"Well, we could eat, and then I could watch how cute you look when you sleep. I may have some questions about limits too," I said.

"Limits, ooooh. Look at you, mister," she joked, "So, where are you now?"

"South Quad, you?"

"Oh, I'm *kind of* close. I'm in the southwest quad. I can meet you at our spot?"

Confused, "Our spot?" I ask.

"Yeah silly, the CCC. I'll be the one waiting for you."

"Ha, you so fuuun-ny." But really, I mean clever. "K, see you soon."

"OK," she hung up. I stared at the phone until the third and final flashing *end call with Camille* and wondered if she did too.

When I got to the CCC, Camille was reading on a bench. She was engrossed and unaffected, almost oblivious but not because I don't think she could ever be considered unaware or ignorant. I grabbed her shoulders from behind and jostled her, and she screamed out loudly.

Looking relieved and annoyed, "Oh-my-gosh! Lewis, don't do that!"

"I'm sorry, you looked so cute, and I couldn't help it."

Standing up, "So that's what you like to do to cute things, scare the hell out of 'em? You got some issues," she sassed.

"I know, *muah ah ah ah…*" I joked, lifting my arms in a Count Dracula pantomime.

"So, where you wanna eat, Count? And you better count fast because I'm so hungry. I could be into cannibalism right now, and did-I-tell-ya you are looking delicious?" she kissed me.

I kiss her back, "So I tried Thompson today, it was OK. Let's try Columbus, I hear it's got everything. I mean the map says, 'Explore your hunger at Christopher Columbus Dining Hall,' I'm not sure they serve human though."

She laughed, "Well, I guess I can make an exception this one time."

Hooking her arm through mine, she rested her head on my shoulder.

"You realize we are crossing the CCC for the first time in our clothes," I said.

"You're right, ugh! You are such a bad influence. I still can't believe I did that, sicko."

"How can I be a bad influence? I guaranteed your expeditious and expedient graduation, and I'm taking you for sustenance after a grueling day. Oh contraire, it would appear as if…as if I'm looking out for you," I said arrogantly.

"Lies! But seriously, I still can't believe I did that. My mom would murder me if she knew-"

"That's the beauty of it, she'll never find out. Also, just FYI, it was my parents who told me about the CCC tradition. They condone it."

"Are you serious? No way! Now that's funny! Talk about parental advisory. You think they actually did it though?"

"Oh, my dad did for sure. My mom though, that's questionable."

She looked at me intrigued, "Why do you say that about your mom?"

"Um, she's just really conservative. It's debilitating actually, she worries about everything. I can't imagine her *not* being afraid of trying something new, let alone being nude in public, which is actually illegal."

"There isn't anything wrong with being reserved and conventional," Camille said. "I wouldn't consider myself to be a risk-taker either. If it ain't broke, you know?"

"I think it's fine and probably necessary to have some structure and routine, but I think it becomes dangerous when you aren't flexible or don't take any risks. And that's just it, how do you know it ain't broke if you haven't tried anything else? Like our meal, we'll probably really enjoy it, right?"

"Yeah," she said looking and sounding suspicious.

"OK, so are you going to be a creature of habit and reorder the same exact thing every time you go to Columbus or try something new?" I asked.

She smirked, "If I really like it, yeah. Why get something, I *may* hate when I can order something I *know* I'll love?"

Playfully bantering with Camille while strolling across campus with the sun setting behind Southern California's foothills was exactly where I wanted

91

to be. The perfection of this moment reminded me of my favorite photograph placed alongside other pictures of perfectly captured moments. How will or can I discern one moment from the other when each and every moment with Camille is equally as perfect as the next?

There was a late afternoon collegiate rush all around campus, but Camille and I remained inside our picture-perfect bubble. Our flirtatious banter continued into the dining hall before being abruptly terminated by a chaotic sea of starving coeds. Columbus didn't serve buffet style, mass-cafeteria-made food like Thompson. Instead, there were multiple themed restaurant stations to choose from like the food court in Vedado Hills Mall. The cornucopias availability of anything a pallet could crave was overwhelming: *Chick-Inn, Exotic Pizza Emporium, Beastly Burgers, The Green Thumb*…Camille and I considered every option before amicably deciding that we wanted Mexican, so we got in line at *South of the Border*.

I sighed, "So look at all the options we have here, you could love many things."

"I see your point, but *will like* my meal versus *could like* something else is not a risk I'm willing to take right now."

Opening my hand toward her, "But you don't know that you won't like *something else*. I mean, you have to take a risk on the very first meal to decide whether or not you like it, right?" I insisted.

"Lewis, why do you think it's so bad to be a creature of habit?" she asked. "And what do you want from here by the way because we're next?"

"I don't care, maybe some nachos," I said.

"Mmm, and a chicken burrito. You want to split both?"

"Sounds good," I kissed her.

We found a tandem-booth behind a large partition separating the dining area from the dishwashing area. Well actually, Camille found it accidentally while looking for the restroom. Considering how busy Columbus was, this area was surprisingly secluded (I'm guessing because people wouldn't expect tables to be behind where dishes are washed). Also, this secret nook was located at the front of the building, so ceiling-to-floor windows spanned the length of the wall.

Exchanging a nod, Camille and I acknowledged our mutual satisfaction with the aesthetic and kinetic comfort of *our* booth. Staking a claim on the booth we began sharing the burrito and nachos, we had exhausted our conversation on risk-taking, so we agreed to disagree—but in a sincere way, not in that condescending way when you just want the other person to shut the hell up.

Our new topic of conversation was the first day of classes, and we were both aghast excitedly competing to recount the events of our college debut. I was pleased to hear that Camille felt less stressed after having met her professors and seen the syllabi. When she asked about my day, I began from the beginning...the 3:00 am move in and window mystery. Her reaction was pretty much identical to Phil's: shock, disbelieving curiosity, followed by a non-negotiable demand of explanation. All of which I have to deal with tonight, and right now I do not want Aden monopolizing my time with Camille.

I changed the subject, "So Phil invited me to this party Friday night. I told him I wanted to check in with you before committing."

"Check in with me?" she said, poorly produced rhetoric masking her blushing. "Lewis, if you want to go, *go*. You don't need my permission, although I appreciate the thought."

"Well, I meant in case you were planning on hanging with me."

"To be honest, I hadn't planned on doing anything, but I do think it's a good idea to mingle and be social. I could see if Sandra wants to do something that night, and you and I can spend Saturday together," she said.

"That works for me, I mean if you're sure you're OK with it."

"Yeah Lewis, trust me, I'm fine. Besides, I'll let you know if there's ever a problem." Camille grabbed a loaded nacho and ate it.

"OK, cool. I do want you to meet Brant's roommate, Phil, eventually. Also, Brant thought you were hot by the way," I took a bite of the burrito.

Through her chews, Camille gasped, "He did? I was a mess. *It* was hot, I was sweating, and I know my hair was –"

"You looked gorgeous," I interrupted, my mouth full of cilantro and generously marinated chipotle chicken.

Smiling, "*Gorgeous*...aww. Not true, but sweet. Thank you. But really, you wanna know what's *not* gorgeous? That chewed up, masticated fowl in your mouth," Camille said, transforming a sweet smile into a disgusted grimace.

I opened my mouth and stuck my tongue out, "AAAAHHHHH."

"Ugh, you're disgusting."

"Yeah, but you love me," I said, immediately realizing the gravity of my words.

Camille didn't flinch, and those invigorating butterflies shot a familiar tingling sensation through my chest and shoulders. I was frozen in time and space, mesmerized by the intoxicating spell cast in her eyes. They had become dancing sapphires again, relentlessly waltzing with my eyes. Camille hadn't said it, but at that moment, I knew that she in fact loved me.

Chapter 9

Sneaker Pimps' song, "6 Underground," resonated through the hall as I approached 1004 Ponce West. I braced myself for the difficult conversation that was about to take place once I opened the door and crossed the threshold. There's no tactful way to address Aden about this, and it's inevitable that I do. So, I turned the key slowly and entered the room even slower, and then I saw him. He stood roughly six feet tall and looked to weigh about 175 pounds. He must have just showered or something because he was shirtless and buttoning his jeans. Awkward.

I noticed the petulant Armani underwear band ostentatiously advertising itself above the designer belt loops of his jeans. Armani...really? And I thought Phil was a freaking Ken doll.

"Hello, I'm Aden, Aden Vanhook," he said extending his hand.

Shaking it, "Yeah, I'm Lewis Lewis, we met this morning, only I was half asleep," I said intentionally unimpressed.

"I do apologize for that, Lewis. And I'm sure you are curious about the window as well," he initiated.

I smiled awkwardly, every wrinkle in my forehead at attention. "Uh...well, yeah."

He looked solemn, "I suppose the most direct way is to just inform you that I have a rare disease. It's called Polymorphic Photosensitivity. It's genetic and extremely fatal if exposure is not carefully avoided."

I wasn't quite sure what polymorphing photograph nativity was, but I immediately felt horrible for Aden in a sympathetic, thank God I don't have that, kind of way. "Oh-my-gosh, I'm sorry but, what is that?" I asked.

"It's quite alright, I've lived with it all my life, but thank you." Aden was smiling, but it was obviously a natural response to my uncomfortable reaction. "The easiest way to explain Polymorphic Photosensitivity is that it is simply just a severe sun allergy. Fortunately, when you are exposed to the sun, the ultraviolet light triggers a molecule that produces vitamin D. That process takes place in your liver and kidneys, but your skin has to come into contact with sunlight first. The vitamin is stored in your blood and helps your liver, kidneys, bones, sensory reflexes, and such. Unfortunately, I have a deficiency of *that* vitamin, so when I am exposed to sunlight, I basically—well I essentially boil from the inside out. It's not pretty or comfortable."

Open-mouthed, "Oh man, I'm sorry, that has got to be tough. I'm so sorry," I offered, feeling beyond asshole for my ignorance and insensitive conversations with Camille and Phil.

"It's OK. Like I mentioned, I've had it my entire life. No beaches, amusement parks, or picnics for me. I'm more than at peace with it. A person doesn't know what they're missing if they've never experienced it."

"Well, if it's any consolation, you don't look sick at all," and he didn't!

Aden Vanhook was probably the most impeccable human I'd ever seen. Looking at him was like looking at a male model's airbrushed photograph in a magazine. What normal teenage guy has flawless skin, not a zit, pore, scar, or spot of discoloration? The difference in my freckled, sun-baked skin versus his flawless, sun-coveted complexion was obvious. I'd stay out of sunlight too if I was a skin crazed narcissist that didn't live in California. And his physique didn't resemble that of a terminally diseased person either. He was 100% anatomically correct and it was envy igniting. I guess being inside all day gave him plenty of time to develop a six-pack and guns. But the weirdest part about this kid was no doubt his eyes. I can't recall ever seeing anyone's eyes this color before—the color of ice. Strangely, the more I looked at them the longer I wanted to stare at their vapid, wolf-like presence. It was all too much: the hair, the clothes, the grammar, the skin, the eyes. He really is a living Ken doll. With the amount of maintenance it's got to take, he must be gay. Maybe he's a fashion design major.

"I'm sorry to sound ignorant, but what are you going to do about classes?" I asked.

"Well, I'm an engineer major and thankfully SoCafo offers—"

Remembering my conversation with Brant, I interrupted, "Night classes, I know. My buddy is also an engineering major. You should meet him sometime you know…if you don't in your classes."

"What did you say his name was?" he asked.

"Brant."

"I'll keep my eyes peeled for a Brant then, we'll have to grab a bite to eat sometime," he said with a smile I can only describe as macabre.

"Well he and his roommate, Phil, invited us to a party Friday night. You can meet him then. I mean, if you're free Friday night and all."

Putting on a cranberry-colored T-shirt, "Ah, but nothing in life is free, Lewis," Aden said still smiling. "I'm off to class, thanks for the invite. I'd love to go."

He turned off the stereo, grabbed his messenger bag, and left the room. Unlike me, Aden was so confident in his appearance that he didn't even check himself in the mirror. I stood there trying to figure out if the conversation was redeeming or not. I had no idea what had just happened.

In mind-blowing situations like this, Dean always seems to make sense out of the nonsense. And given his ability to talk his way out of sticky situations, I'm wondering how he would have handled the conversation I just had with Aden. Not to mention I haven't spoken to him since I got to SoCafo, but that ass hasn't called me either! I need to call him. So much has gone down since I got here, and I know he's not going to believe half of it.

Picking up after the first ring, "Yo! What's up loser?" Dean greeted.

"Dean! Oh man, you are not even going to believe what's been up!"

"Don't tell me you wrecked the jeep! You idiot!"

"*Nooooo*...nothing life-threatening, just life-altering," I reassured him.

"OK, so what's going on?" he asked.

"Well for starters, Camille and I are dating."

"Camille who? Harris? You're right, I don't believe you."

"Wow, thanks, man. What did I do to deserve a best friend like you?" I groaned.

"Wait a minute, you're serious? I don't believe it!"

"Believe it, dude, 'cause it's true! I just got back from dinner with her."

"What? How did this happen? I've been after her for years. Damn, Lewis with the score!" he said, finally giving me some praise.

"Well that's just it, she claims to have been after me for years, so it really wasn't anything I did per se...or you could have done *to score*," I said victoriously.

Dean was quiet for a moment which made me wonder if he knew about Courtney, Deb, or Julie. But that was the girl realm that didn't condone nor require any exploration by Dean or me, or any guy for that matter.

"Well that's awesome, Lewis. I knew there was something going on that night at Sharkey's. Come to think of it, why was she even there? That is so far from her scene."

I knew the answer to that too, but felt to respond would be adding insult to injury, so I changed the subject to Aden. "Dude, and then my roommate!"

"Douche bag or what?" Dean asked.

"*Or what,* for sure!" I said.

"Really? De-da-de-da details!"

"OK, well first of all he moves in at three o'clock in the flippin' morning, totally wakes me up."

"Whaaaaaat?"

"Yeah, and when I get up the next morning the window is gone," I continued.

"What do you mean the window was gone? Like he stole it? There was a hole in the wall? It was missing?"

"No! Like he drywalled over it and it's not there anymore!" I said.

"Shut-up! Dude, you are so full of it. At what point in this conversation are you going to tell me something factual?" Dean asked.

I could tell he was feeling like I was punking him. The irony, he's the one that's always pranking me. "Dean, listen to me! Would I lie about this? He has some kind of Vitamin E deficiency or some shit, I don't know, but he can't be exposed to sunlight or his body shuts down. It's like some sort of genetic photosensitivity disorder," I said.

Dean sighed, "He sounds prêt-ty douche to me!"

"No, but that's the thing, he's not! He's like really well off and probably the best-looking guy I've ever seen in my life."

"Lewis, now that hurts," Dean joked.

"But I'm serious, his body looks like all he eats is protein, and he was wearing freaking Armani, Dean! *And* his skin, eyes, hair, and teeth are unnaturally perfect. It's almost like he's a manufactured droid-alien," I said.

"OK, now I know you've gone postal. Does Camille know you're gay?"

"Dean, it's not funny. I'm serious."

"I am too," he fired back.

"You're impossible! I don't know why I called you."

"Because I've been your best friend since the first grade, idiot," he snapped. "But really, I'm happy for you and Camille, she's a great girl, not to mention hot as all—"

"Dean, c'mon man! Discretion!" I warned.

"Right, my bad. But this sun allergy stuff sounds legit. I've heard of it before, it causes boils and burns, it's pretty grotesque. My dad actually represented a company that was being sued over it. One of their employees had it and could only work the night shift, but when the company restructured, they closed that division and laid him off. He claimed it was discrimination, and they settled for millions. It was pretty messed up, but my dad didn't care, he still got paid."

Half interested I said, "Wow. Well listen, I've gotta run, I've got to get ready for tomorrow. When does UCLA start?"

"Next Monday. Not looking forward to it at all."

"You'll be fine. The moving is the worst part," I said.

"Yeah, I know it. Alright, bro, I'll call you soon," he said.

"OK. Talk to you later man," I hung up.

Being up at 7:30 in the morning after being woken up at 3:00 was brutal, but tomorrow would be a later morning because my first class wasn't until 10:15. After finishing my nightly SSS, I squeaked back to my room to prepare for tomorrow's classes. I swapped my Tuesday-Thursday binder and books with Monday-Wednesday-Friday's and begrudgingly set my alarm clock for 9:50, projecting that twenty-five minutes would be plenty of time to get ready for class in the morning. Unfortunately, I wasn't awoken by the incessant buzzing of the alarm; instead, it was the incessant canoodling of Aden and some girl he had brought back to our room. It was 1:27 am this time, and I was much more awake than I was when he moved in. Damn him, but at least he was courteous enough to leave the lights off again.

I repositioned myself, covering my face with the pillow, but the sounds of fornication were too aggressive to ignore. My pillow-covered head was planted deep inside the mattress, yet the ripping of clothing and screams of pleasure were no less muted. Finally, I heard (what I can only imagine being) Aden and his guest climaxing because it actually sounded more like someone was being murdered. After that, I slowly drifted back to sleep.

***

Restlessness woke me up before the alarm clock, so I took a look at my schedule to figure out what time I'd be done for the day—4:30. I left a note for Aden on the stereo saying that we needed to talk and was 5:00 good. I hope I'm not being a prick, but I really can't go every night with an unsolicited, wee-hours-of-the-morning wake-up call. The window is fine, given his condition I totally understand. Yeah, it still blows, but Aden can't help that, but he can help the nocturnal escapades. And his bed is a single mound, so his female guest must have made her exit after I went back to sleep. At least she knew how to *exit* a room quietly.

I stepped outside into the heavy rain and cursed the damn drywall. I don't mind the rain, but when I don't know that it's raining and step outside unprepared, it's a pain in the ass. I didn't have an umbrella or a jacket, but I didn't want to go back inside and grab it for fear of being late. I managed to make all of my Monday classes on time, so if I make it to my Tuesday courses, I'll be officially and fully enrolled. I pulled my book bag over my head and bolted toward the CCC.

When I got to my Molecular Biology lecture hall, soaking wet, there must have been 350 people in the space. The section was held in an enormous auditorium, and luckily, I was on time because people were standing by for an open spot. The *first-day* attendance process was incredibly intrusive:

Professor Spivey scrolled through course enrollment, which was linked to our passport accounts. When a student's name and photo came up on the huge projection screen suspended above the stage, if they were present, they had to yell 'present' as loudly as possible. There were two boxes beside the passport picture labeled "enroll" or "unenroll." Dr. Spivey would then click the appropriate box on his computer, sealing the fate of the roster. When my picture was flashed, I made sure to yell over the clamoring crowd. Dr. Spivey checked enrolled, and I relaxed into my chair and watched the rest of the charade play out.

This process took approximately thirty minutes. At the end, the standby students were entered in order of seniority, so any freshman hoping to get a seat was pretty much out of luck. Standing by to watch for your passport mugshot was humiliation granted solely to those who arrived on time. Strolling in late meant you traded that minor embarrassment for the major upset, disenrolledment! The begging and pleading in front of hundreds was debasing to no purpose, as Dr. Spivey was unremitting.

Dr. Spivey looked to be in his early thirties and was obviously a strict, unwavering man. His hair was noticeably dyed blonde, and he wore slacks that were too big for him and a button-up shirt with two top buttons hanging slovenly open. His voice carried an air of no-nonsense despite its monotone passivity. Apparently, he was pronounced a science prodigy at age six and came on staff at SoCafo when he was barely twenty. It was all hearsay I gathered from the speculating students sitting around me. But whatever truth may be, he was a great teacher. Once he filtered out the students that were not in the class and delved into Molecular Biology, he magically came to life. Within minutes of listening to Dr. Colin Spivey, it was obvious that he was obsessed with science.

When he dismissed us, I felt cheated because I wanted to learn more. Hands down, Biology was my favorite course so far. After the lecture, we split into labs that were held in the same building. Dr. Spivey's teaching assistants, or TA's as they like to be called, ran these sections. Tracey, my TA, was a blonde who seemed too ditsy to run a Molecular Bio lab, but she knew her stuff. When she got to talking about the dehydrogenized molecule for our next DNA experiment, I had to check the text's glossary for definitions.

There were about thirty of us in the lab, and the class was actually held in a lab—with white lab coats and equipment and chimpanzees and everything. We were assigned partners, and I ended up with an introverted, hunchbacked guy from Washington with long hair and a ton of freckles. Tracey recommended that partners exchanged numbers since we were responsible for each other's grades. He wasn't very talkative at all. In fact, if he had a choice, I'm sure he would have worked alone. Anyhow, he said his name was Tim (no last name), so I got to be Lewis (no last name).

I had one more class after lab, and it was Philosophy 101. I had no idea what was happening in that room. I left more confused than I went in, and the feeling left me without a clue as to why the course was required. Finally, after my useless Philosophy class, I was done. I walked outside to see that the rain had become a light drizzle. The warmth of the day mixed with the chill of misty droplets was actually refreshing.

I hadn't eaten anything yet, so I texted Camille to see if she wanted to meet at Columbus for dinner again. She responded yes almost immediately, so I texted her that I'd meet her at Hoffmann at 7:30 (giving myself enough time to talk to Aden about his nocturnal habits and do some homework).

On my walk back to Ponce, I came upon an unexpected detour. There were half a dozen police cars forming an arch in front of a residential building. The siren lights were flashing, and in front of the cars was an area completely cautioned off with that daunting yellow and black crime scene tape that you see on shows like *Law and Order* and *NYPD Blue*. Quite a few students were lingering about, so I approached the police line to see what I could gather. A much-frazzled girl clenching here elbows, sobbing and shaking her head told me that a female sophomore, Jessica something or another, had committed suicide. She jumped from her window earlier that morning and claimed (in a suicide note) that she couldn't endure another year of the demands of her parents or the world. A male commuter had found her on his way to class. Traumatized, the girl mentioned that the impact had cracked the sidewalk, and when I looked beyond the caution tape, I saw a bloody splotch of concaved concrete enclosed by forensic flags.

I covered my mouth, "Oh my God."

"I can't believe it," she cried, "This is my second day of school! I don't know what I'm going to do."

I put my hand on her shoulder and told her that everything would be OK. I had no idea if this was true, but I didn't know what else to say.

She continued hysterically, "I overheard some of those forensic people saying she stabbed herself in the neck with some sort of mail opener or something, but I don't think Jessica would've done that. She seemed so...so happy," she said through tears.

An eavesdropping fraternity type chimed in, "Forensics couldn't be sure because the body took quite an impact, but apparently she gouged at the arteries here," he touched his neck underneath his right ear, "and then threw herself from that window." He pointed up at an indiscernible (higher than six) story of the building.

"Did her roommate see anything?" I asked the girl.

The frazzled girl wailed, "I didn't hear or see anything!" Frat guy and I both jerked our heads at whiplash speed. "She left for class yesterday afternoon, and that was the last time I saw her. I woke up this morning to the cops banging on my door telling me they needed to ask a few questions." She pulled a tissue that had already been used out of her pocket and wiped her face. "Then my RA said I had to leave the room while the cops went through our stuff and searched for evidence of...of foul play or homicide or something."

"What was her name?" Frat guy asked.

"Jessica Riley. Oh my God," she began to bawl again. I patted her shoulder sympathetically.

Campus security demanded that the scene be cleared for investigation, so I walked around the sea of spectators, slipped through the barriers, and headed home. The past three days have been nuts with change and drama. Without a doubt, the first eighteen years of my sheltered life were dull in comparison to my recent relationship, bizarre roommate, and bloody crime scene experience.

When I got home, Aden was laying in bed, casually dressed, and watching television. "Welcome home, Lewis," he said.

"Thanks, man. How are you?" I asked.

He sat up effortlessly and hit the power button on the remote. "I'm well, thank you. I slept in, got some classwork done. Our first project is a suspension bridge. I drafted a scale and am starting the model tonight."

I nodded, "That's cool."

"How are you?" he asked, but somehow, I felt like he already knew.

I shrugged, "Saw where a girl committed suicide this morning."

His facial expression became grim, yet his eyes did not change, "Really? I'm sorry you had to see that, Lewis. Is that what you wanted to talk to me about?"

I shook my head, "No, I left that note before I saw...all of that. Why would you think I would want to talk to you about *that*?" I asked.

"Oh, I see. I told you I slept in. I wasn't sure when you left the note, but I guess if it was a traumatizing scene, you may want someone to listen really," he said, his tone sincere and understanding. Damn, it's hard to be angry with someone who has the potential to be a pretty decent human being.

"Thanks, I appreciate it, but I actually wanted to talk to you about something else."

Lying back down on the bed, "By all means," he said. He crossed his legs and placed his arms behind his head, "Proceed, Marc Antony, I am your Rome."

I had no idea what he was talking about, but I put my stuff down and sat on my bed facing him, "Aden, you seem like a pretty cool person so far, but I think that if we're going to be roommates, we have to work out our schedules."

"I agree," he said. "What do you suggest?"

"Well, I know you have night classes and will be getting in late, but last night your guest was a bit loud and the night before, you—"

He put his hand up, "Lewis, enough said. I apologize. You are absolutely right. I have been majorly inconsiderate of your sleep schedule."

"No problem. Things can be different on the weekends, it's just on nights that I have class in the morning, I can't keep being woken up in the middle of the night and then struggling to get back to sleep man."

He sat up, placed his elbows on his inner thighs, and leaned toward me, "Let's make a vow. I am accustomed to sleeping all day due to my condition, so your daytime routine is opposite mine. You see how this could get a bit precarious?" he asked.

"Uh, that's what I am trying to say." I thought I was pretty clear.

He continued, "So how about if I promise to never wake you from your sleep, and you promise never to wake me from mine?" Aden extended his perfectly manicured hand for me to shake.

Why are all of my interactions with Aden so damn odd? What is he talking about? Maybe being inside all of his life has caused him to be a social moron. Or maybe he's just a freaking weirdo. He looked so clueless, sitting there with his palm open to me, so I shook it and looked into his unusual looking eyes. They were slit into piercing shards yet still inviting, like crystal. Sensing from my expression that the eye contact was becoming increasingly more difficult to maintain, he winked his blue blood, debonair eyelid, and I knew that we had sealed some sort of strangely fortified deal.

Chapter 10

Tonight Katrina was much perkier than the night of our first encounter. Real talk, when she isn't being nasty, she's actually very good looking, almost striking. Katrina's features were alarmingly handsome: strong jawbone, deep-set eyes that were so dark they sparkled, perfect onyx complexion, and short, jet black hair that followed the contours of her face.

I stopped to show her my passport and commented on the pink mood that she seemed to be in. "Well we're having a good day, aren't we?" I said.

"Well, our class standing was published this morning," She smiled victoriously, "I'm in the tenth percentile. I have my pick of residencies honey," she gloated.

"Already?" I asked.

"Yeah, med-school is not on the same academic calendar as y'all. We are pretty much all year 'round for eight years."

"Ewww. That's terrible."

She nodded, "You get used to it though. Oh, L.L., I'ma call you that," Katrina winked, and I nodded, "this dude came by here to see Camille, and he was FINE! But honey, he was up there for a long time until she walked him to the door and stuff. They didn't kiss or nothing, but I could tell he was feelin' her."

She could only mean Brant, that bowel movement. How could he be both an asshole *and* what comes out of it too? "What!" I said.

She crinkled her entire face into a nasty little grin and pointed at me, "Hmmm, got you joking. I can't lie to you boy! You should have seen the look on your face!"

"I hate you," I smiled, more relieved than humored. "And I hope you bomb your next test," I joked.

"Oh, you lucky I like you! The last fool that said some mess like that to me..." she took her finger and slid it across the base of her neck in a throat-cutting motion.

I laughed out loud, "You're funny," I said while rolling my eyes and shaking my head. "Hey, do you mind if I call Camille from here?" I pointed to the desk phone.

"Sure," she pushed it toward me, handed me the receiver, and dialed 0 *.

I entered Camille's room number. "Hello."

"Camille, it's me. I'm downstairs."

"Oh, OK. I'm leaving now. See you in a sec, bye."

"K." I hung up, pleased at having avoided another awkward elevator ride.

Katrina was tracking me with her eyes, "Y'all together?"

"Yeah, we're dating," I said proudly.

"That's so cute! You don't see enough interracial relationships. And the babies are so pretty too. I got to find me a white boy. You got a brother?"

"No, but I have a single roommate."

"Is he fine?" she asked.

"Um…I really don't know how to answer that," I said awkwardly.

"Y'all men are trippin' pretending like you don't know when another guy is attractive."

I was intrigued, "What do you mean?" I asked.

She sucked her teeth, "I mean men are such physical beings: always want to look good, want a girl who looks good, the car, the house, the job…all got to look good, right?"

"I guess," I shrugged.

"Well, then you know when a man *does* or *doesn't* look good. You know when a man is finer than you, or if you are finer than him, right?"

"Yeah, I suppose," I admitted, thinking about those intimidating, chiseled men on male fitness magazines that I can never decide if I want to shoot, be, or watch having sex for educational tips.

"And you wouldn't hang out with a busted dude with jacked up teeth and no style—like a straight-up scrub."

"Probably not," I said embarrassed.

"Well then stop playing! Is your roommate fine or not?"

Embarrassed, "Yeah, he's fine, I guess. But he ain't got nothing on me," I whispered.

She shook her head, "Oooooh, you are so bad, Camille better watch out. And hook a sister up."

"Alright, I'll bring him by sometime," I lied.

Immediately I thought about how hard dating would be for someone with Aden's condition. Who could date someone that they would never see during the day without feeling like an eternal booty call? Something told me that Katrina would not be down with that. And besides, he doesn't seem to be the relationship type. From my brief experience, Aden Vanhook definitely strikes me as a well-experienced playboy.

The chime of the elevator door distracted me from the conversation with Katrina, and Camille stepped out wearing yellow, low-top converse, a blue tennis-looking skirt, and a flowing flowery top. She was radiant, even in sneakers. I lost all concern for anything that was happening around me. The sight of Camille was literally stunning. Is it possible that a person can become more beautiful in twenty-four-hours' time? She smiled, *the* smile, and I wanted to genuflect. She *is* absolutely, positively, and amazingly gorgeous.

"Hey babe," she said.

Smiling, I shook my head and responded, "Hey beautiful."

Hugging me, "I missed you," Camille said before kissing me on the cheek.

"Ugh, y'all are gonna have to go with all of that," Katrina said putting her palm up.

I smiled, "I thought you liked interracial couples, Katrina?"

"Hmm! From a distance I do. Not all up in my business."

Camille grabbed my hand and tugged me toward the exit, "Bye girl."

"Bye y'all," Katrina said.

I put my arm around Camille's shoulder, "So I've decided," I said.

"What, boy?"

"We are both going to order something we've never tried before."

"You are still on that? Please. I already know what I'm getting," she said.

"C'mon Camille. Just try something different for today? For me?" I stuck my bottom lip out.

"OK, but if I don't like it…"

"Then I'll eat it, and you can get what you originally wanted."

"Deal," she said holding out her hand mockingly.

I swatted it away playfully, "I've been making a lot of deals today," I said.

She squinted, "What do you mean?"

"Well, I had a talk with Aden that ended with a sort of pact. We promised to not wake each other up."

"Aww, that's cute. So, you guys are getting along then?" she asked.

"Yeah, I like him. He's pretty chill. Smart, cool," I teetered my head trying to seem unaffected.

"OK, so what about the window? *That* is just weird."

"Not really, he has some sort of skin disease. Sunlight is really bad for him, like fatal."

She laughed, "What? Is he like some sort of vampire or werewolf?"

"What? Werewolf?"

"Yeah, don't they like worship the full moon or something?" she said sounding totally clueless and adorable at the same time.

"Nooo. They transform every full moon. It has nothing to do with the sun, and vampires are nocturnal, like bats. You're a mess," I laughed.

"I told you I'm not into all that horror foolishness. It's crazy. And please explain why *your* people always want to run upstairs, or they always want to go looking for the killer?"

"What? Oh, that is so stereotypical," I said.

"Well, it's true…at least in the movies."

"OK, so since we're talking about stereotypes, then how come *your* people always want to add their own soundtrack to the movie?" I mocked, "Uh uuuh girl, don't go in there!"

Camille giggled, "Never do that again. But you are so right. It's crazy, right? So, you get your people to stop running upstairs after killers, and I'll get mine to stop commentating," she joked, "And *we* will teach our children not to do both."

"Children, whoa. Slow down Juno," I joked.

She elbowed me, "Hypothetically speaking, stupid."

"I know, I know. So, what'd you want to order?" I asked.

"I was really wanting some yasi yaki noodles from that Hu Sans place," she said pouting.

"Well you order that, and I'll order something you've never had," I said.

"You've never had yaki? Oh, my goodness! OK, so now we need to find something I've never had."

"How about sauerkraut and sausage pizza," I offered.

"Yuck, it would be a first for sure," she admitted.

We went our separate ways once inside Columbus: Camille to *Oodles of Noodles* and I went to *Exotic Pizza Emporium*. We met back at what we were now calling *our spot,* the hidden booth for two tucked behind the partition. Camille was already sitting there with a tray toting a plate full of strange, transparent looking noodles piled up like a small mountain, with squid and shrimp delicately lying on top. I had a pizza stone with a perfectly baked, sauerkraut, and sausage deep-dish pie, steaming hot. I placed it on the table purposely.

"Boom," I said, throwing my hands up flagrantly.

"Oh please," she sniffed the steam rising from the crazy looking pizza, "Emmm, it smells really good."

"Um, wait 'til you taste it, babe," she smiled at the term of endearment. I kissed her on the cheek and sat down. "So, what do we got there?" I asked.

"Yasi yaki, most people call it yak though. My mom makes it with onions, vinegar, and chicken. You haven't had yak 'til you've had hers. But until then, this'll do."

She lowered her head and closed her eyes for about five seconds—I think she was saying a blessing. After lifting her head, she stabbed a defenseless shrimp with her fork, twirled some noodles around it, and extended the treacherous looking utensil to my lips. I opened my mouth and closed my eyes while she fed me.

As it turns out, Yaki's delicious! Surprisingly, the noodles tasted like a salty, buttered pastry, and the shrimp was a perfectly contrasting seafood flavor. "Mmmmm," I opened my eyes.

Camille was smiling, "Right? I told you."

"Give me som'ore of that," I demanded.

She prepared another bite, this time with squid, "Here."

Chewing heartily, "That is ridiculous. I want to dump the whole plate in my mouth!" I said.

"Uh uh, you better not. I want some too. But first, let me try some of that pizza," she opened her mouth and closed her eyes.

I picked up a large slice and put it to her lips. She took a bite and chewed it cautiously, "What the hell? That is delicious, Lewis. Oh-my-gosh!" Camille said showing all of the contents of her mouth.

"Wow, how can you tell? You haven't even stopped to swallow yet, nasty," I teased.

"Lewis, that is sinful, straight up. Honestly, I'd rather have that than the yaki."

"Or we can share again. You could have anything of mine you'd want, babe."

"Oh yeah?"

"Yeah. I want you to be happy," I answered.

She blushed, "I am Lewis, very happy. What about you? Are you happy?"

"No. I'm ecstatic. Who needs light through a window when I have you?"

She leaned over like she was going to kiss me, but then ducked her head down and snarled another bite of pizza. "Thanks," she said, chewing with puffy cheeks.

"That's foul dude, you're fired." I took a bite of the pizza too, "Oh, this is better than back home."

"Hey, you're eating my meal. You're supposed to be eating that yak, which is *not* better than back home," she grinned.

"My bad, food police! Here," I put the pizza in front of her and slid the noodles in front of me. "Did you hear about the girl that committed suicide today?" I asked.

"What? No! What happened?" she asked.

"I'm not entirely sure, I just saw the scene. Police cars and crime tape, the whole nine."

Camille covered her nose and mouth with both hands, "Oh my God, what?"

"Yeah, it was pretty rough. She stabbed herself through the neck and then jumped from her dorm room window. Her roommate slept through the entire thing," I continued. "It was pretty crazy. I had just finished texting you and was walking home when I saw the flashing lights from the cop cars. It was a total coincidence, but I actually talked to the roommate, she was hysterical."

Removing her hands from her face, "Well I would be too. That's horrible. Oh-my-gosh Lewis, are you OK?"

"Yeah, I'm fine. It's just eerie, with the note and all. Apparently, her parents were super hard on her, and she couldn't take the stress of school anymore. It got me thinking about your scholarship and grade point average. I worry about you."

She stopped me by placing her hand on mine and looked at me intentionally, "Lewis, I can understand why a person would, but I *personally* could never do anything like that. You don't need to worry about me."

"I know, but the roommate said she always seemed so happy, so you never know."

"That's true, but I don't think I'd let a scholarship end my life. There are so many other options: grants, student loans, work even. So, what was the girl's name?"

"Jessica Riley, I think."

Camille shook her head, "That's so sad. That poor girl's parents have to come and identify her."

I took her hand in mine, "Yeah, it just kind of makes you think about what's really important, you know?"

She nodded, "It does. But it also may taint the school year for some people, especially administration. They have to deflect the media and calm rising tension without offending families, students, faculty, law enforcement, or maybe even activist groups if drugs or alcohol were involved. It could be a circus around here for a while."

"Such the Communications major," I said, impressed by her insight. "And how would you deflect the paparazzi?" I asked in a cheesy, radio deejay voice (attempting to lighten the mood a little).

She picked up a slice of pizza, "By telling them to eat their feelings away," she took a hulking bite.

"Funny," I began eating again also.

"No, but seriously, there really isn't anything you can do in situations like these. Just let time heal them. The news will go away when the sensitivity of the matter has been diluted by time. It's terrible to think that way because someone lost their life, but to the media, it's just another story. These news people can be piranhas, and they'll feast until the next meal ticket comes along."

"You're right," I agreed.

"Well, you are right too."

"About what," I asked.

"About trying new things," she admitted. "This pizza is everything, Lewis. The company isn't so bad either," she said looking down.

"Hey, watch it, I have feelings here," I laughed, but Camille looked serious.

"You do make me happy, Lewis, *really* happy." She leaned across the table and kissed me.

I must admit, that kiss was more delicious than anything either of us had on our trays.

Chapter 11

Aden was on his computer when I got home from class the following evening. Camille was having dinner with Sandra, so I decided it would be a good opportunity for me to introduce him to Columbus.

"Hey Aden, you hungry?" I asked.

"No, I had a meal not too long ago, but I'll go with you. I could use a taste of evening air before class."

"OK, cool. You ready now?"

He closed his laptop, "Why not?"

Aden stepped behind the door and waited for me to finger comb my hair in the mirror, "Are you pleased?" he asked.

"What do you mean?" I gave myself one last glance. "OK, let's go."

Aden opened the door, but before stepping out he paraphrased his absurd question. "Are you happy with your appearance?"

Moderately offended, "I guess so. I mean, I could use some more muscle mass. My hair is a bit shaggy, and I don't know what to do with it at times. I guess I'm more comfortable in cargo shorts and a V-neck than I am in Armani jeans and muscle T's, if that's what you mean," I said, staring at him blankly.

"Have you ever worn Armani jeans?" he asked smugly.

"No, I can't say that I have."

He shut the door, "Try these on."

Aden walked over to his closet and pulled out a pair of designer jeans. After ripping the tag off, he handed them to me.

"Aden, this really isn't necessary. I mean I have jeans."

"Try them on," he insisted.

Losing the will to argue, I took the jeans from his hand. I really did not want to try them on, but I didn't know how to refuse. Up until now, all of my interactions with Aden have been problematic. One more issue and I could see things becoming full-on hostile. So, I turned my back to Aden and swapped my shorts with the jeans. Surprisingly, putting them on was like slipping into a transformative, magical glove. They fit perfectly. My legs looked longer, my butt looked firmer. I felt hot as hell!

Taking a step back, I looked myself up-and-down in the mirror while Aden watched from behind the door, "Wow man, these do look pretty damn good," I admitted.

"Well then they're yours," he said.

"What? No way Aden, these are brand new."

"Point taken, but that's why they're yours. I've had them for quite a while and never worn them. Besides, they suit you better than me."

"You're a terrible liar. Let me see that tag," he flung it at me from behind the door.

I caught it, "You paid two hundred ninety-eight dollars for a pair of jeans that don't fit!"

He shrugged, "Life is all about paying prices, and nothing is *truly* a perfect fit, is it?"

"Facts, although these jeans are a damn good one."

"However subjective that may be," he smirked.

"Yeah, well I owe you," I said.

"In friendship, there are no debts. Enjoy them."

I looked at him and suddenly felt a bit sorry. He probably didn't have many friends where he was from. Not being able to go outside as a kid had to have murdered his social life. He had to have been homeschooled, and everybody knows how freaky and socially awkward products of homeschooling can be. College is probably his first opportunity to forge real friendships, which is a shame because he's a really nice guy. Too nice. And cool when he isn't trying so hard. I bet if Aden wasn't sick, he would run this place.

"In that case, you just might be my new best friend," I said, knowing that Aden could never replace Dean's position in that role. "Thanks for the jeans, Aden. You didn't have to, but I really appreciate it."

"My pleasure my friend."

"So, you ready to go, dude?" I asked.

He laughed, "I'm waiting for you to finish ogling yourself in the mirror."

"Alright, alright. Let's go." I slipped on my shoes, which now looked pathetic against the three hundred dollar jeans. "Let's go this way," I said, walking toward the side exit. "This will bring us out closer to Columbus. Watch out though, that door is really-"

I was going to say 'heavy', but Aden tapped the metal plate with four fingers and the door flung open. "You were saying?" he asked.

Saving face, "Oh, um…nothing. I was saying that I need to get myself to the gym, stat," I said.

"Why don't we go tomorrow evening when you get back from class? Then we can take you to the barber to get that hair cropped, and if we have time, the shopping plaza."

Walking up the stairs, "What about your classes?" I asked.

"I can skip tomorrow's lab. I got a lot done yesterday and am going in after my classes tonight. It'll be fine."

I looked down at my raggedy sneakers loudly clashing in opposition to the fresh denim, "I guess I could use some new duds. I need to OK it with my girlfriend, but she should be cool."

"Girlfriend? Do disclose."

"Oh, her name is Camille, you'll meet her. We went to high school together," I said.

"That's lovely. You've heard that ancient saying, *Love makes the blood rich?*"

"Yeah, it's so true. I feel like my heart is pumping pixie-dust through my veins."

He laughed, "Feel's delicious, doesn't it?"

"YES!" I jumped and threw my hands and head back. Aden laughed out loud.

"Alright, well I look forward to meeting the lucky lady," he said.

"Oh, I'm the lucky one," I said.

"Well, she will feel like the lucky one once she sees you after tomorrow."

"Alright," I said extending my hand.

He shook it, "We have ourselves another deal."

Although it was dark out, Aden carried himself as if it were day. I guess this should seem appropriate considering that night *is* his day, but his lurid peppiness posed a complete contrast to the gnashing darkness and everyone else, who seemed to be repressed by moon shadows. Oddly *and* inexplicably, his energy made me feel more turned up too. Just being in his presence was thrilling, possibly because his style and poise were so smooth—I don't know. But I did notice how girls could sense him coming from indiscernible distances, even on the sidewalk across the street. Guys passing by discreetly looked him up-and-down with a poorly hidden envy *and* vain pangs of admiration. Yes, guys do envy things that they admire. By default, I was also checked out and made to be an accidental source of jealousy, so I held myself with more confidence to match the wake of Aden Vanhook as he gallivanted across the CCC.

I decided I wanted the sauerkraut and sausage pizza again since yesterday, upon my urging, Camille had totally forgotten the appeal of yaki noodles. Since he wasn't eating, I asked Aden to grab us a table. I thought it would be easy to find him, but after I got my pizza he was nowhere to be found. I became slightly annoyed (carrying a tray of pizza getting colder by the second) looking for him in a crowded dining hall. So, I just decided to go to Camille's and my spot behind the dishwashing partition.

No. Fucking. Way.

I blinked hard to affirm that what I was seeing was not a hallucination. There Aden was! Relaxing into *our* booth with his loafers kicked up on one bench and his arms spread across the back of the other.

"This OK?" he asked.

Concealing my shock, "Perfect actually, this is where Camille and I always sit," I lied. It was nothing but strange and unsettling. There were more people eating behind the partition tonight, but it was not nearly as rowdy as the main section. But regardless, how did he find this exact spot? I sat down, "You sure you're not hungry?"

Aden grimaced, "Not in the slightest," he leaned back and placed his hand over his nose, "sauerkraut huh?"

"Yeah, amongst other things," I said.

Removing his hand from his nose, "Sausage, tomato paste, mozzarella, basil, Italian herb seasoning, flour, and garlic to be exact. Smells good now," he said, "But I'm not hungry."

"So where are you from?" I asked.

"Shasta, up north."

"OK, the mountains. That's cool," I took a bite of pizza.

"Yeah, my parents moved there because it's always cloudy, and the fog runs from the mountains over the city. It's perfect for our condition."

"Oh, that's right. You said it was hereditary. Which one of your parents has—"

"Polymorphic Photosensitivity…both of them."

Swallowing, "Both! What?" I asked, shocked, and incredulous.

"Well, it's a rare disease, but that's also what makes it so hard to have a life. When you meet someone who shares your routine and health needs, it's not only convenient to share a life together, but it strengthens the bond as well."

"Totally," I agreed.

"And that's my parents. We had domestic help that took very good care of us," he said.

"Damn, like a butler *and* a maid? So, you're pretty well off then?"

114

"Well…yes. My father sued a former business partner and did very well in civil court," he said.

"Wow, that's like terrible, and awesome at the same time," I said

"Yeah, it's bittersweet. He loved his work prior to that nasty incident. So, what about you? Where are you from?"

"Vedado, a suburb about an hour outside of Los Angeles."

"And your parents? What type of people are they?" Aden asked.

"They are strait-laced, wholesome Western-American folks. SoCafo Alumni lovebirds, Dad's an architect, Mom was a teacher, but chose to stay at home when I was young."

"Really? They met here?" he asked.

"Yep."

"Now that's a testament to true love. People don't fall in love the way they used to. So how does your mom like staying at home while her degree sits on the proverbial mantle?" he asked.

"She loves it, but I think she gets bored every now and then. She misses teaching the most in those moments. There's only so much cooking and cleaning you can do before *Lifetime* becomes Academy-Award-winning entertainment." I finished my pizza and took a sip of water.

He laughed, "Are you an only child?"

"Yep. What about you, do you have brothers or sisters?"

"Nope, just me," he said, "but I've always wanted a brother."

"I know, me too. Even though my best friend, Dean, is kind of like a brother. He's like a much *younger* brother, even though I'm only three months older. We've known each other for forever, so despite his immaturity at times, we're pretty tight."

"You're lucky then, I've never had friends. My parents thought they could make up for it by buying me jeans that I'll never wear and extremely fast sports cars that don't slow down enough to ask where I'd like to go."

I didn't know what to say, so I nodded a little and continued eating and listening to him vent about his alienated yet affluent upbringing. "I didn't ask to be born into this life. I wouldn't have—it's a lonely life. But it's mine, and I've got to make the best of it. What other choice do I have? That young lady, Jessica Riley, is lucky to be free from the demands of this world, or the next one for that matter."

"That's a demented way to look at it. She could have sought therapy to get well. How did you know her name?" I asked.

"It's been all over the news," he said.

"Oh, that's right," I said, glad that Camille hadn't heard me ask such an asinine question after our paparazzi conversation. "It's just what you said about the demands of this world, I had no idea so many people could feel that way. But I agree, there's such unbelievable pressure to make a life for yourself. I guess I never really thought about it. I don't know what I want to do with my life either," I said.

He exhaled heavily, "Nor should you. Do what make you happy. Feast on the delicacies of life while you can. Let life come to you, Lewis. Once it's over, there's nothing left but loneliness and heartache, for eternity."

I finished my water, "You're right. I could be dead tomorrow, and what can I say I've done but try to please my parents and worried over not having a keen sense of direction in life. I'm excited about tomorrow, I could use a change," I said.

He nodded, "Exactly. You're young, smart, good-looking, interesting...You have the ability to naturally manifest anything you desire in this life. People are always going to want something from you, Lewis, but that will only be debilitating if you don't know what you want from yourself. In order to find *Lewis*, you've got to leave his conditioned comforts and step into the bleak unknown of his intuition. You might actually discover something that you like from taking the risk."

Reflecting on what Aden was saying, I thought back to the conversation I had with Camille about taking risks. How could I ask Camille to try something new when I haven't tried anything? I need to apply my philosophies to my own life. No wonder the first day of Philosophy was an illogical mess to me, I was totally unreceptive to it.

Aden's insight was grim and came from a place of isolation and depression, yet it was understandable. Somehow, I can identify with him. Maybe it was fated that he'd become my roommate? Less than a week ago, I was struggling to decide what needed to be packed for this new chapter of my life. Thinking back to that guy, I would've left it all and not lost a wink of sleep. Today, the risks that I need to take are apparent. In the book of life, SoCafo is a new chapter, one of change and opportunity! I can't let my parents or society author this pivotal installment of my life. Damn it, as Lenny Kravitz is my witness, life *is* going to go my way!

Chapter 12

I awoke Thursday morning having slept soundly through the night, thanks to Aden respecting his end of our pact. Even though these recent mornings have been devoid of sunlight, I didn't miss it, nor did it seem necessary to usher a positive day. Familiar with the room, I felt my way to the sink, where I brushed my teeth and washed my face using the sparse lighting above the mirror. Aden's sleeping silhouette didn't move, so I was relieved by holding up my end of the bargain as well.

After putting on the jeans that Aden had given me, I slid on my nicest sneakers and quietly left our room. Forcing the side door open, I stepped into the sunlight and was taken aback by its blinding brilliance. It took a moment to readjust my eyes before I could see clearly enough to head up the stairs and across campus to Biology.

Dr. Spivey seemed different today. He was much more put together and energetic. His clothes were much better suited for his frame, and he was clean-shaven, and no longer wearing glasses. It's amazing how an SSS had transformed him. Taking note of Dr. Spivey's polished newness, I couldn't help but be excited about letting Aden spruce me up a bit too.

As engaging as Dr. Spivey is, I couldn't think of anything except for what I was going to be doing after all of my classes were done: Camille, the gym, new hair, new clothes, hanging with Aden. I fidgeted through the lecture and after Dr. Spivey dismissed us, I bolted straight to the lab as if getting there earlier would make it end sooner.

Our objective for today's lab assignment was to figure out the molecular structure of an unknown DNA strand, and then identify what ecosystem the organism belonged to. This challenge would have been impossible if it weren't for the bank of choices detailing specific DNA characteristics. We (mostly Tim) settled on our sample being a pelagic organism, so then we were free to go. I had some time to kill before Philosophy, so I invited Tim to lunch. I wasn't expecting him to say yes, but he did.

While on the way to Thompson, I noticed that Tim's fingernails were painted black and that he was wearing the same outfit he had on during

Tuesday's lab. Thank God he didn't smell though, in fact, he smelt a little like peanut butter. His hair was slightly soiled, and he persistently stared at the ground as he walked.

"I guess you'll never step in dog shit that way," I said.

"Nope."

A few silent moments passed, "What do you want to eat?"

"Food," he said.

"OoooK," I said, feeling like retracting the invite. "Thompson it is." A few more silent moments passed, and I realized that unless I initiated the conversation, Tim was silent. And even then, his answers were restricted to a one-word minimum. "So, where are you from?" I asked, trying to test my theory.

"Washington, you asked me that already."

Damn, he's right. But at least I got six words out of him. "Sorry about that, my memory isn't the greatest."

"Yes, it is. We just remember what we want to. Everything else is just noise…" he trailed off into a mumble, "or baggage," he finalized.

I looked at him skeptically. His face was unreadable. There was not one analyzable emotion present, whatsoever. I decided that I needed to shut the fuck up. Without any further conversation, we walked to Thompson. After filling our trays from the buffet, we took a seat and began eating. It was moderately busy, so the dining hall buzzed with light conversation.

I refuse to sit in silence, damn it! "So, what's your major?" I asked in the most chipper sounding voice I could force.

"Coronary Science."

"Hmm, that's ah, pretty cool."

"Why?" he spat.

"Um, because it is."

Morosely staring at his tray, "That doesn't answer the question," he said.

"Well, I guess because you're doing something you want to do despite convention or…or others' expectations. You're a non-conformist. That takes guts."

Tim nodded his head and looked at me, "Very cool, dude." He picked up a piece of square jello with his fingers and put it in his mouth.

Satisfied with his curt approval, I sat and ate the rest of my lunch and didn't utter another word. Actually, it was nice to sit with someone else and not have to talk. Afterward, I was prepared to leave without saying anything, so imagine my surprise when I heard *Tim* say that he'd see me next Tuesday. I felt like I had done the impossible—I broke through!

In lieu of my conversation with Aden yesterday, I promised myself that I'd go to Philosophy with a different outlook. That first class seemed so pointless though, maintaining attention is going to be easier said than done. I do recognize my mistake from Tuesday though, in expecting to gain something from the course, I was disappointed when Philosophy didn't immediately prove itself advantageous to my life. But today, I'm going to follow my advice to Camille and take a risk—and Aden's advice of letting life come to me (which in this case is letting this course reveal itself).

Today I noticed some things that I was oblivious to on Tuesday, for example Professor Lackey was an obese old man, bald, with a beard. At first glance, he appeared to be jolly, but in actuality, he was a coarse, old bigot. His choice of words was purposefully offensive, and he enjoyed exploiting our world practices using what he called 'language and logic.'

Professor Lackey introduced us to the logic tree in which we set out to prove theories based on *logically* connecting one thought process to another. There were many pre-law types in the class which led to heated discussions, so the course had suddenly become much more interesting and combative. As he sat in the center of the hexagonally shaped lecture space, spinning in his cowering chair while it screamed 'bloody murder' under the enormity of his weight, Professor Lackey aggressively claimed that people were esoterically logical, when the moral depravity of our world lent itself to illogical thinking so often.

"And so young lady, you feel that we have a moral obligation to help those in need when all logic, when traced on the logic tree, supports the primal idea of survival of the fittest? Explain yourself!" he barked.

A self-assured redhead spoke up in an English accent, "I don't believe that the logic tree is an accurate measure of what is right, with all due respect Professor Lackey. It simply serves as a tool to separate what is logic from what isn't. Ethics is of an entirely different nature, Professor. One can't view ethics as a logical matter due to the subjectivity of its definition and individual interpretation. Therefore, I can't help but feel that *your* tree is utterly ill-bred and painfully obsolete." Whispers of agreement and rebuttal could be heard throughout the room.

"And that is precisely the type of treacherous thought that gives the tree its power and necessity. It is illogical to think that because you possess stellar ethical standards, that you can solve all of the world's problems. Ethics are illogical on the premise that they are subjective. They are ideas that we see fit to change based on circumstance. Killing for example; yes, that man tried to rape you, bash his head in with the closest weapon you can find. But oh no, that little girl that was struck and killed by a stray bullet is such an awful tragedy. How about we send the gunman to the chair! It's a simple and ethical question, is killing right or wrong? Your illogical thinking makes it subjective when it really isn't at all. Killing is a logical part of living, and therefore it is ethically right! We kill every day...animals, plants, each other!"

"But sir, what you are suggesting is callous and sociopathic," she said.

"You are delusional," he boomed in annoyance. "Tell me something young lady, why did you decide to attend this university?"

Her tone was less confident, "I'm an exchange student, from England sir...Professor...Dr. Lackey."

"And you would come here, with your country's backward and nonsensical ideals and exploit your ignorance at an institution of scholarly thinking?" his tone had become much calmer, almost pacifying, like a father comforts an injured child.

"But I don't think—"

Still soothing, he interrupted. "I'm not finished. What is callous and sociopathic is a country's sport of standing and watching public execution. What is callous and sociopathic is a monarchy that has made a practice of altering their religion to suit their lifestyle, entering into wars for personal gain, involving other countries in their nonsensically callous and sociopathic war efforts, murdering undesirable blue blood, racketeering, and absolute power in disguise as a democracy where unaccountable bureaucrats impose laws upon the less fortunate populace. So you come here with your hypocritical twaddle and try to deconstruct a logic that has made our country, one in which many people from *yours* left to start anew, one in which is more powerful than any other country in the world, and you want to tell me what is wrong with the ethical foundation of this society. What I think is callous and sociopathic, young lady is treason. And if in *your* country, before public execution was banned in 1870, you would have been tried and beheaded in front of the rest of your callous and sociopathic brethren. Class is dismissed."

Professor Lackey had humiliated that poor redhead. I wouldn't be surprised if she showed up to the next lecture with a bald head and an anarchy tattoo. I gathered my things and tried to exit without making eye contact with the huge dictator. Despite my level of discomfort, I was mentally stimulated and intrigued. I couldn't wait to hear the blasphemous things he would say next Tuesday!

As soon as I got outside, I called Camille. "Hey stranger," she greeted.

"Hey. How are you, babe?" I answered.

"Better now. How was Philosophy today?"

"A bloodbath! Professor Lackey is ruthless!"

"Why? What happened?" she asked.

"Oh, he destroyed this know-it-all in a publicly shaming way. I'll tell you about it at dinner. I'll be at the CCC in a few minutes," I said.

"Alright, I can't wait. See you soon," she hung up.

Camille was waiting for me when I got to the CCC. She saw me coming and began walking toward me. "How was your Calculus test?" she asked.

I had forgotten all about it, "Oh that...not too bad. I'll get it back tomorrow and let you know for sure. How were your classes?"

She exhaled, "OK, but I don't feel at all like high school prepared me for college," she said.

"I know! I don't have the stamina to sit through these lectures for hours upon end," I agreed.

"Right! And these papers, already. We went from writing all those argumentative essays, and now everything is research-based."

"We should write a letter to the president and tell him that secondary education sucks in this country!" I joked.

"Or at least ask for reform, damn," Camille was serious.

Continuing to walk and talk, we filled one another in on the day's events before finally arriving at Columbus. Neither of us knew what we wanted to order, so we split up and said we'd meet back at our table. Being that I had lunch with Tim not too long ago, I didn't really have much of an appetite. I decided on a six-inch tuna sub and cream of broccoli soup from *Sub Standard.*

Camille wasn't back when I got to our spot, so I sat down and waited for her before eating. I noticed that there were two gouged out holes in the table on her side. The chunks had been carved out with some sort of sharp utensil, probably one of the knives here. Professor Lackey would have a field day with ranting about *Youth's illogical and incessant need to destroy what someone else's hard-earned money, blood, sweat, and tears had gone into creating!*

Camille came a few moments later, and I could see from the bright red tray that she had decided to order from *Chick-Inn.*

Without noticing, she covered the vandalism with her tray. "What's wrong with you?" she asked.

"Who me? Nothing. I was just thinking about my Philosophy professor."

"Oh yeah, tell me what happened!" she demanded enthusiastically.

"Well first off, Professor Lackey is a total prick. I mean right-wing Republican, sexist, classist, every kind of 'ist you can be pretty much. He's so painfully blunt, and yet there's a lot of merit to what he's saying."

"Wow," she said dipping her nugget into honey mustard.

"You can say your grace, I'll wait," I said.

Camille smiled and bowed her head, "OK, go on," she said after she had finished.

"So, we had a debate about survival of the fittest versus governmental aid. He ruined this poor exchange student, it was brutal."

She sighed, "That's terrible. As a professor, how can you do that to a student? I mean, our minds are in need of nurturing and guidance, not ridicule and shaming."

"I agree, which is why I intend on keeping my mouth shut and being egregiously Republican in all of my assignments," I said.

"Sounds like a smart move, Lewis. Cheers to that," she raised her lemonade to my Sprite for a toast, "fake it 'til you make it," We toasted.

I tilted my head, "Fake it 'til you make it indeed. Why thank you m'lady."

Smiling, "So how are things with Aden?"

"Oh, I'm glad you mentioned it. We're going shopping after we work out tonight. He's got great taste…it's gonna be like a little makeover."

"Oh, wow. Makeover? I don't think there's anything wrong with the present package, but far be it for me to question the master of taking risks," she joked. Camille threw a nugget into her mouth and rolled her eyes playfully.

"C'mon, don't start that. Don't you like these jeans?"

"Yeah, I was going to tell you they look good. Why?"

"Well, they were Aden's. He never wore them, so he gave them to me." My better judgment told me not to disclose the price or that they were brand new.

"That was nice of him. Not to mention it's the least he could do for waking you up every night and covering the window."

"Camille, give him a break. It's not his fault. Wait 'til you meet him. You are going to love him," I said.

"I know, I'm just giving you a hard time. He sounds lonely and desperate for friends in my opinion. I'm glad he has you," she said.

Aden was anything but desperate, but it seemed gainful to let her think him so, "You're right," I agreed, and ate a spoonful of lukewarm, watered-down soup.

Camille wanted to try my sandwich, and I had been eying her nuggets, so we finished each other's meals and continued talking about our classes. After dinner, we walked back to Hoffmann and exchanged what started out as a goodnight kiss. It was a bit too passionate for the public, and then it morphed into flat out sensual and entirely inappropriate for the public, and we both knew it.

Sensing the scrutinizing eyes, I pulled away, but Camille grabbed my hand and said, "Sandra is at class, do you want to come up for a while?"

Without hesitation, "Yes," I answered.

We hurried passed Katrina and Camille waved. Katrina shot one of her *emmm...hmmm* glares our way and I lowered my head in embarrassment. Camille missed it entirely because she was too focused on getting inside the elevator and maintaining her firm grip on my hand. The ride up was awkward because we shared the elevator with a few Hoffmann residents and had to try to fight the temptation to jump one another. All civility ended when we finally reached room 7007.

Once inside, Camille threw her bag across the room and madly removed her shirt. Like a lioness upon prey, she lunged, locking me into a rough and passionate kiss. I clumsily removed my shirt and threw it onto the floor. Kissing ravenously, we stumbled backward until my calves bumped into the frame of her bed. Camille pushed me down onto the soft mattress and ran over to close the door, shutting out the public world. She turned on the lamp above the mirror, and then took off everything except her bra and panties. Approaching me, not breaking eye contact, Camille's slow strides made every second of her seduction seem like a scene from an adult film. I couldn't get enough. Standing over me, as if to confirm that I was a captive audience, she paused before slowly bending down to remove her socks.

Camille mounted me like a world-class equestrian mounts her stallion. Pinning both of my wrists above my head with one, Camille used her other hand to trace my chest. She leaned over and lightly licked my nipple, and I began to feel myself becoming aroused. Camille could too because she looked at me and twisted her lips into a devilish grin, parting it with her tongue.

She slowly released my arms and began to undo my belt buckle. "I bet these jeans never got this much action when Aden was wearing them," she whispered into my ear.

"Not at all," I whispered back.

She kissed my ear and neck and nibbled her way back to my mouth while her hand navigated its way to my fly. She slid the helpless, Armani zipper down and found me immediately. Massaging slowly, Camille gasped, as if pleased with my size. She played with me until I was at full attention, and then slithered her hand down and squeezed firmly.

Grabbing her hand, "No. Camille, stop," I whispered. "We can't do this."

Breathing heavily, "I know, I know, I know, you're right," she said.

"It's not that I don't want to, believe me, I do. It's just that…" Flushed and embarrassed, I drew a blank.

"No, you're right. This is way too fast. I'm so sorry. I don't know what came over me."

She stood up and began to pick her clothing off the floor.

I sat up, "Camille, I'm a virgin," I mumbled.

She continued getting dressed and pretended not to hear me. After she was fully clothed, she sat down on the bed about a foot away from me, "Lewis, why didn't you tell me earlier?"

Buttoning my jeans, "It never came up, and I didn't think it mattered," I said.

"Of course it matters! We're talking about who you've experienced sex with for the first time," she handed me my shirt, "which in this case is *no one*."

"Are you a virgin?" I asked.

"No. I'm not," she admitted.

"Well, that's OK. Do I know him?" I asked.

"Yes," she admitted.

"Who is he?" I asked.

She looked crazy with guilt, "Lewis, I really should have told you this earlier, I'm sorry. I wanted so desperately to tell you when I told you about Deb, Courtney, and Julie, but I didn't know how."

"Tell me what?" I knew what was coming, that she had slept with Dean, but I needed to hear her say it. "Tell me what, Camille?"

"I…I'm so sorry," she extended her hands, palms up, toward me. "I slept with Dean our sophomore year because I thought that you-"

I pushed her arms away and stood up, "What? How could you keep that from me? What the hell is wrong with you! I can't believe this! Camille?"

Instantly, my mind recalled the vile conversations that Dean had had with me after violating his most recent conquest. He never left a detail undisclosed: how he had fucked Deb in her parents' bed while they were away in Cozumel, how Courtney had followed him around school like a hopeless shadow after he came inside her raw, and how Julie let him hit it from the back and screamed from the pain of losing her virginity. But he never mentioned his exploits with Camille, and thank God for that. I don't think I could have handled it had he been forthcoming with that information!

I felt that discouraging lump that materializes in your throat just before a fit of tears ensues. I couldn't let Camille see me this upset and vulnerable, so I fought back the furious tears with all that I had. And I'm glad I did because Camille was actually laughing.

"I can't believe that you could laugh right now! Dean is my best friend!" I said, my voice shaking with anger and frustration.

"I'm sorry, it's not funny. I couldn't resist. I'm just kidding babe, come here," she stood up with her arms still extended. "I wouldn't go near Dean if we were both magnets," she said.

Palming both of my cheeks, she began to kiss all over my face.

"That's not funny, Camille!" I said, firmly.

"I know, I'm sorry babe," she found my lips and kissed them.

Reluctant to believe her, "So are you a virgin?" I asked again. "The truth this time, no games!"

In the dim lighting, the dancing sapphires were matte-quartz. Camille stared at me deeply and squeezed my hands, "I told you already, I have only had eyes for you. I will give you my virginity when and where you decide you are ready to give me yours."

"I hate you for that. You are the worst! *Never* do that to me again, Camille. I'm serious," I warned, the pain of the joke lifting from my shoulders.

Camille threw her arms around my neck and kissed me on the lips, but this kiss was no ordinary kiss. This caressing of our lips was the sealing of a promise that our minds had connected, our souls were bonded, and soon our bodies would experience physical love for the first time...together.

Chapter 13

By the time I returned to our dorm room, Aden was ready—wearing all black workout clothes, fashionable even for the gym. I had planned on wearing my trusty exercise shorts and a dirty T-shirt, so looking at him in his sleeveless lycra with cut shoulders and biceps made me feel certain that I would at least have to put on a clean shirt.

"You ready?" he asked.

"Just about, I need to change," I said.

"With haste my friend, the mall closes soon."

I threw on my shorts and a clean, white V-neck, and we headed into the crisp night air. I was expecting to walk, but when we got outside Aden headed toward the off-street parking lot. The car that Aden seemed to be taking strides in the direction of was a blood-red, Audi R8 convertible. When he pulled the key fob out of his pocket and unlocked the doors, I stopped dead-in-my-tracks. This piece of engineered art actually belonged to my roommate?

"You must be joking!" I gasped.

Smiling, he said, "About what?"

"*This* is the sports car you were talking about? The one your parents bought you? I thought you meant they bought you a Mustang. This is the nicest car I've ever seen!"

"Oh yeah? Would you like to drive?" he asked.

Open-mouthed, "What? Hell yeah!" I said.

I tracked the key-fob as it soared through the air into my hand. Overwhelmed with excitement, I ran around to the driver's side as Aden walked to the passenger's. I felt the superiority of European luxury within seconds of sliding into the lavish vehicle. After adjusting the rearview mirror and push-starting the ignition, I threw the shifter into first gear and cautiously rolled out of the lot. Once I had pulled onto the street, I opened her up, and before I knew it, we were speeding toward the gym at ninety-five miles per hour. A minute hadn't passed before campus police lights flashed from a patrol-bike into the rearview mirror.

In a panic, "Dude, we're getting pulled over," I yelled.

Aden reached into the glove box as I slowed to a stop, "Give him this," he said handing me the registration and insurance.

I sat with my head and arms cradling the steering wheel for what seemed like an eternity, awaiting the dreaded words...

"Son, do you know how fast you were going?"

With my face nestling the horn, "Yes," I said.

The officer sighed, "License and registration please."

Without looking up, I handed him the papers Aden had given me. "Here you are sir," I said.

He fumbled through them, "I need to see your license, Mr. Vanhook."

I lifted my head, "I'm actually not the owner of this vehicle, sir-"

"I am Aden Vanhook, officer." Aden's face was totally calm. "My friend was just taking my car for a joyride and was unaware of the torque," he said as cool and collected as a quarterback. "Thank you for warning us against the dangers of speeding in a school zone sir, we won't let it happen again," I was entranced by the melodious sound of his voice and the look in his crystallized eyes. "We really appreciate the necessity of your vocation, but now we really must be on our way."

"Well then, my job is done here, gentlemen. Mr. Vanhook, here is your registration." The officer handed Aden the envelope over my very confused head. Then the cop looked at me, "Be careful of that gas pedal, son. We don't want you to hurt yourself or anyone else for that matter, OK?"

"Uh...yes, officer," I said.

After tapping the side of the car, the policeman saluted us, and I drove off feeling like I had just witnessed a miracle. "What just happened?" I asked Aden.

"One of my gifts, I don't lie to people. I just thought I'd be honest, and it worked. The virtue of honesty is often overlooked. I've found that most people respond favorably when being told the truth."

"My best friend, Dean, has a similar gift too, but he doesn't use honesty and is never as smoothly well-crafted as you just were. Damn man! That was crazy-ridiculous!" I said.

"So was how fast you were driving," Aden joked.

We both laughed uproariously as I peeled out. I revved the engine back up to ninety-five, recklessly speeding toward the gym.

***

SoCafo's gym was exceptional as far as workout facilities go. It was stocked with all the new Hammer Strength machines and free weights. There was a Crossfit training area, separate cardio rooms with televisions, and ceiling to floor mirrors on every wall. A few seconds after we got inside the weight room, I heard my name called. Turning around, I saw Brant and Phil walking toward Aden and me.

"What's up?" we fist-bumped.

"How are the classes?" Brant asked.

"They're classes I guess."

We all laughed.

"I told you we have English together," Phil reminded Brant.

"Yeah, Dr. Fuck-your-son, right?" Brant asked. Aden laughed solely, as it was his first time hearing the reference to Dr. Ferguson.

"I'm sorry, this is my roommate, Aden," I said.

With a cocky head nod, "Nice to meet you, bro," Phil said as he sized Aden up.

"I've seen you in class, you're in Engineering, right?" Brant asked.

"Yes, now that you mention it, you do look familiar. Lewis mentioned you. I told him we should grab a bite to eat since we have such similar schedules," Aden offered.

"Oh dude, it's crucial. I'm not eating dinner until after midnight on most days. But the silver lining is that the partying is great."

"Yeah, and I get woken up at all times of the morning," Phil said.

"Oh, don't I know it," I said implicating Aden.

Slightly ruffled, "I beg your pardon, Lewis, that was before we made a deal," Aden said.

"What deal?" Brant asked.

"Not to wake each other up anymore," I said.

"I could use that deal," Phil said to Brant.

"It's not because I'm partying *all* the time, sometimes when I get home from class, you're asleep," Brant said.

Phil rolled his eyes, "Yeah, and you're like a bull in a china shop dude," I laughed loudly at the image of Brant's huge frame attempting to stealthily tiptoe around their extravagant dorm room. "Speaking of partying though, are y'all coming tomorrow night?" Phil asked.

Looking at Aden, "I'm in. You?" I said.

"If I'm invited, certainly," he said.

Brant threw his hand back at Aden, "Man, of course you're invited. It's going to be insane."

Aden smiled, "Well then count me in."

"Alright then, we're in," I said.

"So, what are y'all working on tonight?" Phil asked.

"Perhaps chest and triceps," Aden answered.

"Sounds good to me. Let's get it," I said.

"Alright then gentlemen, we'll see you tomorrow night," Brant said, mimicking Aden's tone.

"Are you going to Cunt-Lit tomorrow?" Phil asked me.

I nodded, "You mean Contemporary Literature? You're disgusting, and yes...I'll see you there."

Laughing at his joke, "Alright, see ya," Phil said.

Aden and I headed to the first available bench press and began stacking on weights. As a novice, I was careful not to overdo it, but Aden was a beast. He loaded up the bar with a couple of forty-five-pound plates and lifted them as if they were pennies. When it was my turn, I couldn't lift the bar at all, and we had to put a thirty-five-pound plate on each side (and I could only do six reps with those). For Aden's second set, he stacked two more forty-five-pound plates onto the bar and lifted them as if they were nickels. I stayed at thirty-five pounds.

Feeling like Aden was annoyed that we had to keep removing his weight and restacking mine, "Sorry man," I said.

"About what?" he asked.

"The weight. I'm sure you'd be done with your workout already if you didn't have to unload the bar with my puny thirty-five pounders."

"Not at all. I don't even really have to work out that much. My strength and physique are genetic. I also have a pretty strict diet."

"But you don't really eat that much," I said wiping away sweat.

"No, you're right. The sun takes a lot out of people, and since I'm not exposed to it, I don't need to eat as much. A good meal will keep me satisfied for a while."

"What!" I said, "That's crazy. So, when was the last time you ate?"

"Hmmm, let's see...after class on Monday," Aden said getting into position to spot me.

While I was doing my reps, my mind drifted. Monday night was the night that Aden and his female friend woke me up. Well technically it was 1:30 Tuesday morning, but still, he hadn't eaten anything in almost two days!

Placing the bar on the rack, "Aren't you starving?" I asked.

Aden smiled, "You have no idea," he said.

Wiping more sweat from my forehead, "Well then let's get out of here and get you some food," I said.

"I plan on getting something to eat while you're getting your haircut," he said. "We'll do a couple of resistance exercises, some free weights for triceps, and call it a night. Sound good?"

"Oh, alright then. I'll try, but I don't know if I can endure all of that. I'm dying…and you haven't even broken a sweat," I said placing my hands on my knees. And he hadn't, Aden's forehead was bone dry.

He smiled, "You'll get used to it. Rome wasn't built in a day."

***

As anticipated, shopping with Aden proved to be an eye-opening experience. I discovered that I had absolutely no style at all. Currently, nothing about anything in my closet could be considered fashionable. Aden explained how shopping could be looked at as a serendipitous encounter. At first, I was skeptical, but the explanation was entirely logical. Even Professor Lackey would have been impressed.

According to Aden, when a person buys an article of clothing, a force has placed them in the right place at exactly the right time, like the universe actually intended for them to have the garment. Evidence of a cosmically aligned shopping experience can be seen when one finds something that they love and it's the last in their size or arriving at the register to discover your most expensive find is sixty percent off (as if the cost would deter Aden from making the purchase).

Up until now, I was happily satisfied shopping at Aeropostale, Old Navy, or American Eagle. Aden bypassed all of those places, instead hitting up a high-end department store of which the name, I can't even pronounce. I was amazed at how much more expensive things were, but also at the nicer quality and craft, and how much better they looked and felt on me. Aden offered to put everything on his credit card, but I refused. My parents were probably going to kill me for charging all of this, but at the end of the day, I need clothes, right?

I spent somewhere in the neighborhood of $3000.00, but it all happened so quickly that I couldn't stop. With Aden's approval, I got five pairs of jeans (I know this might sound ridiculous, but they were all different washes, styles, and fits), a couple of watches, three pairs of shoes: sneakers, black boots, and brown moccasins. Aden convinced me to invest in a black, European-cut blazer, and I definitely needed some new underwear considering how hot-n-heavy things were becoming with Camille. I bought a variety of new tops, all different styles and colors. Aden also helped me figure out that I am truly a medium and not a large like I was accustomed to thinking.

Walking in-and-out of the fitting rooms to show Aden everything that I was trying on was kind of annoying. I don't know why, but he didn't want to sit in the dressing rooms despite the comfy looking chaise in front of the mirror. Not to mention that the fashion show was a bit disgraceful because I knew that Aden's approval was necessary before I purchased *anything*. At one point, I questioned whether I was cultivating a style of my own or if I was being puppeteered into decisions that Aden would make for himself. But that moment passed quickly at the thought of what was currently hanging in my closet back at Ponce.

Despite feeling that I had just charged a bunch of things that weren't 100% *me*, my haircut was worth every penny! Aden dropped me off and went to get dinner, leaving me to my own judgment, and I wanted my hair to be as low and low-maintenance as possible. I've always worn my hair a bit shaggy, so this new close-cropped cut was a drastic yet welcomed change. The sun had given the longer, shaggy locks natural highlights, so when all of that was cut out, my hair appeared to be much darker and thicker.

When I walked into the waiting area, Aden was there, and he approved immediately. "Well well, my friend. You look older in an established way."

"Yeah, I think so too. So, you like it then, it's not too preppy?" I said running my hand over my head nervously.

"Lewis, I don't lie. If I hated it, I'd tell you. You look great. So, you ready to get back to campus?"

"Bullshit, you don't lie! But thanks anyhow. I thought you were going to get something to eat," I said.

"I did."

"Where?"

"The local watering hole," he answered.

"A bar? How'd you get in?"

"I talked the bouncer into it. Bars are not my preference as far as places to eat, I hate alcohol. But I'm a creature of convenience, and it was right across the street," Aden said.

"Yeah, I hear ya. But I can smell the alcohol on you, gross. Are you sure you didn't drink anything, *Mr. I don't lie*? You look a little buzzed too by the way." I was joking with him, but he did seem slightly intoxicated. I mean, he wasn't slurring his speech or anything, but he was definitely more tranquil than usual.

He laughed, "Perhaps I did have a little vodka with my meal."

"I knew it," I said.

We both got into the convertible and peeled out. I had a trunk full of new purchases and the wind was blowing through my freshly shortened hair. Aden drove (the speed limit) and played tragic sounding classical music. I turned it down to thank him.

"For what?" he asked.

"For this, I feel like a new person," I said.

"Well, you paid for everything. All you needed was an eye."

"Well, thanks for the eye then."

"Anytime my friend," he turned the music back up.

I tilted my head back and watched the moon and stars race us. My face grew into a satisfied grin at the thought of everything that was bagged in Aden's trunk. Feeling like a brand new person, I couldn't wait to see Camille's reaction to the reinvented me. I know she said she liked me the way I was, but I also know that this is a drastic and much better improvement from the old Lewis. If Camille liked me before, she is going to love me now.

Chapter 14

The next morning, I wore my brand-new distressed wash Seven jeans with a bright green Lacoste polo and sneakers. My hair was short enough that it took no time at all to groom back into the style the woman at the salon had given me. My walk to Calculus was exhilarating; I was amazed by how much more attention I received from girls. I began playing a game of staring at each passing girl, to see how many of them I could get to make eye contact with me. When they did, I flashed my sexiest smile. Most of the pawns lost the game and flashed a demure smile back, but shush, what Camille doesn't know won't hurt her.

I hadn't studied for today's Calc quiz, so it was a little rough. After I handed in my blue-book, Professor Winn returned the last one—on limits. I was free to go. I'd gotten a ninety-three. My first college grade was an *A*...nice!

Now I know that it is majorly counterintuitive for a college student to say that academics aren't really on their list of priorities, but right now I'm more focused on my social life. How could I not be? For instance, my relationship with Camille...we have so much in common and we never fight. And then my friendship with Aden, it's literally given birth to a more fashionable and risk-taking me. So, you can see how hard finding focus on integration by substitution could be when in love and experiencing a much overdue metamorphosis. Besides, I can always just ask Camille for help if my grades begin to slip.

I was excited to get to English so that I could finalize the details of this evening's festivities with Phil. According to Phil, this party was a SoCafo tradition. The first Friday of the school year, a group of fraternities rent out a campsite, buy an obscene amount of beer, and pay deejays to come and spin all-night-long, or until the cops bust the party up. Admission was going to be twenty bucks per person, but that also got you into the party plus an *all you can drink* cup.

In between party conversation, I tried to listen to Dr. Ferguson spewing something about 16th Century European Folklore. Our first assignment was research-based, and we needed to choose an element of the genre or time period to disseminate. So basically, we were charged with choosing a characteristic of the 1500's literature and discussing how evidence of that period could be seen in Contemporary Literature. I heard him say that we had a week before the first draft was due, so I jotted the date down on a piece of loose-leaf and tuned the rest out. Phil and I continued to chat quietly.

"So the space is probably about twenty miles from campus and it's huge," Phil whispered.

"Nice. I can't wait, dude. I've never been to a rave," I said.

"What!" Phil said louder than I had anticipated.

"Philip Stevenson!" Dr. Ferguson yelled.

Alarmed, Phil turned his attention to Dr. Ferguson, "Present."

"Yes, I am aware that you are here, Philip, but I need you to tell me your intended topic for the research paper on the juxtaposition of 16th Century Folklore and Contemporary Literature."

"Huh?" Phil said.

Dr. Ferguson sighed, "Mr. Stevenson, what topic are you choosing? Wizards, Witches, Werewolves?"

"Oh, yes sir, werewolves," Phil answered.

"Thank you," Dr. Ferguson wrote something on a yellow note pad. "And your social networking partner, Mr....uh *Lewis* I believe?"

"Yes sir," I said.

"Well?" Dr. Ferguson boomed.

Frantically I looked at Phil, and he shrugged. I couldn't choose werewolves too. I shouted the first thing that came to mind, "Vampires sir, vampires."

"Thank you, Mr. Lewis. Gentlemen, please remember that you are at this university to learn." Dr. Ferguson scribbled something on his note pad and continued to the next student. Embarrassed, I sunk down into my seat and didn't initiate conversation with Phil for the rest of the section.

After class, Phil and I went back to Thompson for lunch, and it seemed like all he wanted to talk about was my new look and what brought it about anyway.

Chewing a mouthful of lettuce, "So you just spent three thousand dollars on a whim because your roommate said you needed a makeover?" Phil questioned.

"Not quite. I tried on a pair of his jeans, and I liked how they fit. I mean, he definitely has more style than your typical college freshman. I guess I just needed to go shopping with a fresh pair of eyes."

"Yeah, that motherfucker looked like Richard Gere in American Gigolo. Hanging with him has definitely increased your stock."

Swallowing a spoonful of clam chowder, "What do you mean?" I asked.

"Well, look at you dude, you're already like a little clone of him, and it's been less than a week. I mean, the new look is an improvement, don't get me wrong. It's just that I hope this is you."

"But you barely even know me. These are just clothes and a new haircut, I'm still the same person," I said.

Phil put his fork down, "I'm sorry, I'm not being clear. I'm happy you and Aden are getting along dude, and I'm glad to get a chance to get to know him tonight too. He seems like an awesome guy. In fact, hanging with him would increase all of our stock...he's like a teenage James Bond. But, I'm just sayin' these are the most impressionable years of our lives, you know? I just wouldn't be so eager to change myself so quickly because it'll happen naturally over time, that's all."

I nodded, "You're right, but this feels natural to me. It'd be different if I hated it and felt uncomfortable."

"Good point," Phil said.

"These are impressionable times, which is why I think I should capitalize on change. And Aden's a good guy, so I don't really mind adopting some of his swag. I actually felt *more* uncomfortable being around him in basketball shorts and a T-shirt. I guess I'm just being hypersensitive because I still haven't talked to my parents about how much money I spent on all this," I used my hands to scroll down both sides of my upper body.

"Yeah," Phil agreed, "and for the record pretty boy, it's the best spent three thousand dollars I've ever seen."

"Jackass," I said, launching a pack of saltines at him. "I gotta go before I'm late for my next class."

"Alright bro, see ya tonight."

Sociology was pretty interesting today because Sharon Preedy happened to be guest facilitating the lecture, in lieu of recent events: namely Jessica Riley's suicide. We were having a discussion about suicidal tendencies and anti-social behaviors. Sharon Preedy proclaimed that being a female student and Sociology major who was qualified in social-psychological doctrine, rendered her a common denominator, worthy of facilitative rights. I thought back to Jessica's hysterical and sobbing roommate at the crime scene...would she consider any of the tell-tale signs Sharon Preedy was mentioning to be a tendency that Jessica exhibited? I can't be too sure, but a loss of appetite, social withdrawal, depression...I definitely remembered Jessica's roommate saying that she was happy, and I assume that hungry, depressed people with no friends are *not* happy. 'Jessica seemed *happy*' the roommate's words rang in my ears over Sharon Preedy's rattling self-assured theorem.

After Sociology, I came home and looked over my Calculus notes. I intended on asking Camille for help, but I needed to pinpoint the areas where I didn't have a clue what was going on. I was interrupted by a knock on the door. I checked the time on my new watch, 6:03. Aden was still asleep. Who could this be? I opened the door to a pretty and petite blonde holding a folder with Aden's name on it.

"Can I help you?" I said.

"Hi, yes. Is Aden here?" she asked nervously.

I turned my body to the side, allowing her to judge by the covers pulled all the way over his head, that he was still sleeping. "Yeah, but he's knocked out," I said.

"Oh, yeah. Of course he is. My name is Sarah…um Reynolds, I'm an Engineering major. I noticed that he wasn't in class last night, so I made copies of my notes and the assignment, and I thought I'd drop them off."

I extended my hand to take the folder, "Oh wow. I can make sure he gets them. I'm sure he'll be very appreciative."

She looked apprehensive about giving up the folder, "Um…OK. And what's your name?" she asked.

"I'm Lewis, his roommate."

"Right," she smiled nervously, "Lewis, can I ask you something?"

I crinkled my forehead, "Sure, why not?"

"Um, don't tell Aden I asked," she said.

I pantomimed zipping my lips, "OK."

"Um, do you know if he has a girlfriend?"

"Oh, I don't think so," I smiled at her and she blushed.

Her eyes widened, "Really? OK," she said. "How well do you know him?"

"Fairly. Why?" I asked.

"Is he a nice guy? I mean, from what you know of him, does he seem like a decent person?"

"The best. He's an awesome guy," I smiled earnestly. "I'll put in a good word for you, Sarah," I said.

"Really? That would be awesome. Nothing embarrassing, just that I think he's gorgeous."

"No, you're awesome," I held up the folder. "And will do."

She blushed again, "Oh, OK. Thanks, Lewis. I'll see you around."

"Yep, see you later," I closed the door.

Remembering my promise to not wake him, I placed the folder on Aden's desk and took a mental note to tell him about Sarah after I'd finished my pre-party SSS.

***

When I returned from my SSS, Aden was awake and dressed.

"So, what time do the festivities begin?" he asked.

I shrugged, "I'm not sure. It's an all-night field party, so I'm sure we can get there whenever. I'm meeting Camille for dinner; I'll be back in a couple of hours and then we can split."

"That will be perfect," Aden said.

"A girl, Sarah Reynolds, came by and dropped that off," I said, pointing to the folder on his desk.

"What is it?" he asked.

"Might as well be a confession of love in the form of your classwork from yesterday," I joked as I stumbled clumsily into my jeans. "There is some assignment due Monday night, and I guess she figured since you guys don't have a class tonight that she'd bring it by."

As I finished dressing, he picked up the folder and examined the contents. "Confession of love, huh?" he said without looking up.

"Yeah, she's into you man. Great looking too…I'm sure she wouldn't object if you asked her out," I said grabbing a brand new, beige V-neck.

"That's not a bad idea, Lewis, not bad at all. Not that shirt, wear the black Kenneth Cole," Aden said without breaking his attention from the folder.

"Thanks. Well, you look as if you have some work to do, so you'll have a couple of hours to work while I'm at dinner," I said, zipping up my new boots.

"Perfect. I'll see you when you get back. Give Camille my greetings. You do realize that I need to meet her sooner than later. You should invite me out with you two one of these times."

Giving his proposal consideration, "Absolutely, perhaps this weekend," I said checking my reflection in the mirror. I smoothed my hair into place and left the room

With the excitement of seeing Camille for the first time since going shopping and getting a haircut, I walked hastily to Hoffmann. Katrina's head was unhappily planted in a book. I cleared my throat and she looked up annoyed, at first.

"Well I'll be, look at you," she said smiling.

"So, what do you think Ma'am?"

137

"For all that's George and Clooney boy, you aren't playing with it!"

"Thank you, thank you," I blushed.

"Going to see your girl?"

"Yeah," I reached into my pocket for my passport.

Katrina sucked her teeth, "Boy please, go 'head up."

"Thanks, Katrina."

"Mmmhm."

I leaped onto the elevator with a couple of other residents. It was fun to play the eye contact game in passing, but in close quarters it was uncomfortable. I hit the button for the seventh floor, placed my hands in my pockets, and found a nice spot on the floor to observe.

"Hi," a girl in pink, short shorts said.

I looked up, "Hey."

"Going to see your girlfriend?" her friend asked.

"Yeah. Seventh floor," I said.

"Lucky girl," the co-ed in pink added.

I smiled and resumed my position on floor duty. I awaited the beep for the seventh floor and quickly stepped off the elevator. "Bye," both girls harmonized.

"Later," I said.

When I got to Camille's room, the door was open and girly music was softly playing in the background of the scene that she and Sandra had created by being sprawled out on the floor studying. I knocked on the doorframe, and as Camille lifted her head, her mouth dropped open. The look on her face was one of simultaneous shock and excitement. This look, I bet, grazed her face the night she was announced Prom Queen.

"Can I help you?" she joked. "Sandra, do you remember my boyfriend, Lewis?"

Looking up, "Um, I remember meeting your boyfriend, and that *is not* him girl," Sandra said.

"Ha ha ha, very amusing ladies."

Getting up, "I love it, baby," Camille said. She put her arms around my neck and kissed me.

"That's more like it, come here," I said, kissing her back.

Sandra groaned, "OK, gross. Now I remember him," and went to sit at her desk.

"You hungry babe?" I asked.

"Yeah, can't you tell she wants *you* for dinner," Sandra replied.

"Don't hate girl," Camille joked. "You want anything?"

"Where are you guys going?" Sandra asked.

Looking back at me, "Columbus?" Camille asked.

"Actually, I was thinking we could go to Reno Hall tonight," I said.

"Reno Hall? How romantic," Sandra teased. "I'm good, thanks though. You guys have fun."

"Alright, see you in a bit," Camille said. Turning back to me, "Reno? Wow."

Reno is the fine dining facility on campus. Not that cost matters because we both have meal plans, but the restaurants are higher scale and have a wait staff. I was craving Italian food, so I hope Camille won't mind pasta tonight.

"So, what are you in the mood for?" I asked.

"Pressing question. I could ask you the same thing," she said pressing the down arrow on the wall panel.

"I'm thinking Italian," I admitted.

"Well, Italian it is. See how easy I am," she said.

I made a face and rolled my eyes, "I already knew how easy you are, I'm the one that stopped you, remember?"

She lightly backhanded my arm, "Don't go thinking you're all of that just because you got a cute haircut and some new shoes."

"Yeah, but you love it though. You can't help but sweat this," I flexed my biceps and smiled.

"OK, that's quite enough. I think I just lost my appetite," she turned back toward her dorm room, but I grabbed her hand, pulled her in, and kissed her.

The elevator door opened and the same two co-eds from my ride up were coming back down. They had seen the kiss and suddenly were not as social. In fact, as we stepped onto the elevator, they were looking Camille and me up-and-down as if it smelt like we hadn't showered in days. I could sense that their hate was making Camille feel uncomfortable, so I clutched her close to me from behind and began a monotone dialogue into her ear.

"So yes, to Italian?" I asked.

"Yes, I suppose."

"If you want something else, tell me, babe," I said.

"I'm fine with Italian, just not your attitude," she mumbled, "thinking you're all-of-that."

I kissed her cheek and whispered, "You know you like it," as the elevator door opened.

"I do," she said as we left two nasty bitches fuming on the elevator.

Walking passed Katrina, "Bye y'all," she called.

"Bye Katrina," Camille said as I waved.

"So, who's all going to this thing tonight?" Camille asked.

"I'm going with Aden for sure, but I'm not sure if Brant and Phil are coming with or meeting us there. It's a huge party, why don't you come? Aden is dying to meet you," I said.

"Maybe next time, I've got so much work to do."

I put my arm around her, "OK, but next time I'm not taking no for an answer," I said.

"OK," she smiled.

"Also, I could use some help in Calculus, you wanna go to the library Sunday?"

"Sure," she said, "what are you working on?"

"Integration," I cringed.

"Oh man, OK.," she said. "So, tell me more about Aden."

"What do you want to know?"

"What's he like?"

I shrugged, "I don't know. He's like that cliché guy that every dude wants to be and every girl wants to be with," I laughed, "Minus the photosensitivity stuff."

"Right," she grinned. "So, he's fine?"

"What is with all you girls asking guys if other guys are hot? Chill," I said half-serious and half-joking.

"What are you talking about?" she asked.

"Katrina asked me the same thing about him."

"Well, is he?" Camille looked too interested in the answer.

"Hey! No Ma'am, you're my girl. I'd have to kill him, poison him with some sunlight or something."

"Easy killer, I'm just playing…but what else?" Camille asked.

"He comes from money, his dad is a millionaire from Shasta, and they have a maid and butler and shit."

She laughed, "No way!"

"Way. Guess what kind of car he has."

"Ahh…BMW?"

"A freaking brand-new Audi R8! That's like a one hundred twenty-five, thousand-dollar car."

"You're lying!"

"I drove it to the mall yesterday!"

"Oh my gosh, Lewis. What do his parents do?"

"Well, apparently nothing now. His dad was unjustly terminated from a fortune 500 company or something. So, he sues, right, and wins a multi-million-dollar settlement."

"Wow. Well, is he nice?" Camille asked.

140

"Unbelievably. I told you he just gave me those jeans, right?"

"Yeah…well, that's cool that he's so loaded and still so grounded slash cool," Camille said.

"Well, I mean you *can* tell he's loaded. He's kind-of-a label whore and speaks all proper – it can get annoying at times," I say.

Camille twisted her mouth in judgment, "Have you seen a mirror today?" she says back.

I rolled my eyes, "It's different Camille, just wait 'til you meet him yourself, you'll see. You just better not like what you see," I threatened flirtatiously.

"Oh, so you *don't* want me to like him?" she flirted back flashing a calculating grin.

"You know what I mean," I said smiling.

Camille and I walked into Reno Hall and got in line to be seated at a restaurant called *When in Rome*. A hostess greeted us immediately as the wait staff flanked left and right taking orders and carrying trays of food and drinks. I'm sure that anyone having trouble with tuition, room, and board, or books would love a job like this. I assume they're making minimum wage, plus tips, not to mention they probably get to take home a ton of free Italian food.

The tables were dressed with a white, linen cloth and were accessorized with either a votive or flowering cacti and silverware. We were taken to a cozy candlelit table for two where we were given menus. Shortly after, a bubbly, southern waitress came to the table and introduced herself.

"Hey, y'all. My name's Casey, and I'll be takin' care of y'all t'night. Is this y'alls first-time heyer?" she asked.

"Yes Ma'am," I said.

"Well welcome. Would you like to hear our specials?"

"Sure," Camille said.

"T' night we have what we call Rome's Grand Prix 'cause you get an appetizer, entrée, and dessert for one price of twenty-six ninety-five. You can choose from any of the items on the menu insert."

Camille opened her menu, "This flappy thing," she asked.

"Yes, darlin' that there. If I could recommend the spinach or lobster stuffed ravioli, it is to die for. A little heavy on the garlic if ya' ask me, but some folks like that."

"Yum…the lobster stuffed ravioli sounds delicious. I'll take that," Camille said.

"Alright dear, um…what appetizer would you like with that?"

"Oh, umm…" Camille scanned the insert. "I'll try the calamari," she said.

Writing down the order, "Excellent choice, and you sir?"

"I'll take the spinach stuffed ravioli please, and for my appetizer, I'll take the garden salad with garlic and herb dressing," I said.

"Alright then, that takes care of that. I'll leave one menu for y'all so you can decide on your dessert later," she said grabbing Camille's menu. "Can I get y'all anythang to drank?"

"I'll have water with lemon please," Camille requested.

"I'll have the same."

"Y'all are easy. So I'ma go put you'alls order in and bring your water and garlic bread to the table, emkay," Casey smiled.

"Thanks, Casey," I said.

Still smiling, "You're very welcome," she said, and then turned and hustled off.

"She's sweet," Camille said.

"Yeah, but not as sweet as you."

"Oh, I guess my meal comes with extra cheese," Camille joked.

I smiled jovially, "So what time do you want to go to the library Sunday afternoon?" I asked.

"I dunno, whenever."

"How about around three? I've got to do some research for my Contemporary Lit paper and then study for Calculus."

"I have a paper too," Camille said sticking her tongue out and coyly looking at the ceiling. "Sounds like a plan."

I took her hand and watched the flicker from the candle dancing in her eyes. Camille tilted her head to the side and smiled softly. I shook my head at her.

"What?" she asked.

"You're beautiful."

"So are you," she said.

I smiled at her earnestly, "So…I've been looking at these dessert options and I have one question for you."

"Oh yeah?"

"Yeah—crème brulee or cheesecake? Go!"

"Cheesecake," she said immediately and blew a kiss across the table.

Chapter 15

When I got back home after dinner, Aden appeared to be ready to go, but the vibe was weird, like something about my presence was agitating him. From the moment I stepped into the room, he kept his distance from me. It was bizarre. I don't know what could have happened since the time I left for dinner and now, but he stepped away from me so violently that he backed into his desk knocking something off of it. I couldn't see what they were, but he grabbed them before they hit the floor and then quickly covered his nose.

"Is everything OK?" I asked.

He cleared his throat for an unusually long time before responding, "Yes, I'm fine. Did you eat Italian tonight?" he asked.

"Yeah, how did you know?"

Waving his hand in front of his face, "I can smell the garlic," he said.

"Oh damn. Good call, let me brush my teeth really quickly. Thanks, man, I'm glad you caught it before I offended someone tonight," although he was definitely overreacting.

"No worries, I'll wait for you outside," Aden said.

"I'll only be a minute," I said watching the door close behind him.

I brushed vigorously and swished around some mouthwash before leaving. Aden wasn't in the hallway, so I went out the side exit and up the stairs. When I reached the top step, Aden was waiting for me in his car across the street, with the top down and that same dreadful, classical music blasting. I ran coolly to the passenger side and hopped over the door.

Blowing at Aden, "Better?" I asked.

Nodding, "Much better. Now, Mr. Lewis, our public awaits," Aden said, slamming the gear shifter into first and speeding off.

"Hey, how can you see anything out of the rearview mirror with it tilted down like that?" I asked.

"I can't," he said. "I just turn and look. I hate the glare of the headlights too."

"Too?" I asked.

"Yeah, too many questions," he tilted his head back and laughed maniacally.

I laughed too, "Alright. Brant keeps texting *where R U*, he's probably well past wasted."

Smiling, "Good," Aden said.

***

It took us about twenty minutes to get to the campsite, and the party was well underway. A system of flashlights directed us down a long and dark dirt road behind a slew of caravanning partiers. Aden and I ended up having to park further away than I thought we would, so we followed the music, crowd, and flashing lights toward the entrance. We paid, got our hands stamped, and were offered plastic cups. I took one, Aden declined his.

Brant and Phil were wasted by the time Aden and I ran into them by the main stage as the deejays were transitioning from trance to house music.

"Yooooo! Lewis! Aden! Over here!" Brant slurred, "Took you punks long enough! Give me your cup," he said.

I handed him my plastic cup, "Thanks, watch the head though." Brant pumped the keg and filled my cup slowly.

"Hello there Mr. Lewis," Phil said in his best imitation of Dr. Ferguson.

I laughed, "Well hello there, Philip," I joked back. "How goes it, man?" I shook his hand.

"I'm great…This party is awesome, right? What's up Aden?" Phil asked.

"Hello Philip, how are you this evening?" Aden asked.

Brant interrupted, "Blah blah blah…here, take your beer. Aden, where's your cup bro?"

"Oh, no thank you, Brant. I don't drink alcohol," Aden said.

"Oh c'mon, pussy. It's a freaking party dude. Why don't you-"

Aden interrupted Brant, "I'm designated driver tonight," looking directly at Brant, Aden smiled.

"Oh, well why didn't you say so? I'm sorry man. I totally wish I had your temperance. I respect that," Brant said.

"What? Since when? Who *are* you right now?" Phil asked. "You're the biggest alcohol pusher I know."

Confused and disoriented, Brant turned toward the stage. "Whatever. Here…drink this," he said handing his cup to Phil and walking away.

Phil and I stared at one another for a moment, and then we all followed Brant through the crowd toward the front of the dance floor. There, a bleached blonde deejay with a tattoo complexion and numerous piercings

144

was spinning funky house music. Brant began to jump around and shake his head uncontrollably. In awe of his freedom from concern or judgment, I noticed that this dance must've been contagious because shortly thereafter, Phil joined in too. I turned to find Aden to see if he had caught the *bad dancing bug*, but he was far removed from its catastrophic grasp. Aden was melodically moving his shoulders back and forth with the driving thump of the bass, his eyes were closed, and he was in the process of spinning around on his heels. Within seconds of putting his hands in the air and moving his pelvis from side to side, Aden was enclosed by at least a dozen entranced, female spectators. Aden opened his eyes and quickly exchanged personal glances with each of his admirers, and they didn't seem to mind the competition or notice each other at all. It was as if they were under a spell. The flashing lights lit up his icy eyes and devilish smile as he continually turned and grooved sensually.

I carefully observed Aden like he was a master of the the-art-of-seduction. He had set his sight on a defenseless brunette and was approaching her suavely. Putting his hand under her chin and raising her head to him, he kissed her rapaciously. How could this be so easy for him? While continuing his voracious kissing with the helpless gazelle, Aden took the cup out of her hand and threw it on the ground. Seconds later, he was expertly leading her off the dance floor.

Phil and Brant were Tweedle Dee and Tweedle Dum, jumping and bashing around, so I followed Aden and his conquest through the sea of twirling glow-sticks and plastic cups. Aden had his arms around the slender shoulders and sloppy torso and had no idea that I was following him. I have no idea why I followed them, to be honest. I suppose I wanted to see Aden's game in action. I guess I also wanted to see where and how far they would go, but I decided I had gone far enough when Aden disappeared into the woods with the enamored figure.

I turned and went back to Phil and Brant who were still dancing (badly) in front of the main stage.

"Hey, Aden totally just hooked up with some hot brunette! They went into the woods together," I said.

"What? That's awesome!" Brant yelled, still jamming.

"Right on!" Phil agreed.

Without a choice, I let the contagion of the horrific dance take control of me too. I could feel the splashing of beer on my hand from the wild jumping, but I have to admit, it was a shit load of fun!

***

On the way home, Aden seemed to be a little buzzed again. "You alright to drive?" I asked.

"I'm as fine to drive as I was the other night when you thought I had been drinking, my friend. I told you I don't drink alcohol. Are you alright to ride?"

"Yeah, I'm not gonna puke if that's what you mean. I could have gotten a ride with Brant and Phil if you wanted to make a night of it with that brunette you went off into the woods with."

"What? How did you know where we went, Lewis?"

"I kind of followed you," I said.

My head and chest swung violently forward as Aden abruptly slammed on the brake and swerved the car off the road into an access lane. When we had stopped, he shifted into park roughly and turned toward me, "You followed me?"

"Yeah," I said nonchalantly.

"Lewis, I'm...uh...*fucking* serious right now," Aden said in a raised voice.

Surprised by hearing Aden say 'fucking', "Wow dude, calm down. It's not like I saw you nail her or anything," I said.

"What did you see?" he asked.

"I told you, nothing. I just saw you go into the woods and then I went back to find Phi-"

Aden interrupted me, "Don't ever follow me again," he said.

"What?"

"Promise me you won't ever follow me again," he repeated, shoving his hand into my chest.

"Listen, I don't know what kind of freaky stuff you're into, I was just checking to make sure I still had a ride, OK. You're obviously upset about it, so I *promise* I won't follow you, dude. But look, I don't appreciate being spoken too like some sort of goon or something. No one speaks to me like that, you got it?" I said raising my voice, "I'm your friend, not your lackey."

"I'm sorry, you're right, Lewis," he said. His hand was still hovering in front of me, and I was still pissed, but I shook it anyway. "I just don't like being followed," Aden said intently.

"Yeah, dude, whatever," I said solemnly and let go of his hand.

"So, are we reconciled?" Aden asked. "I'm sorry I yelled. It just took me by surprise. And I'm sure that you wouldn't extend an invitation for me to follow you and Camille," he said.

I could see Aden's point. Just the presence of other people at the Cascades was enough to irritate me. I'd never want anyone to follow Camille and me. I nodded to abash the tension and said, "You're right. We're good, bro."

Putting the car into gear, Aden spun over rocks back onto the paved road.

Chapter 16

Lying awake in the pitch-dark Saturday morning forced me to realize how much I missed the sunbeams through my window. The glow on my arms warming my skin was etched into my brain, but still no substitution for the real thing. And not having to go to class made my restlessness even more annoying because I had no idea what I was going to fill the day with. I mean, is it raining outside? How do I know it's really even 9:38 like the alarm clock says? What if the power went out and it's really three a.m. or something?

I got up and turned on the light. Checking my reflection in the mirror, my eyes were totally bloodshot, although I didn't feel too terribly hungover. I splashed some cold water in my face and brushed my teeth. It was 9:39 and Aden was still knocked out with the covers pulled over his head. The concept of a sun allergy is understandable, but I'm having trouble grasping not being productive during the day. If I hadn't promised not to wake him, *would* he be opposed to a game of pool in the rec room, or watching a movie? He could even do homework or call his parents? But to sleep all day, I would go crazy.

I guess I could walk outside and call Camille and see what she's doing for breakfast. I'm starving and could use some cheesy eggs in the worst way.

I took off my exercise shorts and put on a pair of new jeans and a V-neck. Slipping on my flip-flops, I grabbed my keys and wallet and headed out. As it turned out, the sun was brilliant. Yes!

I sat down on the stoop in front of the side exit, but just as I was pulling my phone out of my pocket, I was also receiving an incoming call. It was from *Home*. I picked up instinctively. "Hello," I said, not sure which of my parents was calling.

"Hey, champ! I was beginning to think you had forgotten about your folks with all the collegiate excitement."

"Hey Dad," I said, "Not at all, just busy. How are you?"

"Great, we got a closing set for the Emerson building, so after this month, things will slow down around here."

"Yeah, you always say that, and then you get your next project. But that's great news, Dad. Congratulations," I said, feeling a jolt of sadness. The three of us always went out to eat in celebration of Dad's building openings. This would be the first time they would celebrate without me.

"Thanks, Lew, but you know these commercial real estate companies and their lawyers. Pray they don't move the closing back so we can celebrate!"

"I will. How's Mom?" I asked.

"Mom's keeping herself busy: gardening, baking, all of that. She's been talking about subbing part-time."

"Oh yeah?" I knew it, "And how do you feel about that?" I asked.

"Umm, I think it'll be good for her. It'll keep her from worrying about you!" he laughed.

"True, but she also hasn't worked in over ten years, how do you feel about her reentering the workforce?" I said.

He lowered his voice, "Between you and me, I think these kids will eat her alive."

"No way Dad, she loves teaching!"

Raising his voice, "Ahh, champ…I smell a wager."

"Nope, not taking it. It's unfair, you've known her for longer."

Dad laughed, "And better, boy!"

"Well, I hope so, you married her," Mom's voice was becoming audible in the background. She was asking Dad who he was talking with.

"It's our son, Patricia," he said.

Mom's voice shrilled, "Ooooooh. Let me talk to him."

"Lewis, hold on a second, your mother wants to speak to you, so I'm going to pass you off to her, OK? It was good to hear your voice, son. Don't be a stranger."

"Alright Dad, love you."

"Love you too, champ."

"And congratulations on the Emerson closing," I said.

"Thanks, Lew. Take care of yourself, champ. Here's Mom."

I heard the shuffling from the phone changing hands and then, "Lewis! Hey dear, how are you?"

"Hey Mom, I'm great. How are you doing over there?"

"Missing you, but your father is keeping me company."

"That's good, Mom," I said not knowing what to say next.

"So did your roommate ever move in?"

I had forgotten that I told her about that, "Oh yeah, Mom, he moved in *really* late on Sunday."

"Oh, that's wonderful. I was worried you were going to be all alone out there. So, tell me about him, where's he from?"

"He's cool. He's an Engineering major, from Shasta," I said.

"Shasta!" she said alarmed.

"Yeah, Shasta. Why?" I asked, but my question fell on deaf ears.

Mom was yelling at Dad, "Cliff! Isn't Shasta where all of that stuff is happening with those deaths and missing persons?"

I didn't need to hear Dad's confirmation to know that she was right. I specifically remember watching that with them on the news after I got back from meeting Dean at Sharkey's.

"You're right, Mom. It was some sort of mountain lion or something, right?"

"Yes, yes! They issued an animal watch and curfew. I wonder if they captured that thing…whatever it was? Oh dear, that was awful."

"It's strange that Aden has not mentioned anything to me about it," I said.

"Well honey, what do you expect him to say, 'Hey nice to meet you, I survived the savage massacre in my hometown?' I'm sure it's a very traumatizing experience, especially for someone so young."

"Yeah, I guess. I wonder if he knew any of the victims."

"Oh, I'm sure he lost some loved ones in a small town like that," she said.

"Oh-my-gosh, I'm going to ask him? This is crazy!"

The thought of knowing someone that left an area where multiple deaths occurred in such a brief amount of time fascinated me. I know it may seem a little callus, but there is something tragically seductive about all of this death. Not to mention the city of Shasta, Aden's hometown, carrying this mysterious plague/curse.

"Don't you dare, Lewis!" Mom forbade, "it's sad enough as it is! If he brings it up, then, by all means, be a good friend and listen, but I wouldn't go asking questions about a tragedy like that. Especially with him moving in late, I'm sure it was related to that citywide curfew."

"But mom, how traumatic can it be for him? I mean, *he's* still alive?" I said.

"Lewis Emmanuel Lewis! I'm astonished at you! How can you say such a thing? Think Lewis, think! The media has turned that quaint little town into a freak show, and with all the looming deaths, you know he probably lost a friend or relative. I swear you and your father can be so insensitive sometimes."

"OK Mom, I swear you can be so dramatic sometimes. But I won't say anything unless *he* brings it up."

"I'm sure he'll appreciate that too," she said.

"Hey, listen, I'm going to call a friend and see if she wants to grab breakfast. I gotta' run."

"Already? Oh, OK…is this a *girl* friend?"

150

"Bye Mom," I said, not allowing her gratuitous prying.

"Lewis!" she insisted.

"Love you, Mom, bye!" I resisted.

"Oh, alright, love you too. Call us soon."

"I will," I said.

Immediately after pressing END, I wished that I hadn't told my mom that I wasn't going to press Aden about Shasta's death toll. I've got to figure out some way to get him to bring it up. But in the meantime, I need eggs and I hope Camille does too.

***

Evidently, Camille was as hungry as I was because we sat across from one another at Thompson, silently enjoying the comfort of eating together. I was preoccupied with devouring my cheese eggs, and Camille had taken a break from her oatmeal to text with Ebony.

"What's up with Ebony?" I asked.

Still texting, "She hates Stanford. She wants to leave."

"Really? Why? She hasn't even given it a chance," I asked.

Looking up, "That's what I'm trying to tell her too!"

"Well, tell her I said hey."

"I will. So how was last night? By the look of your eyes, it was pretty fun," Camille joked.

"Oh, I'm sorry…I didn't know you had even looked up from your phone for long enough to see my eyes," I reached over and put my hand over the screen.

She yanked the phone back, "You suck! I'm almost done, I just need to tell her how much of a—" she mumbled something that I couldn't make out, "my boyfriend is."

"What?"

She roared with laughter, "How much of a sweetheart, babe," she said texting furiously.

I snatched her phone and read the correspondence. Camille had actually typed that she didn't like SoCafo either, but that she didn't want to be anywhere else because I was here too.

Still reading, "Aww, how sweet," I teased.

"Lewis, give me my phone," Camille said sternly.

I handed her the phone and she snatched it out of my hand, "Ass."

I grabbed her hand, "I wouldn't want to be anywhere else either," I said.

Her lips melted into a vulnerable smile, "Thanks," she said.

151

"You're welcome."

"Lewis, if I tell you something, you promise not to laugh?" she looked pitiful, a look that I would have argued Camille Harris incapable of displaying.

"Why would I laugh at you, babe?"

Looking down, "Because it's so embarrassing, and kind of crazy," she said.

"Well, now you *have* to tell me," I said genuinely intrigued.

"Noooo," she pouted, "you have to promise first."

I feel like I've been making a lot of promises lately, but unlike my promises to Aden, I don't feel like this one will come back to bite me. "I promise, Camille. What is it?"

Still looking down, "Well, when I heard you were applying to SoCafo, I applied here too. I was offered a full scholarship to a few other schools, but when I found out you were definitely going here, I decided to accept SoCafo's offer," Camille admitted. "I didn't even know a soul here or anything about the school. All I knew was that you were coming here and that was all I needed to know," she rolled her eyes and bit her bottom lip, "how crazy is that?"

Everything about what Camille had said made my heart feel like it was going to lunge out of my chest. I reached over and squeezed her hand, "Camille, that is the most awesome thing anyone's ever said to me."

She smiled a comforting grin and her eyes sparkled, "Really?"

"Really. You just might be **it** for me. Everything about you, you're the total package. Sweet. Smart. Understanding. Funny. Beautiful. Humble. Cool. Patient. Sexy."

Camille writhed her lips, "I was worried you would think that was weird," she said.

I laughed, "Well it is a bit stalkerish and weird, but you're weird, so I forgive you."

"I hate you," she said.

"You love me," I said.

"No, really I think I do, Lewis."

"You think you do what?" I knew, I just wanted to hear her say it.

"I love you," she said.

I smiled, "I love you too," I admitted.

After we finished breakfast, Camille said she had to go back to her dorm room to study, so I decided to call Brant and Phil to see if they wanted to work out. They agreed to meet me at the gym, so I ran home to change before heading that way. Aden was still asleep, so I tried to be as quiet as possible, and I was doing a great job until I stepped on something that sent a sharp pain through my barefoot. I yelled out loud before falling over onto the floor. What the hell was that? I felt around for the object until I found this odd-looking piece of wood that looked like it was drilled out of something. It must have been there from Aden's drywalling extravaganza that night he moved in. I cursed it and threw it into the trash. I checked to see that my holler hadn't woken Aden, and when his silhouette under the covers didn't budge, I finished getting ready and headed to the gym.

Brant and Phil were already fifteen minutes into their workout by the time I got there. They both had found row machines in front of the jumbo flat screens, and were profusely sweating out the alcohol from last night.

"Isn't this dedication?" I joked.

"Yo! Where's Aden?" Brant asked.

"In bed," I said.

Phil stopped rowing, "Still? He doesn't even drink dude."

I realized that I hadn't disclosed Aden's illness to Phil or Brant, and I thought it may not be my place to. "Yeah, he sleeps in late, even on school days. It's like his routine."

"I hear that, this Engineering schedule is killing me," Brant said.

"Yeah, but you're getting used to it," Phil looked at me, "I literally had to drag his ass here this morning," he said.

"True story," Brant agreed, "hop on this one dude," Brant motioned to the empty row machine next to his.

"So, what's on the tube?" I asked.

"Um, college football, more college football, and the news," Phil said bored.

I began to row steadily, "So what time did you guys leave last night?" I asked.

"We took off around two-thirty or so, shortly after you and Aden," Brant said.

"Cool. I had a blast man, so did Aden. Thanks for inviting us."

"Anytime man, are you kidding. We're going out again next Saturday, to the bar though. You guys in?" Brant asked.

"One-hundred percent," I said.

"Holy shit!" Phil yelled. We all stopped rowing.

"What?" Brant and I asked.

"Look! Monitor three, the news! Oh-my-God." Phil's face was colorless.

We looked at the huge television where the police could be seen removing a blurry, censored image amid thick woods. There was a salt-and-peppery, middle-aged, male reporter divulging the details of the chilling scene behind him.

I'm here at the site of Southern California University's traditional 'Back to School' field rave where a good time has gone horribly awry. Third-year student, Kimberly Dawson's, body was found in the brush just off the campsite where the party took place. First responders told authorities that her neck appeared to be broken in two places. Similar incidents have occurred where campers have gone off alone to use the restroom and unable to see, tripped, impaling themselves on boulders or exposed tree roots. We are awaiting the coroner's full report and will have updates momentarily. Ms. Dawson was twenty years old and a Political Science major. I am Ted McCaig, reporting live from the scene, Channel 11 news.
Thank you.

"What the hell?" Phil gasped.

"What do you think could have happened?" I asked.

"Who knows dude, but those girls get so plastered that anything is possible," Brant said.

"Hey, I know this is going to sound messed up, but Lewis, didn't you say you saw Aden going into the woods with a girl?" Phil asked.

"Yeah, but… What are you saying?"

"Maybe he and that girl saw or heard something."

Brant interjected, "That campsite is so huge, and thousands of students go to that party. That girl could have been in any wooded spot on those hundred or so acres. Aden and his ho were probably nowhere near where that happened."

"You're a pig," I said beginning to row again.

"What? It's true," Brant replied.

"Yeah, but why does the *ho* have to be a *ho*?" Phil joked.

"You're both pigs. Better yet, Tweedle Dumb and Tweedle Dumber," I joked.

"Hey, I resent that. Which one am I? Tweedle Dumb?" Brant asked.

"Why does it matter?" Phil asked flatly.

"Because my grade point average is higher!"

We all laughed at the ridiculousness of the joke, but despite my laughter, I felt a stemming awkwardness. My mom has always told me that death travels in threes, and so far, there have been two. In the pit of my stomach, I had an eerie feeling that the third death was imminent because Mom's theory has always proven itself true. When I was in seventh grade, Grandma had kidney failure, Sean Slade had that weird, rare heart attack, and James Stein, after missing most of the 6th grade, finally lost his battle against Leukemia. Then in tenth grade: our Chow-Chow, Bear, died, our neighbor in the back, Mr. Ross, got bitten by a snake hunting, and then my Latin teacher, Mrs. Frazier, got some sort of blood poisoning and kicked out-of-the-blue.

"Guys, what if more people die?" I asked.

"What do you mean?" Brant said.

"Dude, it's not like these are homicides. I mean, the Suicidal Sophomore and the Jolly Drunk Junior?" Phil said laughing.

I was beginning to think my mom was right about men being insensitive, two people had lost their lives and Phil is joking about it. Death seemed to be all around me, and it was not something that I wanted to make the brunt of crude and tasteless fraternity jokes.

I felt a surge of anger shoot through me, "You mean Jessica Riley and Kimberly Dawson." I got up from the machine and walked away.

"Dude, where are you going?" Brant asked. I ignored him and walked out of the cardio area. As I exited, I could hear Brant calling Phil a total douche. Angry as I was with Brant too, I was glad that he at least agreed with me on his opinion of Phil at this moment.

I was pissed at Phil, but not shocked. I haven't known him that long, but from what I did know, he wasn't the most respectful of souls. I flung the door of the gym open and tried to let the fresh air calm me. It wasn't working, so I called who I always call when I'm pissed, Dean.

"Yo, what's up kid?" he answered.

"Dude, I hate when you call me kid, I'm older than you, idiot."

He laughed, "I know, that's why I keep doing it, kid."

"Dean, not today."

"OK, OK Lewis. I'm sorry. I forgot it's your time of the month, isn't it?"

"Dean! Can you be serious for once in your life?" I yelled.

"Whoa man, alright. Whose ass do I need to come out there and kick?"

"Gosh man, nobody's," I said.

"Don't tell me you and Camille broke up already."

"No, just wanted to talk."

"Bout what?" Dean asked.

"Two girls have died since I've been here and it's starting to freak me out a little."

"What? Two," Dean asked, "What the hell is in the water?"

"I know! It's craziness," I said relieved to finally be getting somewhere serious with him. "And these two guys I've been hanging out with just totally pissed me off by making light of the whole thing."

"What happened?" he asked.

"Well, we were working out and the news –"

Dean interrupted me, "You work out now? Seriously, what is in the water, dude?"

"Dean," I said sternly.

"OK, OK. Go 'head man, I'm sorry."

"So, the news comes on, and this party we were all at last night is the feature story. Get this, some girl was found dead in the woods! And before that, a girl jumped out of her window! On my way home from class that day, I walked right by the blood-stained spot in the sidewalk."

"Oh man, I'm sorry. That's pretty heavy. Are you OK? I can come out there if you need me to."

"Nah, I'm OK. Just frazzled, I guess."

"How are things with the agoraphobic roommate?" Dean asked.

I laughed, "Dude, he's not homebound, he has a vitamin deficiency."

"Right, right, like the guy out in Shasta that sued the company my dad represented," Dean said.

"Wait a minute Dean, where did you say that was?" I asked.

"Shasta, you know, where they've been under a curfew for months," Dean affirmed.

"No, that's what I thought you said. Aden is from Shasta."

"Who?" Dean asked.

Frustrated, "My roommate! My roommate is from Shasta," I yelled into the phone.

"OK, chill out dude. I got it. Is his name Vinhook or something?"

"Vanhook," I said.

"Yeah, Vanhook! That's the name. How could I have forgotten that name?" Dean said.

"What do you mean?" I asked.

"Uh, my mom and dad, don't you remember? Dad stayed over in Shasta working on that case, and Mom thought he was having an affair. They fought constantly; remember your parents letting me crash with you? Vanhook this and Vanhook that, it was the worst. I can't believe you don't remember! And then when Dad lost the settlement, and he had never lost as much as a dollar bill, that was the most peculiar part to Mom. Dad claimed that Vanhook guy and his attorney had won the settlement board over somehow and then he was home again, and everything was back to normal."

156

It was all coming back to me, "Yeah, I remember that," I admitted.

"Why ya' bringing it up anyway?" Dean asked.

"It's weird, but I'm pretty sure that guy is my roommate's dad. I mean, Aden said his dad sued his former business partner, he's from Shasta, and also has the same illness—which is genetic. It has to be, right?"

"Dude, I'm sure it is. Just ask him," Dean said. "But I'm not quite sure what this has to do with the dead girls." Dean was right, what did ancient legal history have to do with Socafo's current death toll?

"Nothing really, I guess," I agreed.

Suddenly I felt totally baffled. There was so much happening, and I couldn't quite put my finger on the catalyst. College, Camille, and Aden had come into my life and with them so had change, love, and death.

Somehow, this conversation with Dean had left me less enlightened and more confused.

I needed to be alone.

I needed to clear my head.

I needed to think...I ended the call and headed to the jeep.

Chapter 17

Smashing Pumpkins, "Bullet with Butterfly Wings," blasted through my speakers as I sped down Campus Concourse Boulevard on an aimless journey. I didn't care that I didn't know where I was going or that I was traveling twenty-five miles over the speed limit. I hadn't been inside of my jeep in a week. I had forgotten the thrill of ownership over its newness, and it reminded me of home. Aden's car was by far the superior vehicle, but my truck was a testament to my parents' love for me, which made it invaluable.

Luckily, I escaped campus without being pulled over and was now a little safer to speed on the open highway. I turned the GPS off and decided to let the road navigate my trip. I must have driven for fifteen minutes before I saw a familiar-looking sign. I was very close to the campsite from last night's party. Possessed by curiosity, I suddenly turned the steering wheel onto the campground.

Things looked very different in daylight. There were so many side roads that I hadn't been able to see the other night. I didn't remember taking any more turns after that first one, so I remained on the long and windy dirt road. My SUV handled the uneven terrain much better than Aden's sports suspension. I could have been coasting on a cloud through the air. After a few moments of coasting, I came to a clearing about the size of a football field. There were trees all around the perimeter, thicker than the woods at the Cascades. This must have been the parking area. It was completely deserted, so I drove until I couldn't drive any further. I parked the truck and decided to see if I could figure out exactly where I was last night. Brant was right, the enormity of the campsite was overwhelming.

Following my poor sense of direction, I slowly walked forward and began to see strange impressions in the grass from where the platforms were laid, presumably for a stage or dance floor. In an attempt to find my bearings, I turned toward the trees and realized that I was not alone. Through the thicket of woods, I could see another small clearing where media vans and curious campers were huddled around something. Walking toward the small group, I realized that I was leaving where the keg and main stage were! The direction that I was heading was leading me directly to where I had seen Aden disappear with that brunette! I continued to follow the small path through the trees…it all felt so familiar until I couldn't walk any further because of the crime scene quarantine.

The déjà vu was incredible; all I could think about was Jessica Riley. People were lingering and speculating just like they had at Jessica's death site and here I was, again. Right now, *I* seem to be the common denominator, but what could I possibly have to do with these deaths? I inched in closer, and then I couldn't see anything at all!

Something was covering my eyes, temporarily blinding me. I tried to yell, but my mouth was being muffled by someone behind me. I jerked desperately, but whoever was restraining me was too strong. I was being dragged away from the scene, and I couldn't see by whom, nor could I yell for help. In a panic, I dug my heel into the large, male, black combat boot, and thrusted my elbow into the gut of someone wearing red and black flannel.

I heard the sigh of pain and then a familiar voice say, "Lewis, it's me…Tim."

Tim? From Biology Lab? I turned around, and Tim's hands were above his head in the surrender position. "What the hell is wrong with you?" I yelled.

"Shhhhh…keep your voice down," he warned.

"Why? What is going on here?" I demanded.

"Crime scene investigation," he said, "Very restricted access. People without clearance are being taken in for questioning."

"What? Crime scene? The news said that this was an accidental death," I said.

"Of course they did. You believe everything you see on the news? I thought you were a non-conformist."

Shaking my head, "Well how are you here then?"

"Remember? I'm a Coronary Science major. The department sent me to assess the cause and time of death. It's actually for course credit. We get called every time there's a death in the town," he said.

"Really, that's sucks."

"Not really. But the news doesn't know anything. I mean, her neck was broken, but that's not what killed her," Tim said.

"Now I know you're crazy," I said, "how could anyone survive a broken neck?"

"You are as dumb as you look. She was dead before whoever *broke* her neck *broke it*. The broken neck is a cover."

"What are you talking about?"

"Well, I got a call when that girl supposedly jumped out of her window."

"Jessica Riley," I offered, trying to sound knowledgeable.

Tim nodded, "Yeah, her. Anyhow, she had these wounds on her neck," he touched below his right ear, "and so does this chick."

"Kimberly Dawson," I corrected.

"Yeah, Kimberly Dawson. Anyhow, I don't think that Jessica threw herself out of a window, and I don't think this girl tripped on any tree root or whatever they're telling the public. I think they were murdered. And I think it was a vampire."

Tim looked to be seduced by his own ridiculous, theoretical deduction. "Dude, lay off the drugs," I said.

"I don't do drugs," he said.

"Well then change your major to Psychology. A vampire, really? I'll see you in the lab." Rolling my eyes at his supernatural conspiracy, I turned toward the crowd.

"Lewis, don't believe me—fine. But don't go that way. Go back the way you came unless you want to spend the next four hours answering questions. And judging by the looks of it, your eyes and the stamp on your hand place you at this party last night. I hope you have a good alibi."

Tim was crazy, but he had a point. I quickly ducked back through the woods, across the vacant lot, and climbed into my jeep.

My heart was racing from the anxiety of thinking that I was being kidnapped and now the possibility of getting caught and becoming a homicide suspect. I made it safely off the grounds and headed to campus. I felt a bit stupid for driving out here in the first place. My heartbeat slowly began to subside from the shock, so I turned on some music and rolled the windows down in hopes that the wind would blow away my anxiety.

Biology Lab was definitely going to be interesting now considering that my partner is a gothic psycho, obsessed with death and imaginary predators, with an all-access coroner's pass to whomever becomes case number three on the SoCafo death toll.

I fastened my seatbelt and looked at my eyes in the rearview mirror. Tim was right about one thing; they *are* still bloodshot.

Chapter 18

As disgusting as the showers are in Ponce, I really enjoyed my shower tonight. I let the steaming water rinse away all of the confusion that had clouded my mind over the course of the day. All I could feel was sympathy. Sympathy for the Riley and Dawson families that had to come and identify their daughters. It's got to be emotionally devastating to walk up to a body laying on a metal slab in a cold room to claim that the person is, or was, someone that you've known ever since they took their first breath.

Heaven forbid this heavy consignment lay upon my mother's shoulders—what would she say? What would she feel? Or what, in God's name, would she do? Accident or not, death for anyone, especially a parent, is probably never easy to cope with. It's not like a doctor says, *I'm sorry to inform you that your daughter lost her battle with Cancer, but at least she wasn't bludgeoned to death.* Or a grieving wife says, *My poor husband had a heart attack, but I wish it were a car accident that took him from me.* Death is death.

I hate when people ask dim-witted questions like, *What would you rather die from, drowning or fire?* I'm usually like, "Um…I'll take *neither* for five-hundred please." Idiots.

Death is a curse that makes life seem like it's not worth living sometimes. I don't ever feel this way until I'm confronted with it. The virus eats away at the living, consuming their thoughts about mortality and fate. Wouldn't it be nice to have a death due date much like babies have a birth due date? Then we could prepare a little bit better: take more risks, take fewer risks, laugh more, cry less, love like there is no tomorrow, and hate less like there is.

Don't get me wrong, I think that life is wonderful, I just haven't always understood my purpose in it. Perhaps that's why I'm enjoying the newness of college, Camille, and Aden. Maybe I need them to fulfill this uncertainty in me, or maybe they can help me discover what my purpose is. Could the void in my life be so easily filled just by being a SoCafo student, or someone's boyfriend, or a friend, or roommate? If so, what does that say about me?

I turned the water off and dried myself lethargically before walking on wet flip flops back to the room. Aden was in the process of putting his boots on when I walked in.

"Hey," I said.

"Good evening, Lewis. How was your day?"

"Not so good man," I said.

He glanced up at me and stopped, "Why, what's the matter?" he asked.

"I don't know dude; it just seems like everything is falling apart. Well, not my relationship, that's the one thing that is keeping me together right now. But another girl was found dead this morning."

"I know," Aden said, "Did you know her?"

"No, but she was at the field party and broke her neck that night. I went out to the site today, and my Biology Lab partner attacked me."

"You were attacked? Why?" Aden asked.

"Well, supposedly I wasn't supposed to be there, but the guy is absolutely nuts! I'm talking like a possible terrorist. He starts calling me stupid and a conformist for listening to the news when, in his mind, it's clear that both girls were attacked by vampires. Vampires! Can you believe that?"

"What's his name?"

I fully intended on answering Aden's insignificant question, but I wasn't done with my personal-pity-tirade. "And then Phil turns out to be the biggest prick of all time. I mean, we are in the gym working out, and he totally showed no compassion for Kimberly Dawson."

"Kimberly Dawson?" Aden asked.

"Yeah, that's the girl they found this morning."

"Oh, of course."

"I mean, he referred to that brunette you met last night as a ho, and Kimberly Dawson as a drunk. Basically, he all but said she had it coming. And dude, my foot is killing me, I stepped on some wooden drill bit you left on the floor, and it stabbed the crap out of me. I'm not sure if you need it, but I was pissed and threw it in the trash. Oh, and my best friend Dean's dad was the lawyer for the company your father sued." I took a deep breath and tried to read Aden's face. He was surprisingly emotionless, after everything I just spewed.

"OK, I'm going to have to take a moment to comprehend all of this because you just disclosed a lot of information, Lewis. Now let's go back: Philip said that the girl that was found in the woods was a ho? What is a ho?" Aden asked.

I looked at him in disbelief, "You're joking, right? You don't know what a ho is?"

162

"No, I don't. That's why I'm asking for clarification." Aden's expression gave no sign of folly.

"Ho is short for a whore, like a hooker or a-"

"Lady of the night, prostitute, madam...I got it, continue."

"Yes, that, and no. He said the girl I saw you going into the woods with was a ho."

"Right," he shook his head, "and that the girl that was found dead was intoxicated and probably had it coming," Aden clarified.

"Yes," I confirmed.

"OK, got that. Now what's this about your best friend, Dean, his dad represented the CBC when Father sued the britches off of them. What a coincidence. How did you figure all of this out, Lewis?" Aden asked skeptically.

"Dean and I tell each other everything, and when the settlement was happening, his parents talked about it all the time. Anyway, I was telling him about you, and he recognized your last name. What is the CBC?" I asked.

"It stands for California Blood Commission. It's a medical affiliate that stores and distributes blood to hospitals for transfusions, surgeries, disaster relief...you name it. They organize donations too, like the Red Cross, it's just not a non-profit like the ARC. It's like a pharmaceutical company, just specializing in plasma and blood."

"No wonder you're loaded! Your dad sued the freaking California Blood Commission?"

"Well, it's not something that I like to talk about if you can understand. But this Philip sounds like a real, *prick* you say," Aden sounded incredibly awkward attempting to speak as if he spent his afternoons on the beach and his mornings at soccer practice.

"Yeah, just a total ass. I don't know what I'm going to say to him in class on Monday."

"And, who is your crazy Biology partner that ah...attacked you?" Aden asked.

"Oh, some lunatic...Tim, I don't even know his last name," I said.

Aden hissed oddly, "Well that's a shame," he finished putting on his boots. "Well, I have a date, so I'm off."

"A date? Who with?" I asked.

"Haha, wouldn't you like to know. Actually, it *is* someone you know."

"C'mon, tell me. Who is it?"

"It's not the brunette," he smiled.

"C'mon man, don't be like that."

"See you later, Lewis." Aden grabbed a black leather jacket off of the back of his chair and left the room without answering me.

Chapter 19

The Library at Southern California University looked like it should have been Architectural Digest's building of the millennium. From the moment Camille and I walked in, we were completely in awe. The open atrium was at least fifty feet high and had an arched glass ceiling which allowed a magnificent light to illuminate the entire foyer. The light continuously ricocheted off of the marble floor, causing the bronze accents in each tile to sparkle. The walls were adorned with ancient alumni portraits, school donors' plaques, and SoCafo awards and honorable mentions. One would think that to put sitting areas in this huge and ornate lobby would distract from the grandeur of the space, but the furniture actually made it seem more intimate and inviting. The people parked in these seats were so absorbed by their reading that they didn't even acknowledge that Camille and I had entered their space.

A mahogany information desk rested at the center of it all...with its 360-degree views and stream-lined wood finish, this spot would be Katrina's dream-come-true. By the time Camille and I finished gawking and made it to the information desk, I had to remind myself that I was in a library and not a museum.

"What floor do we need to go to?" Camille asked.

"I need to eventually do some research on sixteenth-century folklore. Where would I find stuff on that?"

She laughed, "Google."

"I know, really...but Dr. Ferguson specified in the syllabus that all research had to be P&P."

She sucked her teeth, "I hate that. Well go to Google and find something *published*, and then *print* it out!"

I put my arm around her shoulder, "And from whose lips? Certainly not my graduating class's Valedictorian," I joked.

"I'm kidding," she pointed to a stack of pamphlets on the information desk. "Here, let's check out the directory."

"Good call," I said, watching her open the tri-folded piece of waxy paper.

Reading, "Lewis, this library has eight floors and a basement with newspaper archives. This is insane," Camille said.

"What? How am I supposed to find anything in here?" I asked.

"Calm down, each floor is themed more-or-less. So, let's see, if you need history there is a floor for that, and it is…four! According to this, there are study islands on each floor and then study peninsulas! This is so cute!" Camille said in whispered excitement.

"What's the difference between the study island and peninsula?" I asked.

She read on, "Um, basically a study island is separate from all sources and you have to use your passport to get access to them. They are completely silent, so you'll have your law and med school, psyche, kind of independent study going on in there."

We looked at each other incredulously, "And the peninsula?" I asked.

"You still have access to books and computers in the peninsulas. It says here that you can't use your cell phone, but the academic conversation is allowed."

"Peninsula," we whispered in unison.

Camille and I laughed out loud together, and the sound reverberated throughout the open space. An older woman, who had remained invisible until now, peeked up from behind the information desk and her floating spectacles to shush us.

"Sorry Miss," Camille said, "Um, could you tell us where the elevators are?"

She used both of her hands to scan the perimeter of the atrium. There were five solid gold, elevator doors that were designed to be virtually invisible, and from a distance, they appeared to be decorative plates. There was a camouflaged crease that followed the separation of the doors, which were linearly blended into the creases of the wood and tile panels on the wall above.

"Thanks," I said before realizing I still didn't know where we were going. "Which elevator do we take?" I asked, and the woman pointed to the pamphlet in Camille's hands and looked away. "Thanks again for all of your help," I joked.

Reading the directory, "OK, so the north elevator will put you out in the resource section of each floor," Camille assessed. "Northwest are the islands, and the northeast elevator will take us to the peninsulas. In between are media centers where the computers are and you can use your cell phone, or tutor, and things like that. So, I say we go up on the northeast elevator to the fourth floor. We can set up in the peninsula, get Calculus out of the way, and then you can get your books while I finish up my work."

I looked at her in admiration, "You are so wonderful, you know that. It would've taken me an eternity to figure out where I needed to be."

"C'mon fool," she said heading to the northeast elevator.

The elevators whizzed us up to the fourth floor, where we found a vacant, oblong table by an outlet. We plugged in my 15% phone and Camille's laptop.

"This is so nice," Camille whispered.

"I know, I think I may have to come in here every day and just sit and look at shit," I said.

"Seriously," she agreed. "So, you're doing integration and inverse operations, right?" I nodded. "So, let me see your book, I may be a bit rusty."

Camille put a pencil in her mouth and then began to put her hair up into one of those brisk ponytails like the day we went to The Cascades. I watched her as she tilted her head back and collected her thick, healthy locks. Her eyes were closed, and she took her fingernails to groom the hair above her neck before securing it with a little brown thingy she took from off of her wrist. The shorter strands didn't make it all the way through the loop, so they were caught and sprouting out. She must have known this would happen because she took the cute, scallywag hairs and wrapped them around the pencil tightly, and stuck it into the center of it all.

She removed a pair of black-framed glasses from her laptop bag and put them on, and then began to skim through the table of contents in my Calculus book. I was still watching her, amazed by the transformation that had just taken place. Camille had gone from being my hot girlfriend to my gorgeous and scholarly future wife.

"OK, so you need to write this down, or do you know the general formulas for integration?" she asked.

"Huh?" I said. I had no idea what she was talking about.

"Ugh, Lewis…OK, so there are basic formulas for integration or substitution or whatever you want to call it. But Calculus is more complex, so you end up with hyperbolic, exponential, and logarithmic formulas for those operations."

"OK," I said faintly comprehending.

"Basically, if you know the general formulas, you can *substitute* them into these more advanced ones and still do the operation."

"How?" I asked.

"OK, so the whole purpose of using the integration technique is to rewrite the problem in terms of the new variable."

My face was contorted with confusion, "What's that?"

167

"It just refers to the variable that you assign to what you are substituting…So what *that* means is one or more of the basic integration formulas are being applied to the more complex one."

I nodded because it was actually beginning to make sense. "So, I am just taking something hard and making it easier?"

She nodded, "Essentially, yeah."

"OK, so what else?" I asked.

"Well, that's it. All you need to know are the basic formulas and when and how to apply them, the rest is just like Algebra. I mean, this method seems like more work initially, but it will eventually make the indefinite integral much easier to evaluate."

"Um, indefinite integral?" I said.

"Lewis, really? Have you not been to a class at all? That's just what you're looking for, so in Algebraic terms, it's the *x*. So, let's try a problem. Where are your notes from class?"

"What notes?" I said.

"What? You don't have any notes," she began to laugh. She took her glasses off and looked at me, "Lewis, you are going to have to start taking notes during class."

"But she doesn't give us any notes. She just does all these problems on the smartboard," I said.

Camille sighed and put her head down, "Those *are* the notes, Lewis."

"Oh, OK. I can do that," I said.

Camille turned the book around to face me, "Here, do this problem."

It was a squiggly looking sign and a bunch of variables underneath a square root thing, "Can I at least look back in the book for the formulas?" I asked.

"Does she let you use them in class?"

"Yeah, she lets us have an index card with whatever we can fit on it, front-and-back," I said.

She put her glasses back on, "That's smart."

"Why?" I asked.

"Well, because you'll have to actually know which formulas to write on your card in order to pass, so it's like truly testing your understanding of not only the rationality of the operation but usage and application as well."

"Oh, I see your point. That old bag knows what she's doing."

"Lewis, do your work…and yes, you can look at the formulas. Start writing the ones you are using the most down now, you can transfer them to your notecard later. I'm gonna start working on my paper."

"OK," I smiled. "I love you," I said.

Without looking up, "I love you too, fool," she said smiling.

Camille's keyboard began to work overtime as she typed away, into her zone. After a while I had finished a few problems, Camille checked them, and found more difficult ones in the book for me to practice with. After successfully completing a couple of the more challenging operations, Camille showed me how to check my work, which sped me along through the unit. When I felt that I had mastered *integration by substitution*, I made my note card for the test. We worked well together, at least from my point-of-view.

"I'm done," I said.

"Good, how do you feel about it?"

"Oh, I got this," I said.

"Good, I'm excited to see how you do."

"OK, so I'm going to go get some archaic folklore books."

"You want me to come with you?" she asked.

"No, stay here and get your work done. I'll be right back."

"OK. I'll be here." I kissed her cheek and headed off the peninsula into the sea books.

Being in a library, I realize the absurdity of acknowledging how many freaking books there are here…but there's rows and columns upon shelves of books! It took me forever to figure out how they were cataloged. I should have taken Camille's offer to come with me.

Eventually, I stumbled into where I needed to be, and I couldn't help but chuckle at some of the titles: *Warlocks and Witches…Legends of the Werewolf…Vampires; Modern Myth vs. Ancient Fact.*

"Vampires…modern myth versus ancient fact?" I said to myself.

I grabbed the thick, encyclopedia-looking tome and observed the cover page. The V and M in the word *vampires* dipped down like a set of fangs, and the *Modern Myth vs. Ancient Fact* was centered underneath. There was no listed author or illustration on the cover. I began to thumb through for a table of contents. The book was divided into sections, and each section presented the myth on one side of the page and the (alleged) fact on the adjacent side.

"What a crock, ancient fact. I should check this out for Tim," I whispered.

I began to read the prologue which explained the existence of vampires. I wasn't sure if this was the book that I needed, but I didn't feel like looking through the thousands of books in front of me. I headed back to our table, where I found Camille still rhythmically typing.

"Did you get what you needed?" she asked without looking up.

"I'm not sure, going to see if I can use anything in this book," I waved it at her.

"Oh, OK. Let me know if you need any help. I'm in the zone right now, babe."

I smiled at her, "I see. I'll just be here reading *quietly* then," I said.

"OK. Muah," she said without breaking her concentration on the screen.

****

V<small>A</small>M<small>PIRES:</small>

Modern Myth
vs.
Ancient Fact

****

𝕊𝕆ℂ𝕊

Modern Myth

Beginning with Bram Stoker's 1897 novel, *Dracula,* many pop-culture myths began to materialize subjugating the fictional vampire. Since, the inception of a vampire has become fantasy. According to modern theologians, who in this case are authors that perpetuate the vampire character, vampires are "made." This could not be further from the truth.

It is common myth that vampires can choose their destiny. For example, if a vampire wishes a human to become his or her mate, they may acquire this goal simply by transforming the desired human into a vampire.

Many fictionalized accounts of vampires describe them as immortal beings. Contradictory myth then proceeds to detail ways in which to kill a vampire. These types of conflicting myths maintain the delusion that vampires are fictitious. In addition to immortality and self- selected creation, some other common myths about vampires include that they can be killed by ingesting garlic or a stake through the heart, sleep in coffins, can travel at the speed of light, can read minds, don't have reflections in mirrors, can shape-shift, and are demised by the image of a crucifix.

Believing these myths about fictionalized vampires is extremely dangerous, as actual vampires are exceptionally cunning and have been able to keep themselves hidden from society by its belief in these non-truths.

Parallel, you shall see proven fact dispelling the common myth that many people have aloud to cloud their perception on the indisputable existence of these beings.

Ancient Fact

The existence of Vampires can be traced back to Ancient Egyptian civilization. In fact, there is evidence to support that Queen Cleopatra and many of her predecessors and cohorts were vampires, and the pyramids built to protect them from the sun.

Contrary to modern myth, vampires are born of one another in the traditional sense. Female vampires ovulate until their age of maturation, which is about eighty-six years old. Male vampires mature closer to seventy-five, at which point they appear to be what is equivalent to a human in their early twenties.

If vampires are not nurtured by the blood of other non-vampires, their aging process is much more expedient.

Vampires are not immortal unless they continue to drink mammalian blood. They are stronger than humans, although the capacity of this fact has been fantasized. A vampire has the strength of roughly six or seven humans depending on their age and feeding cycle. Vampires cannot travel at the speed of light, although they can move six or seven times faster than a human. Although they can be injured, vampires also heal that many times faster. In the same manner, it takes a vampire much more strenuous activity to break a sweat due to their higher basal metabolic state.

Although garlic will not kill a vampire, the smell is repugnant. They can conceal this by plugging their nose with an unmalleable object such as metal or wood. Vampires do not sleep in coffins however they do prefer dark spaces such as closets or basements. They sleep with their eyes open and are easily woken…

𝕊𝕆ℂ𝕊

The book went on to explain how vampires do have reflections in the mirror but avoid them at all cost for two reasons: because they see the souls of the people that have fallen to their feeding, and because the appearance of their true age is reflected in the mirror.

I have to admit that the juxtaposition of myth and fact was pretty interesting, especially the part about how vampires *cannot* read minds but just temporarily control them on some frequency. And get this, that same frequency inhibits vampires from *ever* being able to think of or utter a non-truth!

Interestingly enough, some myths actually turned out to be fact according to this book; like vampires do have to be invited places since their kind was excommunicated during the Crusades. If they infringe upon any home, church, or social gathering without invitation, they will be unable to breathe until they exit.

"Camille, this book is wild!"

"That's nice. Keep reading," she said engulfed by her work.

I buried my head back into the book at which point things began to get increasingly ominous. The next section discussed vampires' aversion to the sun. They do not have the ability to synthesize sunlight into vitamin D like humans, therefore exposure is fatal. I continued to read on about how a vampire's genetic pool is superior to a human's because they have bred out all undesirable characteristics over thousands of years. Vampires also depend on their relationships with their human sponsors. The human is typically unaware of the vampire's true identity and nature, however, in some relationships they are privy. The myth about these persons is that they are considered to be the vampire's goon or slave, but in modern times this person can be a secretary or assistant, maid, butler, or friend.

My mouth dropped open from the shock of what I was reading. I thought back through the events from yesterday, and all the way back to Aden's arrival. Tim's assessment of the deaths suddenly seemed rational. I've never seen Aden shower because he never sweats, his classes are at night because he can't go out during the day, and neither can his dad, which he admitted, probably because he cannot lie! Oh my -gosh! He didn't come into the fitting room or the barber because of the mirrors—In fact, he has always avoided the mirror in our dorm room! I've never seen him eat, although he did come with me that one time, I had the pizza…with garlic!

I flipped back to the section where the book described a vampire's repulsion to the smell of garlic and how they can mask it by plugging their noses. Suddenly I remembered the two holes in the table! How could I have been so clueless? With the strength of seven men, Aden could have easily dug two pieces of wood out of a table, and *that's* what I stepped on yesterday!

My mind thought it and then I said it aloud, *Aden is a vampire.*

Camille looked up unexpectedly, "What?"

"Oh-my-God Camille, Aden is a vampire," I repeated.

"Oh, you're joking," she sighed. "Lewis, I really need to get this done before tomorrow or-"

"No, I'm not joking, listen…He's allergic to the sun, and so is his father, and his mom too."

"Um, Lewis, this isn't funny."

"I'm not trying to be funny, I'm dead serious!" I said.

"I thought vampires didn't have parents, don't they like…bite each other or something?"

"No! That's a myth, Camille, Look," I began to read from the book, "A vampire's fangs secrete an anesthetizing toxin into the bloodstream, and once they have bitten into their prey, death is imminent. Vampires will often mutilate and/or position caucuses to look as if the death was accidental in order to conceal their identity and hunting patterns," I looked up, "Don't you see? That's why Jessica Riley and Kimberly Dawson's deaths were…Oh my God, Kimberly Dawson was the girl I saw Aden go into the woods with, and Jessica Riley was the girl that woke me up!"

"Lewis, I don't know what this is all about, but I don't have the time or patience for these games. OK? This is *not* funny."

I was shocked that Camille couldn't see and hear my seriousness, "Camille what is wrong with you? Can't you see that I'm not trying to be funny? I'm serious!" I said flustered.

She took off her glasses, "Yes Lewis, it's funny that you are being seriously inconsiderate to the fact that I helped *you* prepare for your math test tomorrow, and you can't even stop this stupid joke for long enough to let me finish my paper, knowing how stressful this year is going to be for me! Now can you shut up and let me write?"

"But Camille, Aden is a fucking vampire!" I yelled.

She began packing her things, "That's it Lewis. I'm out of here. You clearly need to be alone right now and," she shrugged and looked at her computer, "so do I."

"Camille, please listen to me," I begged.

"Lewis, a very smart person, if they knew me at all, would just be so, very quiet right now." The sapphire in her eyes was gone and there was nothing but disappointment and frustration. I watched her pack her things, and then she left me alone in the peninsula feeling like I was stranded on an island.

Chapter 20

Alone in the peninsula study area, I continued to broaden my understanding of Vampires. So many of Aden's behaviors were beginning to make sense now. I've been a complete idiot. But idiocy faded and mortification set in when I read more about vampires' human sponsors.

ℰᴐᏼᎡ

Ancient Fact

A vampire's human sponsor is someone in which the vampire has placed and sealed a trust. This deal is solidified by a verbal pact and physical contact; male vampires will typically handshake while their female counterparts prefer to embrace their human sponsors. European vampires, regardless of gender, will kiss their sponsors on both cheeks.

The acceptance to be one's human sponsor and ally is a deal to never awaken the vampire whilst they sleep. This is important because it is also an allegorical agreement that neither party will attempt to kill one other. This guarantees the human's life, and the vampire's safety. These deals cannot be broken due to the supernatural Law of Obedience. Just as we acknowledge natural laws, there are supernatural laws that we are ignorant to. For example: if an egg falls from a table, the natural Law of Gravitational Pull states that that egg will plummet to the ground and subsequently break. If a vampire or human attempts to break their pact, they will not be allowed to engage in the endeavor because of the supernatural Law of Obedience.

A bond between a human sponsor and a vampire is two-fold. The human (or goon as referred to by modern myth) has two main purposes: One is to complete daylight endeavors for the vampire, and the second (primary) purpose is to solidify the vampire's meals. Because vampires need invitation, their human sponsor provides them access to social gatherings and other opportunities to prey. The human is rewarded by the vampire's ability to make them more desirable. Vampires have the ability to seduce humans regardless of their age, gender, or sexual identity; this skill comes in handy for the human sponsor by influencing their personal ambition and temporarily transfixing their human peers. A vamp (female vampire) is particularly good at this and can compel humans to even feel sorry for them. It is fact that more men are sexually attracted to female vampires and more women desire to befriend them, than their male counterparts. However, vamps and vampires typically travel together either as husband and wife or a relationship unknown to the humans in their community.

ജ⃝ഇ

What the hell? This is too much information. Where do I begin? Clearly, I am Aden's goon or human sponsor or whatever the hell it is, which means I can't kill him! But this explains everything: the speeding ticket he seduced the cop out of, the massive bench pressing without sweating, the physical flawlessness, and of course needing to be invited to the field party—through me, where he preyed on Kimberly Dawson. No wonder why I felt like the common denominator in these deaths, I was…Or was I?

Shasta, California! Aden is from Shasta, so that's seventeen deaths that I had nothing to do with. Oh my God! I can't let what happened in Shasta happen here! I quickly gathered my things and left the library without even checking the book out.

Thank goodness Tracey made us exchange numbers for Biology Lab! Tim isn't a crazy person, he's the only person who will believe that my roommate is a vampire. *The* vampire!

"Hello."

"Tim! Oh-my-gosh, everything you said is true, those girls were attacked by a vampire, and I know who it is!"

"Whoa, slow down! What are you saying, Lewis?"

"I'm saying my roommate is a vampire!"

"OK, OK. Where are you?" Tim asked.

"Leaving the library," I said.

"OK, I'll meet you at Thompson in five minutes," he hung up.

***

176

Sitting across the table from Tim, I explained everything so quickly that I hadn't breathed and was winded by the time I was done.

"OK, so your roommate is a vampire, dude! That's awesome," he said.

"That's not the reaction I was hoping for man."

"You're right, sorry. There's more too, Lewis."

"What do you mean more? More what?" I asked.

"Death," he admitted.

"What are you talking about?"

"I got called to the morgue yesterday, some drunken dude in the bathroom stall of a bar across from Nicky's Salon, you know, by the mall? They initially thought it was alcohol poisoning, but the sorry bastard had those same wounds on his neck as the girls."

"Oh no," I said, but I wasn't really surprised because I knew it was Aden. "It was Aden!" I blurted uncontrollably and annoyed.

"How do you know?" Tim asked skeptically.

I pointed to my head, "I just got my haircut at that place. He didn't come in, obviously because of the mirrors, but afterward, he was acting really weird, like he had drunk a ton of alcohol. But he doesn't drink."

"That's not weird at all dude, he's a vampire. He gets his nutrients from the blood. If he drinks the blood of someone who's drunk...you do the math."

"Holy shit! You're right. So that's the third death," I said.

"Third death? Try fourth," Tim said.

"Fourth?"

"Haven't you been watching the news? Some freshman girl, an Engineering major, they found her body, with no id, inside of the movie theater by the mall, and guess what?"

"What?"

"Same broken neck, same wounds here," he touched below his ear.

"Tim, do you know if her name was Sarah Reynolds?" I asked.

"That'd be the Jane Doe I got the call for, yep. Sarah Reynolds...how'd you know?"

"She came by the room to deliver some work to Aden and I told him she was interested. Oh my God, it's all true," I said, putting a hand over my mouth that I wished would suffocate me. "I've been lining up meals for him this entire time." I hung my head in shame, finally realizing my role in his feeding cycle.

"You didn't know. But now that you do, what are you going to do man?"

I shook my head, "I don't know." Tim's question sent me into mental despair, and I suddenly couldn't think straight. "I gotta get out of here. Aaah, thanks, Tim."

"No problem. Let me know if I can help in any way," Tim offered, but I was too frazzled to respond. I just ran out of the dining hall, clutching Pandora's Box in disguise as a book.

The assurance that Aden couldn't kill me gave me the courage that I needed to run home and confront him. My heart was beating one-hundred miles per hour, and I had no idea what I was going to say, but I knew that whatever I asked him, he had to tell me the truth. But did I even want to know the truth?

I forced the key in the door and nearly broke it trying to unlock it. I flung open the door to find that Aden was not home. I hid the book in my bag and then paced the room nervously until an idea (that I couldn't decide was good or bad) struck me. I never promised Aden that I wouldn't go through his stuff. His laptop was locked, so I couldn't get access to his personal files or emails. I rummaged around on his desk for something…anything.

There was nothing that could potentially help me convince the police that he was a vampire.

I backed up to the sink and began to think about how absurd this whole charade was. What if I was wrong, what if these events were all coincidental. But how could they be, there has to be something. My heart was beating out of my chest, so I put my hand over it to suppress the thumping. Collecting myself, I thought of any possible place where Aden would have hidden incriminating evidence about his true identity. *His* chest! I threw myself on the floor in front of his storage chest and raised the hatch. Viola! Inside were a coiled up body pillow and most of his clothing. If his clothes are all here and this pillow is not on his bed, then where does he sleep?

I closed the hatch to the trunk and slowly stepped toward his closet. Could he still be asleep in here? Deciding to test this *Law of Obedience*, I flung the doors of Aden's closet open. There was a space on the left with nothing hanging and a few items of clothing on the right. This has to be where he sleeps! But this won't prove anything to the police. I need more evidence, better evidence.

Suddenly I heard a key rustling inside the keyhole and shut the closet quickly. I ran over to my desk, sat down, and typed *Calculus* into the web address bar of my laptop. Aden may not be able to lie, but I sure can.

He walked in slowly, "Hello Lewis."

I composed myself, "Hey Aden. What's up?"

"Not much, you?"

"I just got back from dinner with Camille. Where you been?"

"I just had dinner myself," he said. Damn, that's death number five.

"Oh, cool. What did you have?" I asked.

"Oh, very rare meat."

I should have known he'd be good at this; he's had years of experience. That's it! He won't be able to lie about his age, "When were you born, Aden?"

"May 21st. Why do you want to know my birthday?"

Damn! How can I get him to tell me his actual age? "No, I mean, what is your actual age?" I said, and I knew from his expression that I had him.

"Lewis, I'm 108, can't you tell?" he answered. Yes, he was good, but I was better.

I made an incredulous face, "108? No, I'm serious, how old are you? I'm eighteen. You've got to be around my age. I bet you I'm older. Tell me…how old are you?"

"You're not older than me, and I'm not eighteen. So, what did you do today?" he asked.

I got up and went over to the mirror, "Oh, I just went to the library and dinner with Camille. She told me my haircut was uneven in the back, can you look at it and tell me if it looks jacked-up?" I placed my hand on the side of my neck and pretended to be unable to see the spot.

Aden stood away from the mirror, "It looks fine," he said.

I motioned him over, "You can't see it from over there, you have to come closer dude." I turned to face the mirror, "Come look."

"I'm not a hairstylist, Lewis. It looks fine to me," he said and sat down on his bed.

The butterflies began their breakdancing, and I immediately knew that I was tired of playing games and needed to assert myself. I faced Aden, stared directly into his arctic eyes and said, "I know what you are, I know that you can't kill me, and I know that you have murdered four people here and have something to do with the seventeen deaths where you came from. Now, you can either tell me what you are, or I will ask you point-blank because I also know that you cannot lie."

Aden's eyes confirmed what I knew to be true before his voice did, "I am a vampire," he admitted. "How did you discover me?" he asked. I took the book out of my satchel and threw it at him. He caught it and observed the title. "Hmm. So, what do you propose we do now?" he asked.

"I don't care what you propose, I'm going to the police! You're a murderer!" I yelled.

"Lewis, keep your voice down and listen to me. You're right, I cannot kill you, and being locked in a cell without feeding would definitely kill me, but if you read this book, then you probably know that vampires don't travel alone."

"Yeah, so?" I said confidently.

"So, I may not be able to kill you, but my vamp certainly can. So, if you value your life Lewis, contacting the police would be the worst move you could make."

He was right, "Well I hope you don't expect me to keep on letting you kill people."

He smiled, "You don't have a choice. In fact, you have promised to help me do it."

I sat down on my bed across from him, "So I'm trapped? Do I have to help you? Forever?"

"Noooo Lewis, you won't live forever. Think of it as a fruitful arrangement for the time being."

"You bastard," I said.

"How correct you are Lewis, that is why I am here."

"What?" I asked.

"Yes, my parents are dead. That damn curfew kept all the humans inside, and as I am sure you learned from your precious literature; we cannot go where we please without invitation. Our last meals were those of our maid and butler. Being that Mother and Father couldn't kill them, they sacrificed them for us. I'd like to say they volunteered willingly, but as you know I cannot lie."

"So, you are referring to you and your…your vamp feeding on the maid and butler?"

"Yes, I am."

"So, if you have to be invited everywhere, how could you come here?"

***

Aden went over to his desk and grabbed a piece of paper. He flung it at me, and after I read the first three lines, I knew…

> **Congratulations Aden, you have been *invited* to attend Southern California University. The school of engineering is proud to offer you a spot in their program for this academic school year. We hope that you are as excited as we are to make SoCafo your new home…**

My heart sank and suddenly there was a knock at the door. I looked at Aden, and he spoke to me without saying anything.

Do not reveal me to whomever is at the door. Now answer it.

I did as Aden wished. It was Jonathan Green. He looked desperately in need of sleep or coffee. His hair was disheveled, and his clothes were wrinkled.

"Hey Lewis, Aden. How are you guys?" he said.

"Well, thank you," Aden answered. I remained silent.

"That's good. I've got some bad news guys. The school is issuing a lockdown. No one is allowed out after dark in *the* light of these recent deaths. If you are caught out, then you will be taken into custody by campus police. I don't know how long this will last, but I'm required to inform all residents. It's for the best guys, you will be safer in your rooms than out there. Check the news for more updates, or call me if you have questions. Alright, guys, I've got to tell all the residents in Ponce so goodnight for now."

I closed the door and considered the irony, "Safer in my dorm room, locked in with the killer," I said.

Aden laughed, "You know I can't kill you."

"Yeah, but you are responsible for these other deaths!"

"Am I? Who invited me to the field party, who made Sarah Reynolds a menu item?"

"NO! That's not fair, I didn't know! And you cannot blame me for the guy in that bar, or Jessica Riley."

"Lewis, you are just as responsible for those deaths as you are the others. I couldn't have gotten into that bar with an id that says I'm one-hundred eight when I look like I'm eighteen. I told the bouncer I was waiting for my friend to get his hair cut and just wanted to get something to eat because I was famished, and his response was simply 'Come on in,' and even I can't will a human to extend an invitation. And the girl that woke you up, had you actually gotten up and seen her face, instead of putting a pillow over your head, I would have never killed her."

"Shut up!" I yelled.

The thought of being an accomplice to murder made my stomach turn. I began to feel the chunks rising in my throat, and before I could make it to the trash bin, I began to vomit. Aden was not as fast as the speed of light, but he was definitely fast. Before the first chunk escaped my throat, Aden had grabbed the trashcan and placed it under me.

"It's OK. You'll get used to the idea of death," he said.

Still spewing my guts out I managed a weak, "No way."

"You'd be surprised," he said calmly, like a serial murderer on trial. "It's a natural part of living, death is," he said, sounding like he was quoting one of Professor Lackey's lectures.

Looking up from the trash bin, "You say that because you're soulless," I said.

"Perhaps you are right my friend. But do you blame me? I've never had an identity, so I use my victims if I need to. It's the balance of my life; they die so that I may live."

"So then why me? Why here?" I asked.

"Now you are asking the right questions. Well, it was never my family's preference for murder, but after my father lost his job at the CBC, we didn't really have a choice...now did we? That job was perfect, the endless supply of blood without the unfortunate loss of life."

"How can you sit there and act like you aren't even sad that your parents are dead," I said wiping my mouth, "you're a monster."

"Well, we certainly have been depicted that way. We, vampires, mourn in our own way. The death of one of us is a bittersweet necessity. The fewer vampires there are, the better quality of life remaining vampires have. My parents were over 300 years old; they were tired. When they weren't able to feed anymore, they looked and felt 300 years old. They made a necessary sacrifice for me, and my bride. So, *why you* and *why here*? Look at us, Lewis. We have more in common than you think. I don't know what I want out of life sometimes either. Do you think I *like* being 'a monster' as you say?" he laughed, "Being the topic of these books," he held up Pandora's Box, "and the villain in your stories and movies. No, it's a reducing life. Contrary to what the rest of the world thinks of my fictional counterparts, I didn't ask to be born. Just like you, my parents gave me this life. So please, don't judge me."

Aden looked desolate, but I still couldn't pity him. "I do understand, but I don't agree."

"And I don't expect you to. But you are bound by the Law of Obedience, so even if you didn't want to, you naturally and irrevocably would. In fact, you have just as much chance of defying this law as you do of jumping from the roof of this building and levitating."

"I don't believe you!" I said.

"Well you should," he teased, "because you know that I can't lie."

"Then prove it," I challenged.

"OK, follow me down the hall and I'll show you," he said.

Aden opened the door and walked out of the room. I got up to follow him, but I couldn't. I felt as if a stone barge was pressing against my chest, overpowering me. Ossifying me. My legs felt like they weighed a ton a piece, and my arms refused to move forward despite my brain commanding them too.

I struggled against myself as I listened to Aden beckon from the hall, "Are you coming, Lewis?" he walked into the room, and I collapsed backward onto my bed. "You can't can you?"

"But why?"

"Don't you remember? You promised to never follow me."

"Holy shit! You asshole!" I screamed.

Aden shook his head and sucked his teeth rapidly, "Lewis Lewis, I warned you that nothing in life came without a price the very first day we met. Please don't be alarmed or think ill of me." An awkward silence permeated the tiny space for what seemed like an eternity before Aden broke it, "I'm going back out, and it's just too bad that *you're* not invited." Aden glanced up at the ceiling in admiration of his own cleverly ironic joke. "I've always wanted to say that to a human," he smiled wickedly and left the room.

Chapter 21

I woke the next morning with a foul feeling in the pit of my stomach. The Law of Obedience definitely worked its nasty magic because there was no logical explanation for how I was able to sleep through the night considering all that had transpired yesterday. And today was not going to be any easier: I had a situation to reconcile with Camille (or potentially not), a Calculus test to take (or potentially fail), and a bloodthirsty vampire to stop (or potentially get killed). And Aden hadn't even bothered with putting the body pillow on the bed. I guess there isn't any more need for civilities now that I know he isn't civilized.

Making my way down the hall to the showers, somewhere in-between sleep and consciousness, I began to think about how I could mend things with Camille. I can't blame her for not believing me, I had the same reaction to Tim when he told me he thought a vampire was loose on campus. And I can totally see her point about feeling like I wasn't respecting her workload after she spent a couple of hours helping me with mine. I suppose the best strategy at this point would be to pretend like I was joking and apologize. At least that is what Dean would tell me to do.

There was also Brant and Phil...I couldn't tell them about Aden either! They would definitely think I was crazy. I guess I could say that I was hypersensitive about the deaths and overreacted. I could handle Camille and the guys, but what the hell was I going to do about Aden? The fact still remained that my roommate is the bloodthirsty murderer responsible for all the deaths on campus.

As I pushed open the creaking door to the shower area, I shook my head in the anguish of the mental dead-end that I kept arriving at. How could my life have gone from the highest high to the most catastrophic low in such a short period of time? I've always tried to be a good person; I'm nice, honest, and morally consistent...most of the time. What the hell did I do to deserve this horrific burden? But hell, more importantly, what can I do to get rid of it?

I tiptoed around the puddles of stagnant water that were blocking the path to my shower. They were *especially* disgusting today, the rusty metal from the benches had stained the water dark orange. They almost looked like small puddles of blood. This revolting place is a breeding ground for fungal infection, I just know it.

I placed my keys on the bench before turning to get into *my* shower stall. But when I pulled the curtain back, I felt my heart react before my eyes could process what I was looking at! Phil's lifeless body was crammed into the small space, blood-soaked from neck to abdomen, and contorted like a sideshow performer in a circus.

"Oh my God! Phil! Ooooh my God, Phil, can you hear me?"

I stepped beside him and placed two fingers on his ripped-open neck to feel for a jugular pulse. There was nothing. His eyes were open, and the pupils dilated, and it appeared as if he were looking directly at me, begging for help.

I ran out of the shower stall screaming, "Somebody help! Somebody call an ambulance!" I began beating on every door in the hall, "Call 911, someone is hurt! Help!" The charismatic, Asian guy from the meet-and-greet came out first with his cell phone in hand.

"Dude, what's going on?" he asked.

"There's someone collapsed in the shower and…and…and bleeding badly. Can you call an ambulance and the police? I think someone put him there!" I felt like a crazed person, and apparently, I looked and sounded like one too.

"OK, but I need you to relax, slow down, and tell me which stall it is."

"The…the…the third on the left."

"OK," he dialed 911 with a shaky hand.

"Hello, my name is Shunyuan Mills and I am going to need an ambulance at Ponce Hall immediately, there has been an accident, and someone is injured…The showers on the first floor, it's the third shower on the left and hurry! Thank you, Ma'am…No, I didn't move the person, I'm calling for another resident that actually found him…Yeah, his first name is Lewis and his last name is Lewis."

I never imagined I'd experience feeling shock while in shock, but it was pretty damn shocking that he remembered my name. Shunyuan ended the call and made me sit down. All I was wearing was my towel and flip-flops, so he set me upright against a wall with my legs bent and crossed in front of me. Other guys began to come out of their rooms with swollen faces from abruptly waking up.

"What's all the fuss about," a guy in grey SoCafo sweats asked.

"Lewis found someone hurt in the shower, we just called the EMT," Shunyuan said.

"He's dead," I said rocking with my head on my knees. "He's dead." Tears were streaming down my cheeks at an uncontrollable rate, and I just rocked and repeated that Phil was dead.

Guys began to crowd around me, and a few patted my back and said comforting things like, "Help is almost here," and, "It's going to be OK."

The ambulance arrived and confirmed that Phil was dead. Well, the real confirmation came in the form of a coroner, stretcher, and a black bag rolling out of the shower room. I was questioned about everything that had happened, whether or not I knew the deceased, and if I knew anyone that would have wanted to harm him. Up until yesterday, the answer would have been no, but I knew that Phil was dead because of me. I had led Aden right to him. But I can't lead the police to Aden, or I'll be the next one wearing a body bag.

"I don't know. I'd really just like to go and get dressed now," I said.

"Well, I'm Officer Clark. Take my card." Tactlessly, he handed me a business card. "If you remember anything or think of something that may help us figure out what happened here, give me a call."

I nodded, "Yes officer." I had no intention of calling him.

"Shunyuan," I said.

"You can call me Shaun man, it's easier."

"Shaun, can I borrow some clothes? I left my keys in there," I motioned to the shower room, "and I don't think I can go back in there right now."

"No problem. I understand," he said as we walked to his dorm room.

Once inside, Shaun handed me a pair of cargo shorts and a plain white T-shirt and then turned around as I quickly dressed. The shorts were a little snug, but it was probably for the best considering that I was commando. Regardless, it was nice not to be in designer clothes. Everything inside of me wanted to reject all of Aden's influence and hide inside of my old shell.

"You think I can borrow a baseball cap?" I asked.

"Yeah, anything you want. There's one right beside the door," I grabbed a worn-in 49ers hat from a hook behind the door. "It's my lucky hat," he said.

"Thanks…I could use it today. I'll return it to you intact," I said.

"No hurry, just come on by when you feel up to it, I'll have your keys for you."

"I'm done," I said turning to face him.

Shaun turned around, "You need anything else?" he offered kindly.

"No, you're a lifesaver, seriously. Thanks for this, Shaun," I said shaking.

Shaun's face was sympathetic, "No problem at all. But dude, are you gonna be alright?" he asked.

I felt a tear roll down my face and wiped it quickly. "Yeah, I hope so," I said.

I thanked Shaun again and left the room. I didn't know where I was going but it was definitely not back to my dorm room; I needed to get my head together. The only person that I could think of who would be any help was Tim, but I didn't know where he lived or his last name to look him up on the campus directory. I'm definitely not going to Camille's. I want to keep her as far away from this as possible. If anything happened to her, I'd never forgive myself. Brant was out of the question because his place is probably swarming with police officers. I guess I could go to class, but I can't think about Calculus or any other subject for that matter.

My options were sparse, and my nerves were wrecked. I turned back around and walked to the recreation room where I found a spot alone on one of the salmon-colored couches. Lying down on my back, I crossed my legs and arms and began to cry. I didn't even try to stop myself. *I* was a guilty accomplice to murder, the fifth murder. So, another one was coming to fulfill Mom's multiple of threes prophecy, it was just a matter of whom and when.

As the uncontrollable tears continued to flow, a sinister and ominous pain singed my chest because I realized that the next death would be someone that I knew and cared for very much and that I would have contributed to their demise in some way. Because of my blindness and stupidity, multiple lives had been lost, yet mine was spared when all I wanted to do was die! The least I can do is let myself cry.

Chapter 22

Without my cell or a watch, I wasn't sure what time it was when I woke up, but my body told me that I had been asleep for at least three hours. The police should definitely be gone from Brant's room by now. I desperately needed answers to what happened last night, so I headed to Franklin Hall.

When I got outside, the sun was moderate, so my fair guess was that it was probably around three or four o'clock in the afternoon. I walked swiftly to Brant's with my head tucked-down underneath Shaun's lucky cap. When I got to Franklin, I realized I didn't have my passport. This was a newer dorm, so the passport scanner was on the outside of the building. I tried to look as discreet as possible in waiting for someone to come or go before I weaseled my way in. It didn't take long before a group of girls on their way from class came up the steps. I pretended to be tying my flip-flop as the first one scanned her passport and the others gabbed about how hot their Biology professor was. After they all passed, I put my foot in the doorway and slid inside. I followed the group to the elevator and pressed the third-floor button.

When I got to Brant's dorm room, the door was wide open. I could see Brant going back and forth from the closet to his luggage that was half-packed on the floor beside his desk.

I knocked softly. "Brant, it's Lewis. Can I come in?"

"Stay the hell away from me," he said angrily.

The room was nothing like it was the first time I saw it. The walls were bare, the décor gone, and things were packed away in boxes. It was sterile, almost lifeless.

Still standing outside the door, "Why? What did I do? What the hell is going on?" "You're a murderer!" Brant yelled, maintaining distance.

"What? I found him, Brant, I didn't-"

Brant interrupted, "I don't know Lewis, but Phil said he was going out with you and Aden last night, and then I got a call from Stephanie this morning saying the police needed to ask me some questions. The police said *you* found him."

Stepping into the room cautiously, "I didn't go out with Phil last night, there was a freaking lockdown!" I insisted.

"Please," he said avoiding eye contact with me.

"What are you doing?" I asked.

"I'm leaving," Brant said stuffing clothes into his luggage.

"What do you mean?" I asked.

"I mean I'm going home. I can't stay here after this," he said.

I understood his rationale and nodded, "OK, but you can't leave thinking I'm a murderer Brant!"

"Look, I don't know what I believe. I just know the last time I saw you; you were pissed at Phil about the death's, you said some crazy stuff about there being more death, and then Phil turns up dead, and you found him that way. It's all a bit much, don't you think?"

"Listen, I agree it sounds bad, but I'm not upset about all that stuff that happened at the gym. I mean I was, but I definitely didn't want Phil to *die* dude. I want to know what happened last night too."

Brant made eye contact with me for the first time, "Lewis, if you seriously didn't see him last night, then who did?" he zipped up the bag and set it upright.

I wanted to tell him all that I knew about Aden, but I was too afraid. "I don't know, Brant. But you've got to believe that it wasn't me."

He rolled his eyes and shook his head, "I don't have to do anything but get the hell out of here," he said rolling his luggage past me.

"What about school?" I asked.

"I can be an engineer anywhere, and I prefer it to be a place where the death count is zero."

"Can't you give it a little while 'til things cool down? I'm sure there's a logical explanation for everything," I lied, knowing good and well the explanation was totally unbelievable.

He stopped and sighed deeply, "Phil's parents will be here tomorrow to collect his things, and I want to be long gone before that. There is no way I can face them—it's too much."

"I get it, but –"

"Look," he cut me off, "I don't know if you killed Phil, but I think your involvement is fishy as hell. Now I gotta go," he said, storming down the hallway toward the elevators.

I stood in the doorway contemplating my next move. With no phone, passport, or car keys, I'm pretty limited in options. I had no choice but to go back to Ponce so that I could call Tim and figure out how to stop Aden. The

189

sun was beginning to fade, and that only meant one thing…Aden would be waking up soon.

To avoid Brant on the elevator, I ran down the stairwell skipping every other step. I ducked in and out of students, persistently, no, manically checking the horizon. The hue was pink and violet now! This was the first time I ever remember thinking the sunset was hideous. Pushing and shoving my way through commuters, I managed to make it to Ponce without knocking anyone over. I slipped into the main entrance behind a group of guys and ran frantically to Shaun's room and pounded on the door.

"Please be home, please be home!" I said.

From behind the door, I heard Shaun's voice, "Just a second." The door opened.

"Oh, thank God," I exhaled.

"Lewis, hey. How you holding up?" he asked.

"I'm alright, thanks, man. Did you have a chance to grab my keys?" I asked.

"Oh yeah," he turned to grab them off of the hook next to the door, "here you go."

"Thanks. I gotta run, but I really appreciate it."

"Oh, OK. See you later then." I was halfway down the hall before I heard his door close. I felt a ping of rudeness, but presently the urgency of getting in and out of my dorm room before Aden woke was more pressing than neighborly etiquette.

When I got to the room, I was vainly careful not to wake Aden. The tiptoeing, the maneuvering, the nervous charades…all a waste of time. I couldn't wake him even if I tried. The room was cold and unfamiliar. I had no desire to be inside of it any longer than I needed to. I threw a change of clothes into my backpack, grabbed my phone and Pandora's Box and darted out of the room.

Outside, the sun was fighting the moon with all that it had left. From the looks of the sky's purple moon shadows, I probably had less than fifteen minutes before Aden woke up. I pulled my phone out of my pocket and discovered that I had eleven missed calls. Six of them were from *HOME*, two were some local number (possibly Officer Clark), one was from Camille, one Dean, and one from Tim.

I called Tim back first, "Hey Tim, it's Lewis."

"Hey, I called you earlier, I got a call from the Coroner's office, so I kinda heard what happened. You OK?" he asked.

"I could use a place to crash for the night, can I swing by?" I asked, knowing he'd say yes.

"Sure man. My roommate is kind of annoying, but he's cool. We're over in the South Quad, Fletcher Hall, room 121."

"OK, I'll be there in twenty minutes or so," I hung up.

I booked as fast as I could across the CCC. It was almost completely dark, and I didn't want to be out when curfew went into effect. I suddenly felt better about Brant's decision to leave SoCafo because at least now he was one less person that I had to worry about getting killed. Aden didn't know Camille's last name or where she lived, so I felt that she was safe too. Come to think of it, Tim still being alive is a blessing and miracle. Especially considering that before I knew Aden was a vampire, I told him that Tim said a vampire was on the loose.

Tim's side of campus was much older than mine. These were probably the buildings that my parents lived, ate, and went to classes in. Fletcher Hall looked more like a motel than a dorm. The long, one-story building was off of a promenade and so the outside entrance went directly into the living space. There was no passport checker here, which also meant no security. But as long as we didn't invite Aden in, security wouldn't be an issue. I hope.

I knocked quickly, and Tim answered wearing his flannel top and crazy face. "Hey man, c'mon in." He looked like he was about to discover a new precious metal.

"Thanks," I stepped inside the room and threw my bag down.

"Lewis, this is my roommate, Rich," Tim said.

I said hello to a rail-thin guy wearing thick glasses and a Star Wars T-shirt. He was sitting down in front of his computer and peeked his head up for long enough to say hello back. I quickly scanned the room; it was exactly like a hotel room. There were adjacent twin beds, dressers, and desk and one long closet along the back wall. The bathroom was in the back, and there was a mirror with a sink in front of the door leading to it. Megadeath, Metallica, and Rage Against the Machine posters clung angrily to the walls, and the Anarchy symbol had been spray painted, in black, on every wall...overlapping the wall art in some places. Rich looked entirely out of his element in this space.

"I went to the morgue to check on Phil," Tim said.

"Yeah? And two bite marks, right?" I asked.

"No, not quite. His throat was slit from ear to ear. Aden didn't kill him, dude, he couldn't have."

"What do you mean?" I asked.

"Well, as you know Aden is a vampire."

"You think?" I said smugly.

He held his hand up, "Hear me out. If someone gave you the opportunity to tear into your favorite meal, you'd take it without question. No vampire could resist the temptation of blood, it's impossible. I mean, I guess Aden could have still fed off the blood coming from Phil's wound, but when you consider the same markings on the other bodies, it doesn't make sense that he would derail from his feeding pattern now. Phil's murderer was more than likely human, and it was someone who knows you or a lot about you."

"Why do you say that?" I asked.

"Well, they know where you live and they did a pretty darn good job of guessing which shower you were going to walk into, wouldn't you say?"

Tim was right! This was beyond coincidence. Someone was using Phil to send me a message, but who? And why? Could it be Brant? Maybe his accusatory scene today was meant to throw me off or cover for his quick exit. But Brant doesn't know what shower I use, the only person I told that to was...

My phone began to ring. I took it out of my pocket, the call was coming from Camille.

"Hello," I answered.

"Hey," she said.

"What's going on?"

"Nothing, I just wanted to call and check on you. Things are really crazy here right now. We aren't allowed to leave the building, and visitors are getting the third degree from Katrina, you know how she is," she forced laughter.

It was Camille's voice I was hearing, but the conversation was awkward. "So, is there anything you want to tell me?" I asked.

"I guess I'm sorry that I went off the way that I did. Usually, I enjoy your sense of humor, but I was stressed out and I snapped. It wasn't fair to you, Lewis. Then I heard about everything that happened this morning, and I just wanted to-"

"Wait a minute Camille, how did you hear about what happened this morning?" I asked.

"Aden, he's here right now. He –"

I cut her off again, "Wait, Aden is in your dorm room right now?"

"No, he called from downstairs, Katrina's desk phone, you know. He told me he was looking for you and about everything that happened to your friend Phil. I'm sorry, Lewis."

"So, you didn't call about Phil earlier?" I asked.

"No babe, I called to apologize for yesterday. I'm calling now because Aden scared me when he said he couldn't find you. He's on his way up, so

192

I'll let you speak to him when he gets to the room." She paused and then giggled carelessly. "Oh goodness, Sandra wants to know if he's cute."

"Camille, do not invite him into your room, and don't let Sandra either!" I said urgently.

"What, why Lewis?" she asked.

"Camille, there is no time to explain. Just trust me! Aden is not who you think he is. If you love me, just do what I say, please!"

"Lewis, you're scaring me."

"I know babe, but just promise me you will not invite him into your room. Promise me!" I insisted.

"I promise," she said. I heard a knock on the door in the background, "Lewis, it's him. What should I say?" Camille asked.

"I don't know Camille, lie, but just don't invite him in!"

I heard the door squeal open, and then Aden introducing himself. And then he asked, "May I come in?"

"Oh, I'm sorry, my mom *just* called," Camille said, "she and my dad are fighting…I'm on the phone with her right now and I have to take this. If I hear from Lewis, I'll let you know, OK?"

I knew it had to have broken her heart to concoct a lie in which her father was still alive, but she did it! Camille did it! I love that girl, and now, *thank God*, she is safe.

"Camille, close the door," I said.

"I did. Now tell me what is going on, Lewis?" she asked.

"There's no time Camille, just trust me. I have to go, but stay inside and don't let anyone into your room. And don't let Sandra let anyone in either."

"OK, but Lewis you are making me really nervous. Promise me you're going to be alright."

"I promise, babe. Love you."

"I love you too."

I hung up the phone and looked at Tim and Rich who were both staring at me open-mouthed and spellbound.

"Dude, that was intense," Rich said.

I glared at him, "*That* was the least intense thing that has happened to me all day."

Chapter 23

Tim and Rich were at their desks as I sat on Rich's bed and read from Pandora's Box. I was astounded by the myths that people had created about vampires. Like holy water, for example. It was once thought that vampires were demon-possessed humans, so since holy water worked to exorcise demons, people concluded the same for vampires. Not true in the slightest, a vampire could go swimming in a pool filled with holy water (at night) and not be affected in the slightest.

Rich, Tim, and I toiled over what I was going to do about Aden for hours, and we kept arriving at the same dead-end: I couldn't physically kill him, and I couldn't turn him in to the police without risking pissing him off further and ending up dead myself. But what if Aden lied about his Vamp's existence...what am I talking about? He can't lie; there was *definitely* another vampire on the loose, and she could be anywhere or anybody. And God forbid I should run into her; she would spare no mercy in ripping my throat out and draining its fruits for dinner. The only chance I'd stand is never going out past dark and never inviting a female into my room.

"What about the drywall, can't you take it down?" Tim asked.

"Yeah, but what's to stop him from just staying in the closet until the sun sets, and then putting it back up. I mean, he does sleep most of the day anyhow," I said.

"I see your point," Tim agreed.

"But there has to be a reason why he drywalled over the window in the first place," Rich added.

"You think, genius? He's a vampire. The sun'll kill 'em," Tim said rudely.

"That's not was I meant," Rich said adjusting his glasses. "I meant if the vampire dude was going to stay in his closet all day, then what would be the point of drywalling the window? He obviously has moments when he's awake during the day."

"Wait a minute…you're right," I said. "And I am pretty sure he has been awake during the day. If the sun sets around seven and he's up when I get home from class, he *has* to have been up too when it's still lights out."

I knew exactly what I was going to do. I may not have been able to kill or follow Aden, but if everything worked out the way I'm thinking it will, I wouldn't need to.

"You guys, I gotta go?" I said.

"Are you crazy?" Rich asked.

"Yes, I am. But I am also protected by the Law of Obedience, so I think I'll be OK."

Tim shook his head, "That law doesn't protect you from Mrs. Bloodthirsty Vampire. Not to mention there's a human killer out there too."

"There is no human killer. It was her…she killed Phil to send me a message. And whoever she is, she won't mess with me if she knows what's good for Aden. He needs me to feed, especially now that the campus is under lockdown."

"Hold on a second, am I missing something? How do you know it's her?" Tim asked.

"Because I saw Brant, he couldn't have killed Phil. If you had seen the look on his face, he was devastated, not to mention, he had no motive. It definitely wasn't Camille, and she's the only person I told about the shower other than Aden," I said grabbing my things.

"So, what are you going to do?" Tim asked.

"I'm going to end this," I said.

Looking at me through impossibly thick lenses, "Are you sure about that?" Rich asked skeptically.

"I've never been surer about anything in my life," I said.

"Well then may the force be with you," Rich said seriously.

"Or at least the freaking Law of Obedience," Tim added.

"Thanks for everything guys, if all works out, I'll call you tomorrow afternoon."

I left the room as quickly as I had come. Running back across campus, I tried to think through my conversations with Aden. I knew he was responsible for Phil's death. I handed his vamp accomplice Phil's lifeless body on a platter because Aden knew everything! How could I have even thought that it was Camille? I've known her since we were freshmen in high school, and the likelihood of her being an accomplice to murder was as likely as her roommate being a vampire too. And Brant killing Phil, they were friends…true friends. Brant's not a murderer, and he definitely wouldn't kill his friend and roommate.

The campus was a dark and desolate plane. All of the street lights were out, and there wasn't a soul in sight. I bolted across the CCC toward the Upper Quad, and the odd emptiness sent a shiver through my chest. As I approached the front entrance to Ponce, I could see Jonathan sitting behind the check-in desk staring wearily at me through the glass doors.

I walked in, and he sighed dramatically. "Lewis, what the hell man? I told you there was a curfew tonight. What are you doing out? It's past midnight! And especially with everything you've been through today?" he scolded.

"I'm sorry, I lost track of time," I said.

"Where have you been?" he asked.

"South campus."

"What? Why? You know what...forget it," waving me away with his hand. "Alright, well, you're in for the night," he said.

"Goodnight then," I said walking toward my room.

The halls were ominously quiet. I had expected to at least hear groups of people listening to the latest news about the lockdown, but every corridor was its own graveyard. I walked slowly through Ponce until I got to my door. I placed my ear up to the wood and could hear that Aden was inside the room having a conversation with someone. I couldn't make out much, but his tone seemed reaffirming and loving. I turned the key and slowly pushed the door open.

He rushed to end his phone call. "Yes, it's Lewis. I've got to go."

Entering the room, "Hey Aden," I said cheerfully. If I was going to put this plan over, I had to act like everything was perfectly normal and that nothing had happened.

"Lewis, how are you?" he asked.

"I'm fine, just had a long day," I said putting my stuff down on my desk.

"I can imagine. So, where have you been?" he asked.

"Just walking and thinking," I said. "You'd be surprised how clear things can be when there are no people around to cloud your judgment."

"Oh, believe me, Lewis, I know. Sometimes there is nothing more comforting than the companionship of solitude."

"Yes," I said, "and the moonlight."

"That's right," he said flashing his wicked smile. "So, what else were you thinking about?"

I pulled Pandora's Box from my bookbag, "This," I said.

He laughed, "Any new questions you want to ask me then?"

"Yeah, may I see you in the mirror?"

"Why do you want to?" he said.

196

"I want to know what you really look like," I said sincerely, "I mean if I'm going to be your…goon, I would like to see you for what you truly are."

"I prefer human sponsor, we are equals now, Lewis. I mean you no harm, I promise."

I had had enough of his promises, but I smiled anyway, "Thanks," I said.

"I will show myself to you, Lewis because you have shown your true self to me, and I appreciate it."

Aden walked toward the mirror and as he approached, a shadowy hue enveloped the room. I saw the corners of the mirror turn into dauntingly black clouds, and I could only imagine this bleak darkness to be the souls Aden *would* be seeing if he hadn't closed his eyes. He was a 108-year-old coward. I looked at the ancient man in the mirror, with sparse hair and sagging skin, wearing a black Armani polo. It was quite the contrast from the youthful, confident man directly in front of me. Aden turned around slowly, allowing me to see the bald, spotted head and wrinkly crease on the back of his neck. Then he walked away from the mirror, and the room returned to full light.

"Not what you were expecting, was it?" he asked.

Open-mouthed, "Not at all," I said softly.

"Well then I'm glad I could do my part to keep you entertained," he joked.

"So, you don't really have fangs, do you?" I asked.

He laughed casually, "We do, they are more of a hunting adaptation thought."

"What do you mean," I asked.

"Like a cat's claws, fangs retract when they are not being used to hunt or defend ourselves."

"Cool. Can I see?"

Aden opened his mouth wider than I've seen any mouth open as he tilted his head back. Through his gums, on both the top and bottom of his jaws, two tusk-like protrusions with dagger-sharp ends slowly materialized. I wished immediately that I hadn't asked to see them, and shuttered.

"I should have warned you; they can be a bit jarring."

"It's OK," I said, "I asked. So, tell me about you."

"What do you want to know?"

"Your whole vampire history I guess."

Aden began telling his story…he descended from a line of Dutch vampires dating back to the 15th century. At first, I was horror-stricken, but then he explained how one generation of vampires could be five hundred years, and the numbers didn't seem as intimidating. He explained how the

Dutch were colonized, and decolonized, and recolonized, like many countries, I guess.

The Netherlands remained a province of Spain, where his kind flourished under the protection of the Spanish coven of vampires. His grandmother was actually of Spanish descent and met his grandfather during the last days of Spain's authority in the Netherlands. They fell in love and had his father, and his father moved to California during the gold rush after he matured.

I thought this odd too…why would a vampire move to one of the sunniest places in the world? But apparently, California was annexed from the rest of the country at this time and crime was more rampant. According to Aden, many deaths by the hands of greedy criminals and traders went unaccounted for, so it was easier for vampires to feed and disguise the corpses as circumstantial murders. Aden's father met his mother, who was brought to California from France by her human sponsor. Aden's mother's sponsor had heard about the gold and ease of living for a vampire in California, so it seemed to be a great decision *until* Aden's mother fell in love with his father. Her sponsor became outraged with jealousy and threatened to reveal them both, so Aden's father killed her to save them from exposure and potential death by mob execution, which were more common back then. So, Aden's parents baited and changed out sponsors until their last days, where they sacrificed their sponsors for Aden and his vamp (he didn't say how he met her).

"So how does this vamp thing work? You can't travel without her?" I asked.

"Well, it's not that I can't, it's that we prefer not to; it's the principle of companionship. Even humans desire companionship, and your lives are not nearly as long as ours."

Nodding, "I see your point," I said. "Can I ask you one more question?"

"Of course," he said.

"Did you kill Phil or did your vamp?"

"I did not kill Phillip, Lewis…it was she, and that was *one* question," he said firmly.

"Fair enough," I said glancing at the alarm clock. It was 3:37 in the morning. We had talked for over three hours straight. "Um…well, you look good for a 108-year-old, if you ask me," I said.

He laughed, "Thanks, I feel it though. I need to retire, but I am glad that you came to your senses about our friendship, Lewis. It pleases me."

"Me too," I said, "goodnight, Aden."

Walking over to his closet, "Goodnight," he said. Aden opened the door, stepped in, and entombed himself inside of his closet. It was the weirdest shit I'd ever seen.

I went over to my desk, opened a blank word page on my laptop, and began to pluck the keyboard…

MyRoomateisavampire.MyRoomateisavampire.MyRoomateisavampire.M yRoomateisavampire.MyRoomateisavampire.MyRoomateisavampire.MyRoo mateisavampire.MyRoomateisavampire.MyRoomateisavampire.MyRoomatei savampire.

The lullaby of my keyboard continued until I was sure that Aden was asleep. Then I made my move.

I changed into exercise shorts, brushed my teeth, and washed my face…it was time to go to sleep. There was one more thing that I had to do before bed though—set the clock and turn off the alarm. I hadn't made it to any of my classes yesterday, and I was certain to miss them all today too. With it being almost four o'clock in the morning, I needed the sleep. And so, did Aden.

I set the clock back exactly five hours, from 4:03 am to 11:03 pm. I set the time on my phone to match the clock…but I also set an alarm on my phone for 11:30 pm.

***

I woke up to the soft chiming of my phone's alarm. Peeking in the mirror, it was obvious that I was in desperate need of an SSS. I was interrupted yesterday, so it had been over two days since I last showered. After brushing my teeth, I grabbed my toiletries and walked down to the shower room. I chose the first shower on the right, and it was every bit as clean as the third on the left had been. I took a very fast shower and dried off even faster. I had to arrive *home* from class at just the right time.

Like clockwork, my flip-flops slipped and slid as I urgently and nervously trotted back to the room to get dressed. Thank God Aden was still asleep. I threw on a pair of old, cut-off khaki shorts, a faded yellow T-shirt, and my other pair of flip-flops. After grabbing my book bag, Shaun's lucky hat, and my keys, I left the room.

I stood outside of the closed door to Ponce West, room 1004 for a while. Did I want to go out of the side door to really commit to my plan? Nah…

Instead, I turned around and wobbled my key inside the keyhole and reentered the room. I threw everything that I had just picked up *back* onto the floor.

I turned the stereo on, opened up my word document, and began to type…and wait. It wasn't long before Aden emerged from the closet.

"Hey…*Goodnight moonlight*," I joked, "did you sleep well?"

"Like a corpse," Aden said looking like he just stepped off of a runway in Milan. "How was class today?"

"I still hate Philosophy if that's what you mean. But Biology was cool."

"Biology…with Tim…if my memory serves me?" he asked.

"Yep, Tim."

Looking at the clock, Aden changed into a red shirt. "I think I'm going to pay him a visit tonight after class. Thank you."

"Oh, you're welcome. He's weird. Have at it," I replied.

"What do you think about this?" Aden asked, modeling his outfit.

"That's a good color for you," I affirmed.

Aden looked at me and smiled cunningly, "Lewis, I must say, I'm surprised at how well you are adjusting to life as a vampire's cohort."

I looked at him dumbfounded, "Why would that surprise you?" I asked.

"You seemed apprehensive about the entire death aspect, and-"

I interrupted Aden, "I mean, I did tell Tim you were a vampire, and we can't have loose ends running around campus. He's a loose end dude," I said convincingly.

Aden looked at me pleased. "Absolutely. Well, Lewis, I'd love to stay and parlay, but I've got a class to attend, and a lose end to sever. You'll probably be asleep when I get back, so I promise I won't wake you," he winked viciously and strolled out of the room.

I got up and placed my ear to the door. I could hear the heavy side-exit-door slamming shut, so I knew that Aden was in the stairwell. Attempting to open the door, my hand struggled against nothing to even grab the knob. In my mind, I was moving forward, but in reality, I was frozen in space and time. Again, I couldn't go forward! I couldn't follow him! I clamored for the doorknob in vain against the force of the *Law of Obedience*.

I continued to fight, struggling violently until feeling a complete release of resistance. My entire body plunged forward, and I slammed face-first into the door. The pain posed no match for my curiosity. Despite the blood running from my nose, I sprinted toward the side-exit like a crazed person escaping from a mental institution.

I wasn't quite sure what I was expecting to see. I wasn't quite sure that what I was looking at was Aden Vanhook… The 175 pounds of perfection had become a steaming, black, tar-looking mound of rancid smelling bile. Aden was bubbling and flowing over the door's floor panel. I had to kick a disgusting, sullied pair of Armani jeans and a soiled piece of red fabric out of my way so that I could get outside of the building without stepping into the shallow pool of oozing, coagulating, onyx sludge. Squeezing my nostrils, I stared morosely at Aden's remains as he began to seep down the stoop, his plasma's toxic acidity burning through cinderblock and sizzling on the hot concrete below.

Chapter 24

Immediately after the police arrived, I knew that it was a mistake to have called Officer Clark. Because the stairwell was secluded and there were no surveillance cameras or witnesses to Aden's meltdown, all of Officer Clark's questioning seemed accusatorily directed at me.

"I didn't see anything! I was inside of my dorm room," I said.

With authoritative skepticism on his brow, "Son, you do realize that this is the second time that you have alerted the police to a crime scene within a forty-eight-hour period," he said.

Thankfully, this crime scene was so bizarre that Officer Clark, along with his puzzled and nostril clenching precinct, was more fixated on Aden's remains than on me.

The forensic team was also aghast. A few of them gave up on collecting evidence when the still sizzling fluid singed their gloves and burned newly exposed fingers. Forensic surrender was sealed by the screaming and charging toward the special-ops-van for the disinfectant flush.

Tim arrived shortly after the pointless call to the coroner was made. And thank goodness for it because he handled the situation like a professional anarchist.

"You idiots have no idea what you're doing over there in law enforcement!" he yelled.

"Get yourself under control Mr. MacMahan," Officer Clark warned Tim.

"Yeah, that's the problem here," Tim continued, "you tax parasites can't do your job and get this crime scene *under control*."

"That's it, get him out of here," Officer Clark barked at one of his subordinate officers. But no attempt was made to remove Tim from the scene, as every uniformed body present was entranced by Aden's revolting final act of mind control.

"Oh, come on Officer *Clerk*," Tim patronized, "you don't need a team of operatives here, you need some biologists, and that's what my friend, Lewis, and I are. So, can you move your goons aside so we can collect some samples? Coroner's orders." He produced a yellow carbon-paper document from his pocket. "This is an unknown biological hazard. This area needs to be sterilized and samples need to be sent to the Coronary Science Lab for evaluation. Don't tell me you've forgotten protocol?"

"Mr. Lewis, you called me and reported that-"

"There's isn't a body or homicide here or evidence of a crime," Tim interrupted. "So, take your useless team of social conformists, and go pretend to be valuable in the parking lot of a Dunkin' Donuts."

Officer Clark stepped into Tim's face, "You better watch it, MacMahan, I don't give a damn if I *will* be taking orders from you when you finish this stupid program. I'll smash your Goddamn head in and cuff your ass to the stretcher they'll cart you off on, you lousy piece of shit."

Tim smiled, "There you go, from the man himself…great job protecting and serving."

Officer Clark didn't break eye contact with Tim, "C'mon crew. There's nothing here. Let's let this little freak clean up his science project."

"Thanks, gentlemen," Tim curtsied dramatically and waved like a beauty pageant winner until the confused assembly had cleared out.

"Why'd you call him? You said you'd call me!" he said.

"I thought I should call the police; I mean somebody did die dude."

Tim looked down at Aden, "That's not 'somebody' dude, that's *something*."

He removed a small glass vial from his pocket, "Here, take this and try to collect as much of *that* as you can."

"What are you going to do?" I asked. He was already pulling a small canister of something marked flammable from his bag. "Oh," I said.

"Yeah, now hurry and get the sample before somebody sees us."

I set the vial underneath some of the dripping globs of Aden and watched as it oozed nastily into the crucible, fogging up the glass and heating my fingertips. "Ugh, it reeks!" I said, squinching my nose and gagging.

Tim laughed, "Well what do you expect, it's not like he ate his veggies."

"Disgusting," I sighed.

After the vial was full, I capped it and Tim saturated the area with gas. Tim MacMahan clearly had an affinity for pyrotechnics—the cool grace in which he lit and flung the match looked as if it took years to perfect.

We stood back and watched the concrete pyre swell in flames until Aden's toxic blood had burned and the flame vanished. It was over. Aden hadn't lied…he had literally boiled from the inside out.

Chapter 25

Without missing a beat, Tim acknowledged the difficult truth that I needed to concoct a plan that explained the disappearance of my roommate. The totally implausible idea of telling the world that my roommate had been a 108-year-old vampire-college-student responsible for the recent deaths on campus was now chilling in a test tube seemed... Anyway, we decided that on Monday, I would call Officer Clark and tell him that my roommate fled campus after I questioned him about Kimberly Dawson, Sarah Reynolds, and the man at the bar across the street from Nickey's Salon. The story sounded weak at first, but Tim assured me that Officer Clark would take fingerprints from the dorm room, and match them to fingerprints from the crime scenes. And apparently, there were also ways to match Aden's handwriting to that of the suicide letter he had written. And finally, Tim said that I would need to surrender his clothing and car to the police to be entered as evidence, DNA stuff, I don't know.

"But how will I explain the phone call today and the toxic black crud?" I asked skeptically.

"Easy, some fraternity is hazing pledges that live in Ponce by putting a concoction of vomit, urine, feces, and battery acid where they will step and possibly slip and fall into. It's disgusting, but it happens all the time. Anyhow, you saw it, flipped out, and called Officer Clark because you were still shaken up about Phil."

"OK.," I said, relieved to have the solution but depressed by the loss.

"I know," Tim said, raising his pierced brow like a confident mind reader. "And this is the story you'll tell Camille, your family, and every man, woman, and child until your grave. It's for your own good man, trust me."

"You don't have to twist my arm," I agreed.

After I thanked and thanked and thanked him again, I said goodbye to Tim. I decided to take a walk to Bell Hall. I had some school business I needed to take care of.

The Southern California sun was especially bright, and many students were out enjoying it with footballs and tanning oil, or sleevlessly commuting to class. The vibrancy that I remembered from moving in was back again, or maybe it was here all along

Walking across campus, I felt cooler than ever before. But this *cool* was different than that first day with Brant and Phil. It wasn't a shallow cool. I had made a decision that proved my respect and love for human life, and that was cooler than any resistance to peer pressure or acceptance. Despite my temporary loss of good judgment and desperate need for fulfillment, my morality was intact. Maybe this realization is what being a college freshman is all about.

Bell Hall's student affairs center was being operated by a soft-spoken brunette with glasses and great eye contact. "Hi, how can I help you?" she asked.

"Hey, my name is Lewis Lewis. I'm an undeclared freshman, and I'd just like to declare my major. I was told I could do it at any point up to a certain amount of credit hours."

She began typing on her keyboard, "Hi Mr. Lewis, and that is correct, you have until the end of your second semester really," she advised.

"Yeah, I know. But I think I'm ready now," I confirmed.

She smiled, "That's fine too. You can change it one more time after this without additional fees."

"OK, but I'd still like to declare a major today," I kindly insisted.

"Oh, I know Mr. Lewis, we just have to inform everyone of policy and what their options are, you know, university protocol," she said equally as kind.

"Yeah, makes sense. Thank you," I offered.

"So, what major were you interested in, Mr. Lewis."

"Humanities," I said proudly, eager to set purpose to my collegiate journey.

She began typing, "OK, great. I'm putting in the *change of major* request now, so you should receive a letter of confirmation with your new advisor's information within a week."

"Don't you need to see my passport," I asked.

Looking up from the computer screen, she shook her head, "Nope, I got you right here in the system Mr. Lewis. I promise," she said.

I smiled, "OK, great."

She looked back at her monitor, "Your course load is fine for now, but you'll need to begin taking your in-major courses next semester. They should include some Psychology and Sociology classes, but mostly you'll be studying human relations and taking a lot of Anthropology stuff. So, I hope you like people because that's what you'll be studying. I mean, in various contexts."

"Perfect!" I said more excited than I intended.

She looked up again, "Well, that's not even it, you'll be studying abroad your entire senior year, you know? Living amongst different cultures and all of that…it's for your practicum and final thesis."

I nodded in anticipation, "Cool. That's exactly what I wanted to hear Ms…?"

"Vanhook, Joyce Vanhook," she said.

Ha! OK…it's broad daylight and many people have the last name *Vanhook.*

"Cool, and thanks for your help," I said.

I turned to walk away, "Wait," she called out. "What do you plan on doing with that degree, if you don't mind my asking?"

Turning around, "No. I don't mind at all," I shrugged. "I plan on being happy," I said. She nodded as I smiled and walked away.

Mom and Dad would be thrilled to know that I've chosen a major so soon. It'll be the second wave of relief…the first being the phone call from me since the SoCafo campus lockdown hit the news.

"Lewis!"

"Hey Mom, guess what?" I said, pretending like I didn't have multiple missed calls from them yesterday.

"Why didn't you call us back? We have been worried sick," she said.

"I've just been busy, Mom," I answered calmly.

"Busy! With all that's happening? You need to call us; you can't just move away and…and cease communication! We're your parents, Lewis," she said emotionally.

"Mom, I know that. Listen, I love you, but I'm in college now. I can't call you every day, nor do I think it's necessary," I said.

"Lewis! That's not fair. Your father and I heard about the lockdown on the news, *the news* Lewis! Can you imagine how concerned we've been?"

I felt terrible, but I wanted to exercise my true feelings too, "I know, and I'm sorry for that, really I am, but there has been a lot going on around campus, and I needed to take care of myself. I'm fine, I promise," I said.

She sighed in surrender, "Oh honey, I'm glad you're safe. Just don't ever scare us like that again…OK?"

"OK, Mom. Please don't be scared, I should have called yesterday. I just had to sort some things out," I said.

Part of me wanted to tell her about everything that happened, but Tim's advice was paramount. Not to mention that my mom argued the selling points of a minivan, so I'm pretty sure that my roommate being a vampire who tricked me into being an accessory to murder would fall under the category of *things my mother cannot handle*.

"Well, I just wanted to know sweetie."

"I understand. So, I will call you as often as possible, at least once every week, OK?" I bargained.

"Twice?" she countered.

"Once Mom, and a couple of emails," I finalized.

"Deal," she agreed.

I laughed, "OK, good. I love you, om."

"Be careful, son. I don't know what your father and I would do if anything happened to you."

"I will, like I said, I can take care of myself, Mom."

"Oh honey, I know. It's just that you're out there and so far away from us. Are things still going well with your roommate?" she asked.

"Uh, the Southern California sun was too much for his condition, so he withdrew."

"Oh, the poor thing. That's so sad, and I hate to think you are out there all alone."

"I'm not alone, Mom. I have a girlfriend," I admitted.

"I knew it. I knew it when you avoided my questions the other day," she gloated.

I laughed at her, "Questions! Ha, you mean your pries!"

She paused, "So what's her name? What's she like?"

"Camille and she is pretty great, Mom. You have actually seen her before," I said.

"Really, when?"

"Graduation. The Valedictorian Speech that you loved, remember?"

"Oh, yes! She's lovely! When you kids come home for Thanksgiving, we simply must meet her, Lew," she said.

"Mom, let's take things one step at a time. And let me handle the steps when we do take them, OK?"

"OK, fair enough," she sighed. "You just might be growing up, Lew Lew, you know that?"

"Mom, c'mon."

"Well, your father keeps buggin' me to hand the phone over…will you stop pokin' me, Cliff!" she said. "I love you, Lewis. Oh, and promise me-" she alluded.

I wonder what this could possibly be. "Anything Mom," I said.

207

"Make sure you are always with a group of people. Oh, and never travel alone. Statistics show that most missing persons over the age of seventeen were last seen heading somewhere alone. And never invite strangers into your room, even if it is a party, OK honey?" she scolded.

"I promise," I said.

"Thank you. OK, muah…here's your father."

"Hey, champ!"

"Hey Dad, what are you doing home from work?"

"Lost my job, the investors backed out of the Emerson building."

"What!" I yelled.

He laughed, "Just kidding! We closed this morning; Larry gave us the rest of the day off to celebrate. I'm taking your Mom out for sausage and sauerkraut pizza! Sorry, you are going to miss the celebration."

"It's OK, but Dad, you can do better than that, take a risk and do something new. At least try a meal where you'll use forks."

"Give your old man a break. We can't all be Romeo's like you."

I sighed deeply, "Now don't you start," I said.

"Just remember what you are there for, OK?"

"I will," I said.

"Alright son," he said, making me feel like a kid at a T-ball game again.

"I love you, Dad," I said.

"I love you too champ," he said.

"Oh, and next year you're moving me in, no excuses!" I demanded.

"Deal!" he said. "Bye son."

"Bye Dad," I hung up.

Chapter 26

Two weeks later, I was standing in front of Shuan's dorm room holding a clean and folded pair of cargo pants, a T-shirt, and a very soiled, yet lucky 49ers cap. He opened the door almost immediately and looked surprised to see me.

"Hey man," I said.

"Hey, Lewis."

"I just wanted to return these to you."

"Sure thing man, come on in," he said, taking a step back from the door.

"Thanks," I walked into the room. "You have no idea how much I appreciate it, and I do think this hat is *really* lucky," I said.

"Anytime man, I'm glad I could help," he said taking the items.

I cleared my throat, "So we should definitely hang out sometime. My roommate is gone, so I could afford to get out and meet some new people."

Shaun nodded, "Yeah, I saw the news. They still haven't caught him, huh?" I shook my head and fixed the lines of my forehead in the most realistically concerned display I could manage. "For-sure-man," Shaun continued, "a few of us get together every Wednesday night for Speed tournaments. It's a lot of fun. We do it in the rec room, you're more than welcome to join us."

"Speed?" I asked skeptically. "Oh, I don't do drugs."

"The game, not the drug man!" he laughed. "It's cards, I'll teach you."

"Oh," I chuckled, "sounds like fun."

"So, what is the school saying about your new roommate situation?" he asked.

"Well, I talked to Jonathan about it, and with everything that happened, he said he *forgot* to put in the request for a replacement."

"That's awesome dude, you've got a room to yourself! Do you have a girlfriend?"

"Yeah, things are hot and heavy too man," I admitted smiling, thinking about my recently lost virginity and the ongoing practice Camille and I had been getting in my dorm room. "And she has a cute and single roommate…I could hook you up?"

He nodded, "That would be awesome. Put in a good word for me. So, you won't have a roommate this year, that's got to be nice. I'm jealous," he cut an eye at his dorky roommate doing homework, deafened by headphones.

I laughed, "Yeah, it's nice for sure. I'm actually on my way to go see her for dinner, so I have to run. I just wanted to drop this stuff off to you and say thanks."

"Oh, OK. You're welcome, buddy. So, I'll see you Wednesday night?"

"Yeah, see you then." I let myself out.

I walked quickly to Columbus where I found Camille waiting for me at our table. She had already gotten us a large sauerkraut and sausage pizza, and the aroma of the cheese, sauce, and garlic made my butterflies breakdance.

"Hey girl," I said kissing her.

"Emmm," she closed her eyes, "hey boy."

"How was your day?" I asked.

"It's over thank goodness. Yours?"

"Same! My paper was due today," I said.

"Oh, that," she said rolling her eyes. "I still think you should have changed the title."

"Why? What's wrong with 'My Roommate Is a Vampire'?" I said taking a bite of pizza.

"Everything! It sounds like a joke; your professor is never going to take it seriously. I mean, it's a comparative literature piece and you basically turned it into a fiction versus non-fiction parody," she said. "Do you really even believe that Aden was a vampire, like *really*?"

"Well, after he was gone the deaths on campus did stop," I said.

She took a sip of her soda, "Lewis, sometimes I don't know what to think of you, I swear."

I laughed, "I'm joking babe. I think Dr. Ferguson will like the metaphorical analogy. I'm essentially using the beliefs from the sixteenth-century existence of vampires and comparing them to their more contemporary perception. I had to give the paper an edge. I think it makes it more entertaining," I said.

"Well we'll see when you get the paper back," she took a bite of pizza.

"Facts," I agreed.

"And did that hag let you finally retake the Calculus test you missed?"

"Oh. Yes," I said having forgotten. "My advisor approved that pardon explaining what happened when I found Phil—they called it personal grief amnesty. It just sucks that when you find your friend's body, and your roommate turns out to be a killer, the school makes you get a note to make up your assignments."

"I know right! But in her defense, I'm sure many students try to skip class because they are not prepared for those tests."

"But it's her own damn fault! She shouldn't give assessments every day," I said.

"But I thought you said you liked being tested every day and that it helped you prepare more for class. I remember something about," she began mocking me, "Oh, I'd *never* study if I didn't have these test every day, I looooove them, dude."

"Oh, so that's how I sound?"

Laughing, "Yeah," she said rolling her neck.

I shook my head and laughed too, "You're nuts!"

"Yeah but you love me," she said.

"That I do," I said as I kissed her.

We finished our pizza and headed back toward the dorms holding hands. The moon was full and there were stars everywhere.

"Which one do you want," I asked Camille, gazing at the sky.

Looking at me, "I want this one," she said squeezing my hand.

I smiled, "So... Lewis or Emmanuel, go!" I said playfully.

Camille stopped walking and faced me. Her breasts were goose-pimpled from the cool, night air, so I gently placed my arms around her. We found comfort in our gaze and allowed our lips to touch softly. As we stood there kissing, I sensed the luminance of fireflies flickering in our moon shadows.

Camille's tongue lavished mine before she lovingly ended the kiss.

Smiling sexily, "Lewis Emmanuel Lewis," she answered.

Smiling, "So, you wanna come over and roll around a little?" I asked.

"Can't tonight, but you can come over and keep me company while I do some homework," she offered.

"Oh boy! Can't hardly wait," I joked.

She sucked her teeth, "Fine then, go back to your lonely little dorm room and sleep."

"I'm kidding," I said laughing. "It would be my pleasure to watch you do anything, babe."

"That's what I thought," she sassed as we turned toward Hoffmann Hall.

***

Katrina must have had a rough day because when Camille and I walked inside, she was doubled over on the desk with her face buried in one of her books.

I reached across the desk to shake her shoulders a little, and Camille stopped me violently. "No! Don't wake her up," she said frantically.

"Dude, she'd be pissed if she knew people were just walking through here without checking in first," I said.

"I know, but I promised her I wouldn't wake her up," Camille admitted.

"What did you say?"

"Well actually, we *both* promised to never wake each other up."

"Why?"

"I fell asleep studying over there," she pointed to one of the pink sitting areas, "and she woke me up. I was kind of rude to her at first—you know how grumpy I am when I wake up. But then she went into this whole thing about all her medical courses being at night and always being exhausted too. So anyway, we jokingly promised not to wake each other up. You know, she can be pretty funny once you get past all that attitude."

"Camille, what happened after that?" I asked urgently.

"Ahh, what do you mean?" she asked, looking at me genuinely confused.

"Did she…was there…like a handshake or a hug, or any physical contact at all?" I pressed frantically.

Camille looked annoyed and puzzled by my berating attack of questions, "Um…I don't know. Why?"

"Camille, I need you to try to remember. Think!"

"Ugh, OK. Ummm… Oh, wait! Come to think of it, yeah. She hugged me. It was kinda sweet actually."

"Shit! So, *you* told Katrina about our table at Columbus *and* my shower stall?"

Looking defensive, yet slightly embarrassed, "Yeah," she admitted guiltily.

"Damn it, Camille. Why did you do that?"

"Why does it matter? And why are you getting so upset? Calm down. I told Sandra, Ebony, and Olivia too, babe. I think it's sweet that we have our own little spot, and I think your shower stall thing is cute and quirky, and *you*. You have your own little, particular ways about you. It's adorable."

"No, no no-no-no, nooo."

"Lewis, calm down. It's just a stupid story about a shower stall. It's not like I told her that your fugitive roommate is a murderer that you accused, in a college research paper, of being a vampire. Now that would be embarrassing, for both of us," she said.

"Forget about the stories, Camille! Why did you make that promise?" I said, shaking her shoulders.

Camille looked at my hands woefully. "Lewis! Stop it, OK? It was just a stupid girl thing. It's not like it was a *real* promise."

Defeated, I shook my head, "Camille, a promise is a promise."